wants
of the
silent

Part II of the Sun Song Trilogy

Moira McPartlin

Wants of the Silent
Moira McPartlin
© Moira McPartlin 2017

Cover illustration: Graeme Clarke
Published by:

Fledgling Press Ltd,
39 Argyle Crescent,
Edinburgh,
EH15 2QE

www.fledglingpress.co.uk

ISBN 9781912280001
Printed and bound by:
Martins-the-Printers, Berwick upon Tweed

For Colin

Acknowledgements

Book Two of the Sun Song Trilogy has been too long coming and some thanks are overdue. I am especially grateful to my regular early readers Frances Wright and Colin Baird. To Rachel Davidson and Clare Watts who scrutinised every word and to the rest of the Scoobies (SCBWI) and YA crit group who have encouraged and supported me throughout the writing of this book.

There is a smattering of Gaelic in the book and I am indebted to the lovely Maggie Rabatski for checking and correcting that smattering Huge thanks are due to everyone at Fledgling, in particular Clare Cain who took this project under her wing at a particularly difficult time.

Lastly I would like to thank my family for always being there, especially my sons, John and Gary and my sister Liz. And of course love and thanks to my husband Colin, he's the foundation that keeps it all together.

Black Rock Island — 2089

Ishbel

Ishbel huddled on a narrow cliff ledge watching the prisoners escape. The crisp sea wind nipped her face and she breathed in the joy of it. All those years at the Military Base had robbed her of this. She was never leaving the sea again. She watched her brother Kenneth direct the loading of the wasted and mutated prisoners onto boats and submarines destined for the rebel army's HQ. Freed at last from this island of death and experimentation.

She heard him roar, 'This is all going very well.' She smiled. And there was young Sorlie, her charge for so many years looking lost yet tall, older than his sixteen years. Maybe it was the infrared lens he wore over one eye, he seemed alien. He scanned the cliff top as if looking for her, but she knew that was rubbish, he would be expecting her to be on that Northern Archipelago, waiting for the submarines to arrive. How was he to know she had unfinished business on Black Rock? Before Ishbel could stop herself it was done. One short birdcall of the corncrake, her call, the one she knew he would recognise. He lifted his head, she saw his start, his stare, his joy. He had seen her. 'No,' she mouthed and held her finger up to her lips when she saw him move to the cliff. They mustn't know she was there. Vanora would have her arrested and she was not ready to go back yet.

She shooed him away. 'Go, Sorlie, I have work to do,' she whispered. Then putting her thumb and index finger together she OK'd to him and climbed out of his sight, hoping he would get the message. She was a fool to show herself but the shine of joy on his face told her maybe her instincts weren't so wrong.

When the last landing boat left shore Ishbel returned to the cliff. She used the cooling outlet pipe to enter the penitentiary. No one would be expecting that. The pipe was still warm from the escape and now free of algae after the descent of a thousand backside slides scoured it clean. Her coarse uniform and tough boots made easy work as she shucked up the pipe. The alarm that would have sounded during the main breakout had stopped but the main generator lights burned. This she found strange. Why would Davie bother? He would be in his library, she was sure. A prison warden, now without prisoners. She grasped the hilt of the gun in her pocket, rehearsing in her head what she would say just before she put him to death.

There was an eerie air around the reactor room, as if the building was holding its breath. The air smelled of fleeing men, their sweat, their fear. What looked like snail trails of blood painted a pathway on the floor. She drew her gun. On tiptoe, she followed the trail to the control room. She tasted cold and bitter fear in her mouth.

The door was slightly ajar. Again, bright lights shone through, as if someone was afraid of the dark. Sweat ran down her back even though her breath crackled in the chill corridor. She braced and pushed the door. There was a body on the floor. The face was blown off but she still recognised it as Davie, the tyrant of Black Rock and the father she had met only three times. The last time only yesterday. Someone had beaten her to it – her kill denied. She pushed her disappointment behind her as she stepped over the body, just to make sure. What a mess, the top of his skull blown, peppering the walls. That proud silver mane now matted in blood and brains. On the floor beside him lay his old battered gun. Ishbel couldn't believe he'd taken his own life. She lifted the gun with thumb and index then wiped it on the bottom of her coat. This would be her souvenir, her birthright from the father who never suspected their blood tie. She would now never have the pleasure of telling him that after her mother, Vanora, had fled his fist, Ishbel was born and had lived in exile for many years. When mother and daughter returned to the ravaged State of Esperaneo thirteen years ago Vanora provided Ishbel with false papers and arranged her service as a domestic native on a Military Base. Her assigned Privileged family had welcomed her then left her in charge of their precious son Sorlie while they missioned for The State.

It was only later she discovered Sorlie's mother was her own sister, Vanora and Davie's other daughter, brought up Privileged. And Ishbel's charge Sorlie was her nephew. It had seemed so simple then.

Ishbel stood over the brute's body and spat into the gory mess. She hated him even more because he'd robbed her of the pleasure of killing him herself.

The monitors in the control room showed only blurred pictures. She realised she'd been crying, but natives were not permitted to cry. She wiped the tears with the heel of her hand and her nose on a sleeve. The infirmary monitor showed only dim lights. She squinted to make out the shapes. Saliva flooded her mouth; blood on the bed sheets, blood on the floor. Not all the prisoners had made it to the boats. Someone had massacred them, just as natives were being massacred everywhere. There was nothing she could do for them now. Another monitor showed what she guessed was Sorlie's room, untidy as usual but empty. Another pointed to the two doors leading to Davie's surveillance-free library. One was closed, the other open a crack and a ribbon of light shone from within. She couldn't resist one last look. She would take a couple of the rarer books to sell to the Noiri, there was always demand on the black market for books. Maybe she'd keep one for herself.

Vanora's thought-map escape plan of the penitentiary was etched in Ishbel's brain, she knew the way. She crept along the corridor with her own gun in one hand and Davie's in the other just in case the guards woke up.

Someone was near. She could almost hear their breathing in

the pin-dropping silence. The floor covering was soft and yet each toe she put down seemed to crunch like broken glass.

At the side of the wooden door she flattened her back to the wall, melting into her surroundings in the way all natives could. She adjusted her grip on the guns then almost dropped them when a scratchy voice shouted, 'You might as well come in.'

Ishbel stepped into the room and the sight of the small man sitting there almost knocked her back out.

'Oh no, look at you.' She couldn't help herself.

He slouched in a leather chair, a book in one hand, a glass of illegal Mash in the other. The ill-fitting guard's uniform made him look like a rag doll and his stubble, dirty blond hair and walnut eyes did not seem to fit his pasty skin colour. The relief in his eyes showed her he was expecting someone else, but his smile was shadowed in sorrow.

'Ishbel, ah believe.' His voice was slurred and she guessed he had consumed a fair whack of Mash.

'Who are you?' She pointed a gun not quite believing what she suspected.

'Don't you know, Ishbel? It's me, Scud, Vanora's inside man and Sorlie's native after you left him here.'

'No, I've seen your hologram.' And yet there was something familiar about him. She wanted to move for a closer look but the sight of him repelled her. He wasn't right.

He waved a hand down his person. 'Look at me, ah'm Privileged now.' His voice almost sang the proclamation 'The DNA dilution of the native gene. It worked.'

It was true, he had the pale hair and eye colour of a Privileged, but there was still something subservient about his sly look, his skewed gaze, his drunkenness. If this change was the result of a DNA dilution then some of Scud's native Celtic genes remained.

'What are you doing here? Why didn't you go with the others?' she asked him.

'Ah'm going to enjoy being Privileged for a while.' He moved forward in his seat and licked his lips. 'Did my wee man Sorlie make it out?'

'Yes, they've gone.'

Ishbel tiptoed round the room touching the brickwork of books lining the walls. She holstered her gun, stuffed Davie's in her waist belt and touched one book, pushed back another and picked up the heavy tome that lay by Scud's side. It smelled of ancient histories: masculine and rich.

'Ah wrote this book.' Scud's hand wavered towards it, as if afraid a touch would turn it to dust. 'The foremost authority in twentieth century history and yet ah was not permitted to touch my own book.'

'The revolution will change that,' Ishbel said.

Scud snorted in disgust, a drop of spittle ran from his lips. Ishbel forced down her revulsion at the sight of this mutant.

'Ah'm surprised Davie kept it, he had such contempt for me,' Scud said.

'Maybe he had a use for it.' She raked the shelves, selecting a few books. The collection was astonishing. 'Come and help, we can't leave them to be destroyed by the State. We'll take some with us, I'm sure the Noiri would give us good credit for them.'

'Ah'm not leaving.'

'Yes you are.'

Scud shook his head and took a sip of Mash, then smacked his lips. 'Davie had only the best. The State must have been very pleased with the way the experiments were going.'

Ishbel knelt down in front of him and tried to catch his sorrowful eye.

'You are coming with me. Why do you think I'm here?'

'Vanora sent you?' but she could see his doubt.

'No she didn't. She wants you here, I can see it was her plan all along. You were to stay and kill Davie but it looks like he took care of that himself.' She wiped her nose of the rancid smell of him. 'You should have gone with the others.'

Scud put the glass down and sat forward. 'Vanora's plan was not so great. That old bastard nearly killed Sorlie. Was that in her plan? That plug-in he used to open the cells welded him tae the controls. Couldn't move and watched Davie move closer tae murderin him. The wee man must have been terrified. Was that in her plan? What kind of a grandmother is that? Eh?' he said shaking his head.

Ishbel had known the plug-in design was flawed. Even the designer had tried to stop Vanora issuing it but all that earned him was a bullet in the head. Vanora had to have her way.

'Aye.' Scud slurped more Mash. 'But young Sorlie turned it around. Ah don't know what he said tae him but whatever it was it tipped the old man over the edge. Although he didn't have far tae go. Mad as a mozzie in a jam-jar he was.'

'I've disobeyed orders to get here. I've grown up hearing stories of the great Scud. Your sacrifices for the cause, your intellect and humour in the face of adversity. Of how you fought to save your family from being enslaved during the first purge.' Ishbel still couldn't believe Vanora had left Scud here to perish. 'When I was growing up you were a god with a capital G and I'm not leaving here without you.' She could see she had his attention now. 'When I heard you were to be left behind, I defected, stowed away. Stole onto the island. I came to get you. You're right, Vanora has lost her touch. She designed the plug-in so that Sorlie could not move. It was supposed to protect him. But what if Davie had got to him?'

'He nearly did. But you're wrong, Vanora didn't plan to leave me. Ah chose to stay.'

Ishbel shrugged. 'I wouldn't be so sure. She promoted Merj to first lieutenant over me and fell head over heels for his looks and charms, but he was traitorous, I believe a little piece of Vanora knew that. But she didn't do anything to stop him.'

Ishbel kicked herself. What was she doing rambling on about Merj and his promotion? 'No, Scud, if we are to fight this fight we need good honest brains. I need you and so does Sorlie.'

Scud continued to shake his head. 'Very compelling, ah'm sure, but ah don't owe you anything. Ah'm done with it. Ah want tae spend my last few days as a Privileged.' He looked at his communicator as if it told him the time and date of his demise. 'Ah might not be here long but at least ah can have fun. Ah've been a prisoner here for twenty years. There's nothing else going on in my life.' He reached to refill his glass but Ishbel caught his hand.

'What if I gave you a reason to live?'

'And what would that be?'

'What if I tell you I know where your granddaughter is?'

Scud struck her across the face. 'Stop it,' he hissed. Despite his weakened state his blow had clout. 'They're all dead.'

'Reinya isn't and I know where she is.' She held a hand to her hot face. She wanted to hit him back but he looked like he had been through enough. 'And I know how to get her back, Scud.'

Sorlie

The groaning of the bulkhead was a whisper compared to the shrieks of the three hundred escaped prisoners crammed into the submarine hold. Shelves erected onto the heavy metal torpedo racks provided makeshift beds. When we first descended into this sub the men had remained subdued, still dulled with the chemical cocktail Scud had administered before the escape.

The orderly fashion in which guard Ridgeway and I had led the men from their cells into the cooling system pipe, to the beach, was staggering. And even though each prisoner had a deactivated brain function that meant swimming was as a sunken stone, all but a few had calmly ploitered into the water to be picked up by boats and carried to three waiting subs. What wasn't obvious then was the agony they would suffer during submersion. The crew tried to contain the more frantic. Some men thankfully passed out, but that didn't stop the screams.

'Do something,' I said to Arkle, the crewman who seemed to be in charge.

'It won't be for much longer,' he calmly informed me. 'The sub needs to descend deep enough to remain hidden under the tow vessel's wake. Once we're down we can release some pressure.'

He stood with his back to the hatch and his hand on his holstered gun. 'Once the chemicals wear thin, the calm gives way to panic and claustrophobia.'

To look at the unruly rabble it was inconceivable that Vanora had a notion to form them into a revolutionary army, a secret one whose aim was to fight the terror of the Privileged regime, to put an end to native slavery and bring equality to the State of Esperaneo. I looked at this rag-tag mess of humanity, mottled and pigmented through years of DNA dilution experimentation. They couldn't fight a cold, never mind the might of the Esperaneo Military State.

We were heading north to Freedom, Vanora's stronghold, but as soon as the weight of the ocean washed over the decks and pressed us down, the flat palm of the oppression held us lower than prison incarceration had. Ridgeway, the Bas guard turned superhero, said it would take a day to reach Freedom. A day seemed too long. The stink was overpowering. My own clothes reeked of pisshap and the blood and grey matter of Davie's death.

Scud, the only success of the experiment, the only one who truly became Privileged had chosen to stay behind with the twelve drugged guards and the decaying mess of the dead tyrant who caused all this misery. Ishbel would get him out. She had to; why else was she there? The drugged guards would have recovered from their nightcap. Satan's truth, what made Scud want to stay? It wasn't that great being Privileged.

Someone in the corner was spewing in a bucket held by a crewman. Look at them. Vanora had wanted the prisoners released but still they're guarded. Arkle stood smaller than Ridgeway and even though he was Privileged he seemed to give the Bas his place. Ridgeway led the escape but would they see it that way? He was still a guard. Uncle Kenneth travelled on a trawler. All right for him, lording it up there, the compensation for living in a cave for twenty-odd years and not being subjected to the Universal Chipping Programme. Even though our chips were short range, if we were above ground, they would be lighting up command centres all over the State to the point of fuse blowing. We remained undetected underwater and the sub-mariners were busy systematically working their way down the torpedo deck, deactivating the prisoners' chips. No longer prisoners, soon to be an army. Scud had even assigned leaders for the breakout. Where were they now? They had disappeared into this great big, anonymous, needy mass that was at last starting to quieten.

Hours passed in grumblings. Rations were handed out and squabbled over. Groups huddled in corners, cliques formed. Some sort of alchemy was at work as assortments of bodies gravitated, whispering. Some stayed alone, sitting on bunks, knees pulled to chests, staring with murderous distorted eyes towards Ridgeway. One man stepped forward, brazen faced but was dragged back by a gentling hand. Ridgeway walked the length of the torpedo hall.

'Screw.'

'What's he doing here?

'He won't be here long.'

'Bas traitor.'

'Davie's bitch.'

The insults bounced off his back. It was like listening to a giant centipede waking from a hundred year sleep, shaking out its long scaly body, rattling its legs out ready to stamp on whatever lay in its way. The crewmen who weren't deactivating chips stood round the chamber, equally spaced, watching. Ridgeway stood straight and worked his face into calm.

Metal rungs, bolted to the bulkhead, supported the men's bunks. I had an idea.

'Give me your gun, Ridgeway,' I said. 'I need to sort this.'

'Are you mad? Let the crew deal with them. They're restless enough without you wading in.'

'Someone has to do something before there's a mutiny or massacre.'

Ridgeway pulled back his shoulders in that way he does, but I could see from the pinks of his eyes that fear lay just below the surface. But there was something else. He looked ready to drop; I guessed he hadn't fully recovered from his near-death tumble down the cliff before the escape.

'Trust me, Ridgeway,' I said in a clear voice. There would be no whispering in this camp. Whispering was for sneaks and cowards.

As I took the gun I noticed some of the prisoners eyeing it, eyeing me.

There was a box bolted to the middle of the hall that served as a makeshift store for extra life jackets. A vessel this size was only meant to hold a fraction of the men. The cold gun was heavier than expected and I had to heave it high enough to rattle the muzzle on the box. That got minimal attention. I ran the muzzle along the rungs of the bunk casings. A great cacophony sounded, louder than I expected. It tore into the delicate ears of the men, some held their hands up in protection, many growled louder and stepped up to meet me. My back ran with sweat.

'Right, men, stand to attention,' I blustered.

Their recovery was swift. A guard stepped forward but another held him back with a smirk and a nod towards me.

The first snigger happened just to my right but soon it snowballed around the hall, gaining mirth and momentum as it went, until some guffawed. My face whooshed in heat. This wasn't happening. I was still a Privileged in their eyes and they should obey.

'I said, stand to attention.'

'Or what, small fry?' a voice sounded from halfway down the hall. This wasn't the way it happened at Academy training camp. I saw Ridgeway move to join me but Arkle stayed him and took his place.

'What are you doing?' Arkle asked through gritted teeth.

I looked toward Ridgeway: a Bas, a foreigner, neither Privileged nor native. Up until a couple of days ago he was guarding these men and now we were literally all in the same boat. Escapees from a prison, fugitives from the State. I was half native but these men didn't know that. To them I was Davie's grandson, a full Privileged, one of the ruling classes

19

to be served and obeyed by these native slaves. The body of laughing men who stood before us were obviously native full bloods despite the DNA tampering they had undergone.

Arkle's voice was loud enough for all to hear and yet soft, unthreatening. 'These men have been through enough,' he said to me. 'They are tired, they are restless.' He turned to the men. 'You only have a few more hours until we reach our destination. Settle down, get some sleep. The Bas guard will not be harmed.' It was as if he were administering another drug.

Someone murmured, 'Aye well, it's been a while since we've had a laugh, give us that, son.'

Arkle nodded to the speaker as he took my arm and led me back to Ridgeway.

'Ridgeway was in danger. I had to do something.'

'And you are the tyrant's grandson. Why should they obey you?'

'I'm Privileged!'

'And your point is?'

'What the snaf is that supposed to mean?' But Arkle walked away without answering.

A few prisoners lingered in the hall, snarling at me like bears on a chain. Most were herded back to their bunks by crew. One sub-mariner, a native, stepped forward. He had two shiny buttons on his cuffs where Arkle had three.

'OK, men, you've had your laugh, now step back to your bunks,' he said to the bears. 'You'll be organised and debriefed when we arrive.'

As he turned and swung by me he grabbed my tunic and held it a little too tightly.

'Try that again and you will spend the rest of the journey in the head.'

'I was only trying to get some order.'

'Aye, well, that's why we're here, laddie. Vanora isn't dumb, you know. She knows how it is. They'll be disciplined when we get there.'

'How much longer?' My schoolboy shit-whiny voice rose. I checked it.

He consulted his communicator. 'Soon. And you know what that means.' He tapped his ear.

The crew knew what was coming and this time they were prepared.

Most of the men did exactly as they were instructed to do. One ugly guy scarred permanently from ear to ear with a smiley, about Pa's age but taller, strutted along the deck. A submariner shouldered his zap wand but said nothing.

'Hey, boy,' Smiler shouted over to me. 'What's it like to change sides?'

'Leave him alone, he's just a kid,' a small skinny guy with tufted white and black hair chipped in.

I tried to stand straight but the weight of the past few hours withered me in my boots. These guys didn't know I'd watched my grandfather blow his brains out and wouldn't care if they did, in fact there would be celebration. Smiler took no heed.

'Ah only asked a question.'

'Don't you know who I am?' I couldn't help myself.

'Aye, evil bastard's grandson.'

'Vanora's grandson,' I threw back.

The guy invaded my space, his rank breath pushing me back. 'Aye well, we'll have to see what colours you fly, won't we?' There was no mirth in his eyes but his knifed-on smile unsettled me. Then he tilted his head to one side and was about to say something else when a commotion sounded behind him and he shot his hands up to his ears.

Groans rumbled. A sub-mariner led one man to lie down in a foetal position. Two others worked up and down the hall injecting a clear liquid into the necks of each prisoner. My rage bubbled; if they had sedative all along why leave it to the last minute to use? Some pushed their dose away, others helped restrain the more rowdy. The groaning soared to the point where I too pushed my hands over my ears to deaden the pain.

Slowly the noise subsided to the low howl of three hundred stranded souls grieving a massacre of their native peoples. The sound I'd heard that first night I spent on Black Rock all those months ago. Before I knew of the DNA experiments; before I discovered I was not a full Privileged. Before I knew the truth about Vanora, Kenneth and Ishbel; the new dysfunctional family to replace my dead parents. Super.

Soon the sub settled and Arkle led me to the conning tower and for the first time in twenty-four hours we breathed fresh air. I blinked at the brightness. The sky was wide and even though the sun hid inland, the light was startling. We floated on a body of water surrounded by towering cliffs that seemed to rise out of the sea. Ahead of us were two other submarines still on tow. On one of the trawlers, a figure stood madly waving. It was Kenneth, my new-found uncle, kin who had been installed in a cave, twenty-odd years ago by Vanora, to plan this escape. How was he feeling now? Judging by his windmilling arms, he seemed elated. Maybe even a little, what was the word – tipsy?

The air tasted sweet, clean. The sky had breaks of blue slashed across it. Soon we would be meeting Vanora again.

Ishbel

Scud was more sozzled than she first thought. One minute he was squinting at her, next he was slumped in the chair snoring. She had to get him out. She filled her backpack with books.

'Come on, we need to get moving.' She slapped his face but his head lolled. 'How long before the guards wake up?'

'Uh?'

She had no clue where the drugged guards would be but hoped Scud had secured them well. Slap. 'Scud.'

Was it only yesterday when she visited here with Vanora and Merj and planted the drugs for Scud to find and use on the guards? They'd tried to pass the thought map plan to Sorlie, but Davie was having none of it and kept Sorlie distant. Vanora had created a scene, being deliberately obtuse with Ishbel – a little game she was becoming a little too fond of. Ishbel had blotted her nonsense out by studying the books. Selecting the ones she would take when she returned. She had known she would return.

The rucksack was too heavy so she removed a couple of paperbacks before hoisting Scud onto her shoulder.

'Uh, uh.' His hand gestured wildly, drool spilling from his mouth. His book lay on the table. Ishbel dumped him, bagged the book and hauled him onto her shoulder again. Scud's book weighed a ton, she knew she should ditch some others but couldn't bear to.

'Goodbye, dear library.' She doubted she would ever see its like again.

Even in his emaciated state, Scud was still a dead weight; she almost had to drag him the last few metres to the reactor room. She shoved the book bag down the pipe first, then Scud, praying he wouldn't land on it and do some damage.

Scud and the books sprawled on the sand. Ishbel twisted to project her landing away from them. Morning light lazed on the horizon, as usual the cloud cover greyed the day. The beach showed signs of great commotion. Runnels left by the army's feet still raked the shore, even though the tide had tried to smooth out the turbulent sand. Tides were like that, wash and repair.

Scud rolled onto his knees, cradled his head in his hands and his feet dug into the sand. When he lifted his head his face split into a grimace and tears ran.

'See. I told you. Isn't it great to be free?' Ishbel tried to smile but she could have punched him. They'd wasted too much time. When he started shivering she took her waterproof off and pulled it over the wasted body rattling inside the stolen guard's uniform.

'How? Get off?' he slurred.

'Same way I got here. Same way Sorlie and Kenneth got to this beach.' She pointed up. 'Along the cliff.'

'Where are we?' His wide eyes were fearful. 'Sorlie. Davie.' He began to scramble on the sand. He was ravelled with drunkenness or shock, hard to tell. Ishbel dug a vitpill from her pocket.

'Here, take this, it'll help sober you up.'

He shook his head. 'No, the island? Got tae get off the island.'

'I've a boat. I stowed away on the boat Merj used when he tried to abduct Sorlie.' But of course Scud didn't know. 'At first I didn't know what Merj was up to, but he'd been acting strange ever since he'd met Sorlie in Davie's library, so I tracked him and stowed on the boat. I'd planned to intervene but Sorlie did a pretty good job of putting Merj in his place. I just gave him a helping hand.' She laughed at that. It had been such a long time since she'd laughed. What was wrong with her?

'What's funny?'

'While Merj was winded I threw a butterfly bomb in his path. It blew his hand off.'

Scud winced. 'That's funny?'

Ishbel shrugged. 'Come on, let's get going. The vitpill's kicked in now.'

Scud was surprisingly nimble on the narrow ledge.

'Where's he now? This Merj,' he asked as he clambered past a rock fall.

'Dead, probably. At least he looked that way when I left him.'

'And you didn't try tae help him?'

'Why should I help him? Vanora shunted me sideways to promote him.' She worked hard to keep the bitterness from her voice. Natives were not permitted to show such emotion, yet who was going to report her now? Not Scud. 'Come on, the boat will still be outside Kenneth's cave.'

'You're weird, Ishbel, d'ye know that?'

'You know nothing.'

Scud stood still for a minute, his back pressed to the steep cliffside. He seemed to be contemplating. 'Yeah, you're right, ah know nothing. One minute a god, the next nothing.'

'Look, I'm sorry, it's just complicated, that's all. Come on, let's get off this island.'

The boat was gone. The shore came into view as they reached Kenneth's clifftop garden but there was no sign of either Merj or his boat. Even his detached hand was missing.

'Damn and blast it to hell.'

Scud shrugged and sat on the cliff edge. 'So what's plan B?' He seemed almost pleased he didn't have to leave, but Ishbel's brows pringled as she clocked the area searching for answers.

'We use Kenneth's cave, see what we can come up with. If the Military come we'll have plenty of warning.'

'What if the guards set out the seekers? They won't stay knocked out forever.'

'Didn't you lock them up?'

Scud's chin bumped off his chest.

'Unbelievable.' She bit her lip. 'We have to take that chance. How long do we have?'

'Another hour max.'

At the cave entrance Scud dug his heels into the sand. 'Ah'm not going in there.'

'Why?'

He sighed. 'Get real, Ishbel. Ah'll stay out here and enjoy the view.' He sat on a rock facing the sea. They were silent for a few minutes until Ishbel noticed something different in Scud's posture. His shoulders were tense, he was crying again.

'Aw, Scud, don't.'

'Tell me,' was all he said. Ishbel disappeared into the cave and came back carrying skins. She draped one around Scud and settled back on her rock huddled in the none too sweet-smelling skin.

'She's on a prison ship.'

The groan that escaped Scud tugged at her gut. 'How?'

'Scud, your daughter had an addiction problem, you know that.'

'Tig was getting treatment. One of the communications told me that. Vanora had fixed it, but something went wrong. The last ah heard of them, five years ago it was, they had both died of a virus.'

Ishbel sighed. 'That was a lie.'

'A lie?' She could see he didn't believe her. 'Why would Vanora lie to me?'

'Because she needed you here and focused. It was for the cause.'

Anger flashed across his face then retreated as quickly as a wave from the shore. 'If that was a lie then what's the truth?' He rubbed and rubbed his hands down his thighs. 'It's cruel, that's what.' His head went down. She waited. He thumped the sand and sniffed his snot back. 'Are you going tae lie tae me too?'

'No. Never.'

'How do ah know?'

'I'm not Vanora. I'm in deep trouble just being here. She could have me put to death if she chose.'

'But she won't.'

'No.' Ishbel whispered. 'Look Scud, you have to understand what it's like now for natives out here. Life is harder than ever. So many purged, abused, starved.'

'Huh. Hard? Ye've no idea what a hard life is like.'

She sighed. 'No point swapping hardships. The truth is, Tig fell deeper into her rotten world. Reinya cared for her in the Urbans, but Tig got into trouble. Stole some Mash, didn't pay her dealer, got beat up. I don't know, loads of bad stuff.' Ishbel tried to ignore Scud's pinched face; she had to get this tale over with and the quicker the better for them to move on. It was like being back in the Jeep, telling Sorlie his parents were dead and reclassified as traitors. Watching his snivelling pain. She knew she was being cruel but it was the only way she knew how to do it.

'She was sentenced to two years on a prison ship. Reinya was fourteen and was to be taken to the teenage training camp, but she didn't want to leave her mother. She snuck into the Transport with Tig, disguised as a boy. Somehow managed to make it look as though she was shackled to her. They both ended up in the prison ship. You know they aren't too particular about IDs at that stage.'

'We have tae get them out.'

Ishbel placed a hand over Scud's but he snatched his back. 'No sympathy, just tell me.'

She stood and rubbed the palms of her hands, trying to summon some warmth. 'Tig died after only six weeks. Her chemical withdrawal was too severe – they did nothing for her except to give her more of a kicking.' She bit her lip. 'Reinya's alone on the ship with the rest of the wretched.'

Scud was surprisingly calm. 'How do you know all this?'

'You know Vanora has spies everywhere.' Ishbel gave a little cough, 'And I saw them.'

'Tell me.'

'When I brought Sorlie here, we stopped off at the port. Vanora asked me to check they were alright. They were there, we saw them before they boarded Dead Man's Ferry.'

'Why would she ask you tae do that?'

'I'm not sure – Vanora's a control freak. Maybe there was another reason.'

Scud thumped his head with his fist and Ishbel grabbed it, stopped him hurting himself, held it tight.

'They were there on the quay. Reinya was unrecognizable as a girl and she looked tough. She's OK, Scud. All reports indicate she's OK.'

She placed a hand on his shoulder but he pushed her off. 'We'll get her back, I promise,' she said.

Scud's tears dried on his cheeks. With one finger to his right then left nostril he ejected his snot onto the sand, mopping up the dew with the heel of his hand.

'We were so proud of Tig, her mother and I, even though we were only kids ourselves when we had her. We didn't know things would turn out the way they did. One day we had our whole life ahead of us. Ah had a good teaching job at the University of Urban G, and my Jeanie would stay at home with Tig.'

He turned his ragged mutated face towards Ishbel. 'They took me for speaking out. Did you know that historians are the best predictors of the future? We can see the past mistakes and see them happening again. It was all there, you know. Great blind spots in history. Just look back at good people who allowed atrocities tae happen. We're all responsible. The signs were there; the mounting hatred of the immigrants, the growing wealth gap, the total disregard for people's human rights, the media.' He spat. 'The media. Why didn't ah believe they would go so far as tae imprison the academics, the writers? Had it not happened before, many times? The purge and DNA classification, the separation of Privilege and native classes. Ah was blind. Of course they wanted rid of the native intelligentsia. It's a wonder they didn't kill us there and then.'

He gulped a huge breath. 'After ah was taken Jeanie went back tae work at an oldies' care centre, but that closed when the oldies were cleansed from the system. Jeanie and Tig were moved tae a major native camp in the east. Tig grew up in a refugee camp, did you know that?' Ishbel nodded. 'No wonder it all went wrong.' The tears started again but Ishbel held her sympathy.

'We'll get Reinya back. I just need to work out how to get us off this island.'

She retreated into the cave to search through Kenneth's pitiful possessions, leaving Scud with his tears, memories and guilt. She studied the wall paintings and the slaughtered animals hung to cure. Over twenty years her brother Kenneth had called this cave home. In that time he'd accumulated a number of communication devices, each superseding the last; upgraded models, dropped off courtesy of Vanora's boffin disciples. This resource-poor world had still not rid itself of the disposables when it came to communication.

Ishbel knew she need only contact Vanora and they would be off the island. Her communicator had been buzzing red hot until she cut the signal. But then what? Back to base and possibly solitary confinement for a while as punishment? And what fate for Scud and Reinya?

She spread the assortment of devices on the sandy ground and tested each one in turn. Most had been cannibalised for some other use. The prototype tympan was intact, she could contact the moorloggers and still stay undetected by Vanora. One fleet had taken the subs north but she knew of another in the Southern Minch. They could arrive by next nightfall, she was sure. She just hoped the authorities didn't get here first. Of course the guards would wake, but it would take them a while to gather their few brain cells together to work out a plan.

She sat on the sand and sent the signal. But the words churning in her mind were 'Where the hell is Merj?'

Sorlie

She wasn't there to meet us. The great Vanora was absent. Even my tyrant grandfather had met me on my arrival at Black Rock.

The air was so clear and moist it felt like a fresh water cloth had been washed over my face and wrung out in my lungs. Smells of cut grass and salty seaware dizzied my senses.

Arkle ferried me from the flotilla first. Special treatment. Ridgeway and the prisoners remained on board in quarantine until the native doctors checked them. There was no sign of Kenneth and no sign of Ishbel.

It was only now, as he stood by my shoulder, I realised the Privileged Arkle had shadowed me on the journey. We arrived at the jetty at the northern tip of a fjord. A settlement was dwarfed by the steep mountains that hunched over it like a protective cloak. A cultivated land basin lay in the palm of this great amphitheatre. Modified green and golden crops waved and flattened in the sea breeze even though we were still only in the second quarter. Small wooden houses, painted in varying bright colours, scattered around with no formality or order. Species of domestic farm animals, banned by the Land Reclaimists, grazed in safety; some corralled behind fences, while others dotted the lower reaches of the hill side. Kitchen crops grew within hedged fields and my mouth flooded with the delicious anticipation of real food. A rusty engine chunked back and forth in a pasture, ploughing furrows. This looked no more like a revolutionary stronghold than Kenneth's cave had. A chugging fishing trawler wove through the gaps in the subs as if the unloading of these sea monsters was an everyday occurrence. Maybe it was. When the trawler reached the jetty an old man with scraggy beard and ragged coat jumped, with rope in hand, onto the boards beside us. He had the boat secure in seconds and hailed to Arkle in a strange dialect, all yows and hows, to my ears. Arkle nodded and said.

'They'll be gone again by nightfall, Magnus.'

The old man grinned and flapped the comment back. Arkle tapped my shoulder then marched me towards a stone mansion sat back from the rest. It was the style of building demolished in the early years of the Land Reclaimist Regime for being energy inefficient. In the same way that realisation had struck me on Black Rock, I saw there were pockets in Esperaneo that defied the Regime's rules and worked outside their control. Was this why Vanora chose this strange place as her base?

I had no words, no cheek or questions. The fear I felt when I'd first arrived at Black Rock was missing, but the anticipation of what would come next was just as strong. I looked sideways at Arkle's Privileged profile. What was he doing here? He seemed kind, but there was an untouchable strength about him. Maybe it was in his quiet voice, the few powerful words he spoke to tame a volatile crowd. It was only after we climbed the stone steps and Arkle opened the front door with an old key that I found my voice.

'Where's the surveillance here?'

'There is no State surveillance.'

No State surveillance, but he hadn't answered my question. In the Academy we were taught to stop this type of avoidance from a lesser operative. But he wasn't lesser. My Privileged status had been diluted by a tainted ancestry – Vanora. And yet she was boss here. This hierarchy thing was too confusing for my screwed-up genes. As I followed him through the doorway I felt the roof crowd my head. It took a while for my eyes to adjust to the dim light. Stags' heads hung suspended and defeated in the dark hall. Halfway up the hall, a huge gothic fireplace, the kind shown in old horror-casters and much larger than the one in Davie's library, stood cold and unlit. I was led past this into a room larger than our home unit at the Base. This was the kitchen. As Arkle slid back a door, I expected the smell of cooking, but there was none. The rush of musty air cloaked me like earth furrowing over my bones. We descended narrow runged steps into an orange glow of emergency lights.

'Move away from the steps,' Arkle instructed when we reached the bottom.

He pushed the staircase from behind. As soon as it began to move, the wall behind opened. I giggled, I couldn't help it. It was like another scene from a horror-caster. Had Vanora spent her years in exile curled up on a futon, munching popcorn, watching horrors and designing the architecture of her hidden base? Disappointment flashed through me as we stepped into a lift. It creaked and groaned in its descent.

'Don't tell me, an old mine shaft.'

'Why would they build a house over an old mine shaft?' he said, ignoring my mock. 'The house was here first, has been for centuries. The underground base has only been here twenty years. Iceberg architecture – all the rage in the twenties.' That put me back in my box.

'How long have you been in the army?' I asked. He raised an eyebrow, no doubt suspecting another mock.

'I was born into this revolutionary army. I was educated into it.' He looked into his past and must have decided I needed more. 'Vanora saved my parents.'

'Why did they need saved? You're Privileged.'

'Not all Privileged are equal.' And I knew by the square of his shoulders that was all I was going to get on that subject.

We walked through the tunnel for at least a couple of kiloms. The earthworks were supported by humungous beams the size of a Jeep and made from some unidentified material, neither wood nor steel, concrete maybe. At last we reached what looked like an underground cavern and I almost expected to find a lab with a smoking cauldron and a monster with bolts through his neck strapped to a table. But the deeper we walked the higher the ceiling became, until we were in a cathedralesque hall circled with too many people to count, all dressed in identical blue suits. They formed a protective membrane around a nucleus. In the epicentre a transparent ticker wall stretched the width of a room the size of a soccer field. Text rolled across it at a speed too fast to be read by any human. It was unnerving to see those messages. I squinted to read. Impossible. She sat behind a desk, dwarfed by the ticker wall. Dressed in scarlet like some ancient cardinal with the majesty of her empire flickering away behind her. I nipped to tell her red clashed with her skin tone but held my wheesht in this majestic setting.

Wisps of grey hair fizzed around her face but most was tamed by a black ribbon. Red earrings dangled from elongated lobes, a matching tympan protruded from one ear, pince-nez, the type my grandfather favoured, perched on her nose like some fashion accessory. Where was the frail old being who had visited my grandfather's library a couple of days ago? She tapped her fingers on some device on the desk and spoke into the air. I waited for her to acknowledge me. She knew I was there. She footered her hair and batted her eyelashes. 'Affected' Ma would have called her. At last she looked up and those faded green eyes told me it was the same being. Her smile touched her lips and I waited for it to reach her eyes. It never did.

'Well, young man, you've made an excellent start on your revolutionary career. Davie dispatched. Good job.'

Ishbel

Daylight crept over the horizon and with it came the anticipation of sighting the short lights of a moorlogger trawling the depth for a pittance of fuel-picking.

'You hungry?' Ishbel asked Scud.

While they waited for the weak dawn and the moorlogger to reach them she made a stew with the rabbit she'd found hanging in the cave and some stored carrots from Kenneth's clifftop garden crop. He didn't need them now and waste was a crime. She wondered how the escapees were fairing. Kenneth would be well installed in his mother's lair by now and with that thought she felt a stab of unease. She had been her mother's first lieutenant all her life until the charming Merj had entered the scene and stolen Vanora's attention. The old ways were still very much with Vanora and she could imagine her bumping Kenneth, the eldest son, up the pecking order. Where would that leave Ishbel? Nursemaid yet again to Sorlie?

For years Ishbel had been supplying her caveman half-brother Kenneth with preserved food from the Privileged kitchen but she had never met him. She shouldn't have come for Scud. She should be back in Vanora's northern kingdom. Her punishment for deserting was sure to be severe.

They slept, they ate a few morsels. Ishbel fiddled with the tympan. Where was the moorlogger? How many more hours could they risk hiding in the cave? She heated the stew, anything to pass the hours.

'I know this stew isn't up to the usual cuisine you're used to in prison, but you have to try and eat something.' At least he snorted at the irony. He took the bowl and placed a smidgen on his lips but she suspected it was only to shut her up.

At last she saw them. The moorlogger lights seemed hardly to be moving but her shortwave tympan message told her they were headed her way.

'What shall we eat when we're on the boat?' she coaxed. 'I bet they have fresh fish, they always do. I haven't had fresh fish since the beginning of last year.'

'Ah haven't tasted fish for twenty years.' There was an edge to his voice. It wasn't self-pity or bitterness, more like resignation.

'I know, but you're free now, there'll be many feasts ahead and soon Reinya will join you. You can teach her to cook if she doesn't already know how. The young don't know how to cook these days, even the ones in domestic service. It's shocking.' She knew she was babbling but with one eye on the stationary boat she could see something was wrong and didn't want Scud to pick up her concern.

'Aye, and then what?' Scud said.

'Say again?'

He sighed. 'Ah said "then what?" We get Reinya back, ah teach her tae cook, then what?'

'Let's not worry about that. Let's concentrate on now, on getting off and getting her back.'

Scud shook his head. 'No wonder Vanora chose you as her first lieutenant.'

It was Ishbel's turn to snort at the irony.

'Second. I'm her second lieutenant. Merj is… was her first lieutenant.'

Stupid old woman, falling for his sugary charms. Ishbel didn't admit this to Scud, nor the embarrassing fact that at first she too had fallen for him. Her focus was sharper than that of the old woman. She had soon noticed the perfect mask slip.

'Stupid old woman made a fool of herself.' She didn't mean to say this out loud.

'Don't be so sure.'

'What do you mean?'

'From what ah've heard Vanora does nothing without a reason,' Scud said.

They looked back at the lights.

'How long? It seems tae be turning,' he said.

Ishbel stood up. She touched the tympan. 'They've cut the signal. Something's wrong.'

A squadron of lights danced from the southern horizon, not slow boat lights but…

'Oh no.'

The sky exploded in a volcanic burst of light, showers of gold and red shot through the air, blinding them. When they could look again they saw a cascade of light falling to the sea, like molten magma laying down a carpet of fire, consuming everything in its path. It petered out leaving no trace of the exterminated moorlogging trawler. All that was left of the encounter was the retreating lights of the State fighters.

'That's why they turned, they didn't want to give us away.' Ishbel shoved her shaking hands in her pockets. 'It's not fair. They had no guns to protect them. Someone betrayed them. Someone told the State the other moorloggers had helped in the prison escape and if they knew that, they knew the prison was empty…' Her mouth was dry. Those poor souls.

'We have to get out of here,' she said. Scud stared at the now black sea in shock. She looked around. Where could they go?

'Come on – the supply drop off point is on the north of the island. No one else knows about that except the moorloggers and they're not telling anyone.' She helped Scud to his feet and threw the food on the sand for the gulls to enjoy. She watched the carrots scatter like jewels, such a waste.

'Should have eaten your carrots because we're going to have to travel overland in the semi-dark.'

'Old wives' tales,' she heard him murmur, but was more

interested in the other sound she heard. An approaching Transport. So, they had finally decided to come check things out.

Ishbel shoved Scud up the gully to the clifftop.

'They'll check the penitentiary first before coming for us. Only the escapees knew you had stayed behind and no one knows I'm here, not even Vanora. It'll take them a bit to check the cam-record.'

They stumbled along the path, Ishbel often having to drag Scud over difficult terrain, he was so weak and unused to the elements. She would have preferred to carry him but protected his pride; offering a helping hand now and then was better than nothing. As the Transport landed on the H pad on top of the penitentiary crown the perimeter lights switched on, telling them that the guards must have decided to play their part. The light ranged the countryside, but the pair were well outside its beam, they would be OK as long as the guards didn't send out the seekers.

Ishbel had memorised the paths of the island map she was given along with her first assignment. The still Kenneth used to distil his illegal Mash huddled in the crook of a stream junction. The fire long extinguished, it sat desolate and hungry-looking despite its pot belly. Ishbel couldn't help but chuckle.

'That man had some willpower not to drink himself to death in his lonely cave.'

Scud scratched his head. 'Don't know what other damage he did tae himself though, do you?'

She had no desire to explore that riddle. 'Do you hear it?'

'What?'

'Flying seekers. The guards must have launched them. Robotic seekers designed to detect heat and sound. They must know we're here now.'

Scud put his hands up to his ears waiting for their piercing shriek to assault him. 'They'll find us, defo.'

38

Ishbel now knew what she had suspected all along to be true: somehow Merj was still alive. They had all left him for dead on the beach, and now she cursed herself; she should have finished him off. He must have guessed where the butterfly bomb had come from because it was her favoured weapon of choice, after all. The seekers weren't after Scud, they were after her.

'We have to get in the water.'

'Ah can't swim, you know that.'

'You don't need to swim, you only need to stay under the surface until we're clear.' She took her belt off and tied it around Scud's waist. He dug his heels in the peat.

She tugged him on. 'Come, they'll be on us soon.'

'Leave me.'

She dragged him and they both knew she had the strength to make it happen. They ran to the drop-off point. A maddening amount of rubbish was strewn around. Kenneth should have been more careful.

The seeker whirrie increased, heading their way. Scud fell to his knees trying to cover his ears again. The sound was designed to hurt normal hearing to the point of bleeding. Ishbel couldn't imagine how it must be for Scud. She looped her belt round his waist and lifted him into the water with her. He splashed and lashed out and she tightened her grip. She gasped. The water was freezing.

'Take a deep breath.' He shook his head.

'Take a deep breath or you'll drown,' she growled. She waited until she saw him breathe in and pushed his head under the water before he had a chance to think. The action meant she didn't take a deep enough breath herself. She lost air bubbles with the exertion of having to struggle to stay Scud's panic. The cold dragged the feeling from her feet and hands into her core. She almost lost her grip.

She counted the seconds. Her head pounded, her lungs burned. They surfaced together. She shook her frozen fingers until they stung. Scud gulped a mouthful of air, she pushed him under again. In the split second she'd surfaced she calculated the seeker sound was retreating. Ten seconds later she released Scud and held his shaking body to her to calm and warm him. She listened properly this time and there was no doubt the seekers had passed, but the sound had been replaced by another. An alien sound could be detected over Scud's gasping and spewing. Turbulence frothed the water, whipping their legs. Waves churned in a peculiar motion. She dragged the now-unconscious Scud out of the water, but as she pulled him onto the shore a small pin light reflected on the ground in front of her sending her heart plummeting. A two-pronged attack – clever. Now there was no escape. Something loomed up behind them and Ishbel had no desire to face her fate.

When she did pluck up the courage to look, she tasted the salt that cracked the corners of her mouth as she grinned. In front of her was no military vehicle, but a small yellow craft that looked like a toy. A craft that had been extinct since Loch Ness had been drained and the monster myth debunked once and for all. The turret hatch of the mini sub popped and the head of the wily Noiri man, Dawdle, peeked out.

'Well, fancy meetin' yous here,' he said.

Ishbel felt a lump rise in her throat and couldn't trust herself to speak.

'Better get yer arse in here quick, Ish, there's no other cavalry due fur at least another decade.'

Sorlie

The panopticon architecture raised goosebumps over my skin. The regal Vanora sat centre stage, her back to the ticker wall that spewed words no one seemed interested in reading. Who were the authors? Her disciples? Her Vanorettes? And what of these drones fussing about her like insects, what was their purpose in this communication fest?

A monitor wall, filling one quarter of the area, beamed images of many rooms within the complex. From one I could see the prisoners in what looked like a sports hall, lined up in an untidy drill formation, grouped with the same leaders Scud had designated for the escape. Their attempts at organisation were pretty shambolic. They were a rabble and rabbles need to be contained. But this time I would leave that job to someone else. My ears still burned with the scorching I'd received in the boat. Art of War lesson number one according to Sorlie Mayben – leave the organisation to someone else. If only Pa was still alive.

Vanora watched the scene in the sports hall bearing a look of almost contempt. This was the army whose release she had planned and seen executed. She should be pleased. When she stood I realised just how tiny she was.

'Come, Sorlie,' she snipped, and left by a side door.

As we walked deeper into the network of tunnels we passed many open rooms where frantic activity took place. Laboratories, not with smoking cauldrons but with captured animals, electrical experiments. One room behind glass blinked white with no apparatus, two people in white overalls, bent heads almost touching, looked down a tube. This was all familiar, I had watched them from the centre of Vanora's panopticon – glass rooms with no escape from her scrutiny. That was what Arkle meant, no state surveillance but plenty of Vanora's eyes.

Each time we encountered one of her operatives they would stop and bow. I'm sure the smile on Vanora's lips and the slight lift of her hand bestowed more to them than a brief encounter. Creepy or what? As each operative rose from their bow they gave me a shifty look as if to say, 'Don't think you're special, boy.' Paranoia, my next big thing!

The sports hall was closer than I expected and another huge cavern. When we entered operatives stationed in each corner bowed and muttered a chant as if a divine god had moved in its heaven. She glided in and seemed to tower in her tiny frame. The prisoners shrank into the walls.

'Come, Sorlie.' She snapped her finger to me. 'We need to get the men organised.' I was beginning to think she had forgotten about me and now wished she had. These guys were going to rip the piss out of me. Why wasn't she using some lieutenant to help her? It wasn't as if she lacked help, there were hundreds of operatives working away.

When she stretched her neck the red Hebridean hood slipped from her head and hung low on her straight back. Her clothes were crisp and neat, the red stood out in bright contrast against the washed-out black the prisoners wore. The smell of lavender wafted from her in the same way it had from Ma and I wondered at the aroma's significance. Had the scent been passed on from mother to daughter in some secret code? The only difference was that Vanora was here while Ma's body, blown apart by the bomb she strapped to herself, was lying in some foreign land, never to return home with the honours she deserved. Her Hero in Death status meant the State had forced her into a suicide mission. The smell of lavender always reminded me of Ma. Maybe that was all it was; Vanora's intention to unsettle me. Well, it worked

As we moved further into the hall, the rows of ineffective guards stood aside. The rabble wasn't as bad as I first thought from the monitor. The guard, Ridgeway, lurked to one side of the hall. He seemed to have been designated a special role.

'Hey look,' said Smiler. 'It's the wee guy wi the rattle.' His smile stretched to grotesque proportions. 'Where's yer rattle now, wee man. Found yer granny, huv ye?' My face flushed hot but I stayed schtum. Vanora pulled the twin of Davie's ancient revolver from her pocket and pointed it at Smiler. Although his smile remained scarred to his face the set of his brow scowled. Vanora held the gun steady. The silence in the hall hummed. I ticked off seconds in my head. Sweat trickled down the hollow of my spine.

She fired – Fuck! The bodies jumped as one. Smiler remained on his feet, she'd shot above his head. The smell of piss permeated the room. One of the leaders stepped forward. There was a murmur of catcalls.

'Wee sook.'

'Aye, teacher's pet.'

'Aw, who's a pretty boy then?'

Ten or twelve men stepped in his wake, heads bowed to chest. Many behind them laughed in the face of this old woman who had orchestrated their release.

'Is it Vanora then?'

'Aye, boys, it is. It's that wummin, the one called Vanora, she's gonnae save us apparuntly.' The grubby faced speaker turned to her grinning. 'That no so, hen?' They seemed to have forgotten she had a revolver in her hand.

'Whit ye gonnae save us wi?' a ratty man spat through his protruding teeth.

'Make us a pot o' soup.' Someone shouted from the ranks. That raised a laugh.

Another voice, 'Mebbes she's gonnae knit us some decent claes.'

'Aye, come oan, hen, these overalls ur aw scratchie, make us itch.'

'Aye, we aw huv itches that need scratched.' There was widespread sniggering.

Vanora blanked, no scowl or smile, just boredom. None of her soldiers moved to defend her. It was like waiting for a pesky hoard of midges to be blown off course in a breeze. She fired again, closer to the heads this time. She took a barely discernible breath and said in a clear, even voice that travelled to the back of the hall.

'I want you lead men to take your battalion and organise them into two columns. Then I want you to escort them to the quartermasters.' She pointed to a row of tables at the back of the hall where grey-uniformed men and women sat nursing piles of communicators.

'I want you to answer their questions and then they will assign you to your task division. It may take a while so I would appreciate your patience.' She smiled to them. 'The rewards will be worth it.'

The shuffling began again. 'Whit, we no gettin soup then?'

More sniggering then an angry voice sounded, 'Whit task division? We no gettin guns? We no gonnae fight?'

'We were promised jetpacks.' More sniggering.

'Aye, whaur's oor yooniforms.'

Some leaders did as Vanora asked and stepped their men forward. Smiler winked at me before moving into Vanora's space. She didn't even flinch.

'Whit if we dinnae like the task division we're given?' He nodded round the room. 'In fact, whit if we dinnae even want tae be in yer army.'

'If you didn't want to be here you should have stayed in the prison.'

'Aye right, hen.'

'Leave then.'

He looked a bit confused but the smile remained. 'Why should we dae whit you say?'

'You came on my ship, therefore you are in my army. Now take your men and report to the quartermaster.'

He smirked and looked round to his men but didn't move.

'Did you hear the order I gave?'

'Aye.'

'Did you understand it?'

'Aye.'

'Then obey it.' Her tone never quivered, low quiet and strong.

'Ah'm no takin orders fae an auld wummin.'

'So you heard and you understood but still won't obey?' She sounded like a Privileged.

'Aye.'

Vanora lifted the gun and shot Smiler between the eyes. He didn't even have a chance to look shocked. Spray peppered her face but she remained rooted, gun smoking. The rest of the men shook and puddled. I only just held it together.

'Anyone else want to disobey the order?' Vanora said as she lowered the gun to her side. The silence and stillness was complete, like a game of statues.

'Good,' she said and walked from the hall, leaving me behind with the sound of grandfather's mad mantra ringing in my head in harmony with the gunshot. 'Out of the frying pan into the fire.' She had just murdered someone in cold blood.

Ishbel

Scud slept in the bulkhead, curled into a foetal ball under the blanket Dawdle had handed out. Ishbel bit her fingernail and worried his ravaged, Privileged face hid more torture than he admitted to. Had she done the right thing by rescuing him? Not only had she risked her own future, she'd also put Scud through unnecessary pain. Now she had him, she'd no idea what to do with him. Even if he survived the trip north, would Vanora's disciples have the skill to reverse the damage done to his genes? He'd be better off dead. And yet the tug of her native ancestors told her their futures depended on Scud and his historical mind. History was important to the future – she just didn't know how.

While he slept, he had some peace. She stored her unease at his Privileged state in a safe place in her mind, because even though she'd worshipped him all her life, and Vanora had praised his sacrifice as a martyr, Ishbel now faced the reality of flesh and blood and she wasn't sure how trustworthy this new Scud was.

She pressed her head against the pilot seat and closed her eyes. It had been so much simpler being at the Military Base. OK she was a native and subjected to the usual verbal kicking of the Privileged turds, but all natives knew if you kept your head down and got on with things life wasn't so bad. Sorlie might have been an Academy brat but he was bearable – just.

Ishbel pulled her soaked neck-snood over her nose. The sub stank as if the air had been through a male changing room a thousand times. She heard Dawdle beside her, could feel his gaze on her and knew she had to face him. She opened her eyes. He handed her a brew as the mini-sub manoeuvred through the currents on auto route. His hands shook even though his face looked calm

'What happened to the moorlogger?' Ishbel had hoarded the question as long as she dared.

'Betrayed, weren't they?' He glanced at Scud. Weird, did she imagine it or had that look towards Scud held something more than a casual glance?

'I'm sorry.'

Dawdle shrugged. 'Poor bastards did a sound job.' He nodded to the bulkhead even though they were enclosed. 'Moorlogging and their covert operations.' He shook his head and Ishbel could see by the way he stirred the spoon in his brew that he was struggling.

'Did you know them, the crew?'

'You could say so, aye.' He slurped his brew and waved his hand over his mouth. 'Hoat! Too hoat still. Aye, it's gonnae take years tae replace that sort o' operation. Some o' those guys huv been working on the trawler ower ten years.'

'Sorry.'

'Aye. Thanks.'

They sipped the scalding tea, the silence broken only by Dawdle's occasional cooling blow across the top of his mug.

'Where are you taking us, Dawdle? If we don't get Scud help soon he might not make it.'

Dawdle grinned so wide Ishbel noticed he had missing back teeth on the right hand side. Chewing the contraband dried meat all Noiri men were reputed to love would be a real problem for Dawdle.

She couldn't help but smile, there was something so comforting in that grin. 'We have to get to prison ship IV in sector W. Can you take us there?' She was aware she was not now wheedling the usual deal with Dawdle. This was no bartering of kitchen veg for contraband salt or sugar. He continued to grin but said nothing. 'Scud's granddaughter is there, having committed no crime. God knows what might have happened to her. She's only fourteen.'

'She's safe.'

'How do you know?'

'Come on, Ish, you know ah cannae tell ye ma sources.' He waited. When she didn't speak he shrugged and said, 'We'll get ye the lassie but first there's somebody dyin tae meet ye.'

'Who?' But even as she asked unease washed over her.

'Monsieur Jacques.' Dawdle's words echoed her thoughts.

Monsieur Jacques, the Noiri King, the richest and most powerful person in the Esperaneo underworld. Of course Vanora disputed that fact. It was rumoured that he even had the State in his pocket. What would he want with her?

'What about Scud? He needs help. How long will this diversion take?'

'Too many questions, Ish. It may take a while but Scud'll be fine.' Dawdle patted the dashboard. 'Ma wee Peedle isnae as nippy as she used tae be. We'll huv tae take it easy, let her catch her breath now and again so tae speak.'

'Peedle?'

'Aye, Peedle by name Peedle by nature.'

It took aeons. Every few kiloms Dawdle cut to idle to stop the sub stuttering. As soon as Peedle submerged Ishbel's communicator vibrated. 'wt the hell u up to?' Her mother never did mince her words. Vanora had controlled her life since she was born, but the freedom she had while acting as Sorlie's native had given her a strength her mother never guessed at. Vanora constantly underestimated her. When Ishbel was five Vanora had dragged her from a pleasant childhood in the North West Territories, where she could run with the bears and wolves and hunt and fish with other native children. That existence was no good for Vanora, she needed revenge, she needed her army. So she'd dragged her daughter to the Northern Archipelago where Ishbel was given false papers and indoctrinated her into the ways of Esperaneo natives. She was taught the history of their struggles and the history of the state of Esperaneo. At the age of twelve Ishbel was placed into the home of Kathleen and Dougie Mayben and set to work as the domestic native with principle care of their son Somhairle, or Sorlie as everyone called him. What she learned there was that Kathleen was also Vanora's daughter, brought up as a Privileged. She'd been sold by her father, Davie, to the Military. His reward was the noble seat of Black Rock penitentiary. At first Ishbel couldn't understand why her mother had placed her in this home. She'd been there a couple of months before Kathleen told her the truth in an attempt to shake Ishbel out of the sullen bouts of homesickness.

Was she resentful of Kathleen who had been brought up Privileged? She often asked herself the question. Being a native slave in a Privileged home was no easy gig. Maybe resentment had lingered, but only until she saw the life that Kathleen led. The State placed Kathleen under Hero in Death status, a suicide bomber. Who would want that? Ishbel pitied her sister and viewed the State's treatment of Privileged with fresh cynical eyes. Her time with Dougie and Kathleen washed out most of Vanora's influence. She had never carried Vanora's fanatical hatred of the State. She knew the planet was dying and desperate measures must be taken, but the oppression of the native had taken a new turn with the DNA dilution and must be stopped. Even so, Vanora sometimes went too far.

The Noiri seemed to be above the law. Its black market network boasted strength and breadth greater than the Military and the State. The thought of Monsieur Jacques' name churned Ishbel's stomach.

Scud groaned in the corner and placed hands over ears. Ishbel faked a yawn to release pressure in her head. The growing grind of the engine shuddered then thumped as bow thrusters kicked in. She watched Dawdle watch her before he turned his attention to the control panel, open the front screen to show the murky sea part. They surfaced into a black night with only one light shining in the near distance. As they drew closer she made out the shape of the shed Dawdle manoeuvred towards. Judging by the short trees that grew on a hillside surrounding three sides of the loch, Ishbel guessed they were no longer in the High Lands and had travelled south into the Lake Lands.

'Where?' was all Scud managed to utter. His brown eyes filmed over with the grog of sleep and something else. Something milky, sinister.

Ishbel knelt beside him. 'Look, Scud, your granddaughter is safe, but we need to go somewhere first before we fetch her.'

'Not him.' Dawdle's voice was quiet but sharp.

'What do you mean?'

'He stays here.'

Ishbel felt her mouth dry as she watched Dawdle chain Scud to the bulkhead.

'Don't.'

'Nae choice, Ish.'

Scud shrugged, looked at Ishbel with pleading eyes and a defeated look.

'You can't leave him here alone.'

'He's no alone, there's plenty folk kicking about. They'll hear if he needs onything.' Dawdle nodded to Scud. 'Just shout if ye need onything, china, eh?'

Scud shrugged again. 'My life from now on.' The resignation and accusation in his voice was thrown Ishbel's way. Disappointment clouded his face.

'Come on Ish, we cannae keep the man waiting. He'll know we've docked.'

He thumped his fist against Scud's shoulders. 'No hard feelings bud.' Then he turned just before they left the sub. 'Bring ye some rock back, yeah?'

'Rock?' Ishbel asked.

'You'll see.' Dawdle laughed.

*

Dawdle ushered Ishbel into a parked white van as if she were royalty.

'What a mess.' Sometimes Ishbel wished she wasn't quite a native, always tidying, always cleaning.

Dawdle began gathering scraps of paper. He threw scummy brew dregs out the cab window before stowing the clarty mugs under the seat. Small embarrassed dimples appeared on his cheeks.

'Sorry, ah didnae expect this call.'

Ishbel remained silent. Her jaw clamped shut. The cab stank of male. She thumped the button of the window but nothing happened. Dawdle leaned across her and the smell of his spicy cologne replaced the stench in her mind. He stabbed the window button hard with his thumb and it opened, releasing the smell. He seemed to linger a few seconds before he moved back to his seat.

'Sorry,' was all he said, but they both knew what he meant. 'It's not far,' he added.

They drove for half an hour and in that time the only vehicles they saw were military Jeeps. Each one flashed a friendly headlight and Dawdle replied with a flick of a switch at the wheel which lit up the road in front.

'Why don't they stop you?'

Dawdle grinned. 'Now why would they dae that? What harm am ah daein?'

'You must be stealing military fuel.'

Dawdle arched his brows. 'Am ah?' Then he laughed. 'And how would they get their cigs, their meat, and their native booty.' Ishbel winced. 'Sorry. Their bits and pieces.' Dawdle settled back in his driving seat, arms fully stretched towards the steering wheel. 'We don't steal fuel. We barter fur it. The Military worked out a long time ago that we're a necessary evil. Part o' the economy. Let's just call it an unwritten agreement. If we aw stick tae the rules we can exist side by side.' He flashed her that grin again. 'Just play cute.'

After a few more kiloms they transferred to a launch and buzzed out to a structure towering in the bay. It appeared not as tall as it had been before the flood but it was still an impressive structure, similar to the one that dominated the Capital. In the past ten years all available metal had been requisitioned by the Military. Railings cut down, cars crushed and remoulded, scrap of any kind melted down. In fact it was this very production that gave the Noiri its initial foothold into the underworld. There had been calls for the Capital to dismantle its own iconic tower but the symbolic significance was not overlooked. The State realised it could impose many hardships on the lives of the Privileged, but to take their precious tower was a step too far, it would lead to mass disobedience. Half the world could be starving, natives and oldies could be dropping with unchecked suspicious viruses, but take away the metal tower of the Capital and all hell breaks loose. While all this was going through her mind, Ishbel stared up at this miniature version, with its small lights evenly spaced up its legs, and wondered again at the power of Monsieur Jacques to keep it here.

They clambered up a makeshift ladder and entered a rickety old lift that should have been scrapped years ago; its concertina door clacked closed in front of them. Their images distorted and grotesquely reflected back at them from the tired and battered fake gold interior. One side was made of glass and as it ascended as if into the air, she wondered how Sorlie would cope with this exposure to the outside. Many times she had tried to help him conquer his fear of height. Often she would take him swimming with her to the high woods with the other natives. There was an old stone monument to some forgotten warrior, perched on the tip of a crag. The natives had all but pushed Sorlie to the edge, had persuaded him to climb the monument. 'What sort of Privileged do you think you are?

Can't even climb,' they had goaded him. Ishbel remembered his bitten lip, his wee determined face; the eight-year-old had started up the steep stone spiral steps. He got as far as the tenth step and froze. He could neither move up nor down. Ishbel had to carry him home. He never spoke of the incident, he never told his parents, never made her suffer, as many Privileged children did with their native. It was as if he had wiped the memory from his mind.

She stared back at the sea below and realised she missed Sorlie, and wondered how he was fairing in the domain of Vanora. The yank of the lift coming to a sudden stop pulled her back. She stood with her back to the windows and lulled her mind to expect whatever came her way. She was sure it wasn't death, but even if it was, it was something she had been trained to accept.

Dawdle tugged the door open and ushered her into a large room with a glass floor. Even in the dark Ishbel felt an unease in her belly. Music played in the background. Oldie music: folky, rocky. Something from the last century. The sound of the lift descending and then returning sent her, despite the unease, into the corner of the glass room.

Monsieur Jacques was a name, a legend; some even suspected he didn't exist. No one knew what he looked like, or his age. In her mind she expected him to be middle-aged, maybe a bit wily, a bit like Scud before the change, perhaps. Clever, smart – you don't get into this position without being smart.

She didn't realise she had been holding her breath until a whistle escaped through the gap in her front teeth the moment the doors to the lift cranked open.

A giant entered the room, making her take a step back. Satan's truth, she was in a giant's lair. Privileged, definitely Privileged. And well over two metres tall. His hair was receding to almost bald, apart from a crescent of snow-white tuft that cradled his skull. His broad shoulders seemed to push the door open beyond its grinding hinges. His blue eyes twinkled as if enjoying her scrutiny of him. They were not the ice blue of Davie's, but warm blue in his broad moon face, if such a thing existed. There was a crater in the middle of that moon face as if something had punctured it long ago and it had healed over but now it looked like an extra eye that was scrutinising her in return. He smiled, his teeth good, strong and white. He held out his hand to her, a huge paw that was soft and wrinkled and it was these wrinkles that gave the game away. He was old. His face was modified, the skin tightened or maybe even replaced, giving him the look of a giant plastic doll. His hands were old.

'Ishbel. Enchanté.'

She opened her mouth to speak then realised she didn't know how to address him. 'Enchanté,' she said. This was how she had taught Sorlie to address people for the first time on meeting and she remembered the pride she felt when he said this to Vanora in David's study. She always loved the greeting since she had been taught it by the people of her home in the North West Territories. Homesickness stabbed her. Monsieur Jacques held her hand in both of his, obviously pleased to see her. Still she said nothing. And then he realised.

'You must call me Monsieur Jacques.'

No informality here then, she thought. She didn't know why this bothered her so much but it did.

The demarcation line drawn, Privileged and native and yet, when she looked across at Dawdle he was grinning with indulgence as if he had just delivered the greatest prize of his life.

Sorlie

I sidled up to Ridgeway to get out of her range. 'What the snaf? She's just murdered someone in cold blood and we're trapped on this island with her.'

'It's called the Art of War, show them who's boss.'

'Show them who's mad more like. What are we going to do?'

'Maybe wait and see what's happened to Kenneth before we decide.'

'Where is Kenneth?'

Ridgeway looked towards Arkle who nodded. Ridgeway took a deep breath. I thought at first he was going to tell me he'd died.

'He's being deloused and rehabbed.'

'What? Why?'

'Maybe you didn't notice his disintegration. You can't live in a cave for twenty-odd years without some ill effects. He should be set to rights in a couple of days.' He couldn't look me in the eye.

'What are they going to do to him? Not tamper with his brain?'

'He's being well looked after,' the smooth Arkle said, then motioned to the queueing men in the sports hall.

'When this is done we'll begin streaming them into skill sets, they'll be disinfected and allocated.' An echo of history niggled at my mind. The simple words, 'disinfected' and 'allocated', chilled me; the picture of the men in the prison infirmary, slaughtered by my grandfather, still filled my mind. The ones who were destroyed. Yes. Out of the frying pan indeed.

The tangy deodorised smell of cut grass wrinkled my nose to

sneeze-ready as soon as I entered the room. A pre-oldie sat at a desk, writing or drawing old-style on textile. His salt and pepper coloured hair was banded back from his brow and a neat pencil line beard covered only the bottom half of his chin, a classic style that made him look like a philosopher. At first I thought he was unaware of my presence until he cranked his head in my direction. He rose to a slight stoop, placing the palms of his hands on his back to straighten. When the groan escaped him recognition kicked in.

'No way!'

But when he smiled and held his hands out in a "ta da" gesture there was no denying it.

'Satan's truth, what have they done to you?'

Kenneth's grin widened. 'Pretty neat, eh?'

How could this smart, intelligent-looking person have lived underneath the mouldy, decrepit exterior of this erstwhile hermit? He scratched his neck where the busy beard had once grown, while rubbing one foot up the back of the other leg.

'Being clean is more itchifying than I remember, I think I'm allergic to these new-fangled bio soaps.'

'Have you seen Vanora yet?'

His smile wiped. I wanted to know if he knew how crazy she was. I wanted to say 'she's just killed a man.' But the worry wart in me stayed my tongue on that one.

'Have you worked out where all the surveillance is yet?' I could detect a number of possible points in this room.

There was no hint of suspicion in his eye when he said, 'You don't need to worry about surveillance here. You're free.' As if to demonstrate the point he half-pirouetted, half-juddered on the spot. 'Doesn't it feel great?'

Ridgeway joined us. He seemed less surprised by the caveman's transformation. The two men kissed one cheek and the other, then Ridgeway held him at arm's length.

'Unbelievable. You look ten years younger, Ken. Just like your old self, eh?'

Kenneth groaned again. 'I don't feel ten years younger.' He shook his shoulders loose like a cat fresh from a drooking. 'But I will have to get my vitality back if I'm to help Vanora in her revolution.'

The words threw a thick blanket of hush over the room. All three of us stood kicking imaginary sand, waiting for one of the others to fill the silence. I obliged.

'What exactly are we doing here?' I tried to ignore their puzzle. 'I don't know about you but I find this set up all a bit weird.' The statement came out of nowhere, but now it was out I realised it was true. On Black Rock, even though I was shut in a room, at least I had Scud and my lessons and in the afternoon the freedom to explore Grandfather's library. It might have been routine but it was what I was used to. And then, when I was finally allowed outside with Ridgeway, I could explore the island, look for the extinct corncrake, breathe in the sea air, avoid the seabirds dropping their heavy cargo. That was a kind of freedom, wasn't it? Here in Vanora's lair we had found what Pa described to me as his fabled Freedom, but if this was Freedom, why did I feel so trapped? I chose not to burst Kenneth's bubble by telling him Vanora was mad. But I couldn't help wonder why we were even here.

'Well, Vanora's army…' Kenneth stuttered. 'I am sure we'll be given instructions soon.' His stumbled words did nothing to help my frustration.

'What if we're surplus to requirements now we've completed our task?'

Kenneth gulped so hard his newly-visible Adam's apple somersaulted.

'Sorry, I josh.' I added, not wanting to send him off on one of his rants.

'You're not here to josh.' Vanora's voice gave me such a gliff I

57

stumbled back, knocking Kenneth's table, splaying his writing implements to the floor. She stood by the door all regal and showy. She'd changed into a gown trimmed with animal fur. The guns were off camera, the blood washed from her face

'Kenneth.' She held her arms, fingers fluttering, out to her son who looked only a few years younger than his mother. He went to her and although he had to stoop into the embrace, the stiffness of his back and the rigidity of her grin was as mechanical as a soldier's salute.

'Vanora.' Kenneth straightened with a grimace but held his groan in check. 'Long time no see.' They both began a sort of forced laugh that fooled no one.

Still with her eyes on Kenneth she held out one hand to the side. 'Ridgeway, my dear.'

He took it with a bow and kissed it as he was expected to do.

'I'm so glad you played your part in the plan.'

'I told you she arranged your transfer to Black Rock.' Kenneth spoke in a whisper.

'But of course.' Her affected voice was even more pronounced than it had been in the hall earlier. A tiny pinhead of blood had been missed from the side of her nose.

'Why did you kill that prisoner just now?'

Kenneth's eyes flashed a mixture of shock and warning to me but I didn't care. I'd stood up to my grandfather and now I would stand up to her. No tyrant would rule me again, even if it meant death. This was not the Freedom I'd signed up for.

Vanora took her time turning to me. 'Sorlie, you look so like your mother.'

'She's dead.' Was that a wince? Hard to tell. She put her head down for a nano. When she looked up she smiled and held my gaze.

'So I heard. How unfortunate.'

'Why did you kill that man?'

Her smile never faltered. 'Now, Sorlie, you must be hungry,

why don't you and your uncle go for some food?' Her hand gestured vaguely to the door. 'We have a wonderful Bistro, supplied with the best the Noiri can find.'

'You won't answer my question?'

'Leave it, Sorlie,' Kenneth said as he scooped up my arm in his.

Vanora narrowed her green eyes to me and through gritted teeth said, 'Because you have no idea how to run operations. I wasn't going to bring this up, but it seems you insist on embarrassing yourself. I heard what happened on the sub. Your arrogant, childish attempt to quieten the mob. Fool. This is no child's Academy now.' She moved into my space. She seemed to grow, her face to mine. I took a step back to reclaim my space. 'War is not easy, you will learn that sometimes we make difficult choices for the greater good.' I thought she'd finished but she lifted her chin, smoothed her feathers and said in a grandmotherly voice. 'And never forget, this is war and in wars people die.'

'Like my parents.'

This time she'd been expecting it. 'Yes, like your parents.'

'Where's Ishbel?' She'd been expecting that too.

'Ishbel has some business to attend to.'

'When will she be back?'

She shrugged. 'When I order her to come back.' There was something unsettling in that shrug.

'And what's to happen to us?' I swept my arm round the room to include Kenneth and Ridgeway who lurked like a couple of stooges. Why wasn't Kenneth asking these questions?

Vanora smiled. 'So many questions, Sorlie. You know you can leave whenever you like.' The tack she took with Smiler just before she blew his brains out. Ridgeway bristled beside me.

'But where would you go?' she said. 'Back to your Home Base? I'm sure they would love to welcome you back to train you as a suicide bomber, just like your ma.' The hiss she placed in the word suicide made me blink. 'Maybe they'll give you your parents' unit to live in until your mission.'

She was goading me; she knew Ishbel had rescued me from that fate. She knew I had nowhere to go. I'd never be able to leave. I knew where her base was, I'd seen her operations room, that huge ticker wall with the millions of redeye communications from her millions of Vanorettes. She watched me like a scientist with a trapped rat. Then she smiled and placed her arm through mine, her lavender scent enveloping me.

'Oh, it is so good to have you here. My very own gorgeous grandson.'

Kenneth shifted.

'Oh, and my long lost son and his trusty friend.'

'Not lost, displaced,' Kenneth corrected her, but she dismissed him with a finger flutter.

'After your meal we will have a summit.' She hugged me. 'Just a tiny summit. We don't want to cram too much into your tired little heads.'

I looked around me. Yep, I wasn't the only one who felt patronised. Ridgeway was trying hard to hide it; Kenneth glowered. Out of the frying pan indeed.

She turned and floated from the room, saying, 'Why not try the roast turbot? The most delicious thing; I believe we had a fresh delivery this morning.'

'I don't like turbot,' Kenneth sulked.

'Nonsense,' she threw back over her shoulder, stealing the last word.

Kenneth let out a breath when the door closed. 'I told you she was a control freak.'

Ridgeway flopped in a seat. 'I wonder where Ishbel is. V wasn't too happy when you mentioned her.'

'What are we going to do?' I asked.

Despite the tension between us during the prison break, I

now felt these two lovelies were my only hope of remaining sane and alive.

'We play along, we help with the army, we do what Vanora wants us to do.'

'Within reason,' I added.

'Yes, within reason.' Kenneth scratched his neck. 'We go with the flow…for now.'

Ishbel

'Vanora,' Monsieur Jacques began, his huge hand hovering at Ishbel's back, ushering her to a seat. 'I know she's your mother but she's become an embarrassment.' Ishbel remained quiet, her eyebrow raised slightly as she wondered where this was leading.

'A little out of control – non?'

He snapped his fingers at Dawdle who seemed to know the score and began preparing drinks from the bar suspended against the window, a balcony of stained glass bottles embossed against the black night sky on the other side of the glass. Dawdle handed Ishbel a crystal tumbler, still grinning as if he couldn't quite believe she was there. Jacques looked on like a benevolent father. Ishbel raised the glass towards the old giant.

'Sláinte,' she said in her old language but didn't sip.

'Santé,' he said in his.

'So, we talk. Your Vanora,' he paused, Ishbel swallowed her surprise at his irreverence. 'She has gone a little mad, I think.'

'She's not my Vanora.'

He nodded. 'But mad, yes? Her next decisive strike against the State is madness?'

'I know nothing of that,' she said. She checked her suicide pill was still safely lodged in her teeth.

'You know nothing? Do you know the Land Reclaimists are weakening? The eastern border is defended by a bunch of Academy boys. Forces loyal to the Purists are creating havoc from within. The Noiri and the NFF should be sitting back. Let them destroy each other but Vanora is interfering. Sending her insurgents in Esperaneo Major to destroy supply routes. And now I hear her focus is on the Capital. Why?'

'Vanora's last cyber-attack…' Ishbel began.

'Her last cyber-attack on the professional's comms – worked well, yes? The whole professional classes ordered to stay home – destroy all their sensitive files. Very effective. Oh, the State may have been thrown into confusion for a short while, but it could have had dangerous repercussions. Many thousands of infirmary patients died as a result.' He sipped and looked at her, waiting for a reaction she wouldn't give. 'You knew this?'

'Yes.'

'Vanora will become unpopular if she tries a stunt like that again. The State has ramped up their security in all cyber areas. Her actions are beginning to affect my operations.'

Ishbel looked at Dawdle, his face was in shadow but his stillness unsettled her. They were his operations too.

'She is planning something big and from what my spies tell me it needs to be stopped.'

If Jacques thought about torturing her she could end it before it began.

'I realise the Capital is a Military as well as governmental powerhouse,' he continued, 'but it is my home. It is one of the oldest, most important cities in the world. Its classical architecture, its monuments are unparalleled.'

Ishbel listened. She'd never been to the Capital but she understood what Jacques was saying. She studied the man, this legend who now sat in his tower with his back to the sea. It was reputed he had a bigger army than Vanora. Not a fighting army with physical might but an army who fought with their wits. A supply army. There are more ways to skin a cat, Vanora often told her.

'Are you kidnapping me?' Ishbel asked.

His laugh was genuine. 'Non, ma chérie, I am not, I want your help. I need you to contact Vanora. Help me to stop her plan.'

Ishbel felt her heart beat rise. Her palms begin to sweat.

'I cannot do that and you know it.'

'Oh, I know you won't betray her, but we could maybe persuade her it is not such a good idea, this plan of hers to attack the Capital. She could attack Beckham City instead. It is after all, strategically important for this island state.

Ishbel shook her head. 'Beckham City has lost its usefulness. It's dead, full of pumped-up has-beens who never really embraced the true nature of Esperaneo.' S'truth, she sounded like a Ganda-Ad.

Jacques' smile remained benevolent but Ishbel detected a hardening round the edge.

'Very well. But you will send a message from me.'

'Why should I do that? You could send her a message through your network.'

'Because it will be more powerful coming from you. She'll realise I am not messing. And why should you cooperate?' He signalled her over to the window that faced south to the promenade canal and the invading sea. The broken pier jutting out of the bay like an oldie's arthritic finger pointing to the past. 'Because I have something that you want.'

Ishbel stopped breathing. 'What?'

He ignored her, leaned back in his chair and placed his hand comfortably on top of his old-man belly as if it had been designed for such a purpose.

'You know my dear, you are quite a formidable woman.'

Her face remained rigid. Flattery was the oldest trick in the universe, he really should know better.

'How so?' she said.

He took a sip. 'Well, you've led a double life. You are not yet twenty-two years old and already first lieutenant in the NFF.'

'Second,' she corrected him, then mentally kicked herself. Merj was history, she should remember that.

'Second,' he nodded. 'Still pretty impressive. And let us not forget, you are half Privileged and yet seem content to live a native life.'

Ishbel had nothing to say to this. The Privileged genes she

received from Black Rock Davie were alien to her. She wished them diluted, the reverse of what happened to Scud. She was native and would always be native.

'What do you really want from me?' she said, placing her drink on the bar.

Jacques' eyes widened, but she'd had enough of this cat and mousiness.

'Ish...' Dawdle began, but Jacques held up his hand to stay his words.

'It is good.' He stood and walked to the corner glass, and seemed to examine her from the reflection. Then turned.

'D'accord, I will not beat about the heather.' These guys were priceless, Ishbel thought. 'Your mother manages her empire, and I manage my empire.' He waited.

'My mother would disagree. You have a rabble of white van men. That's not an empire.'

'The Noiri is more than that and she knows it.' His smile somehow made worse the bite of his words.

'Does she know of the new kid on the block?'

'What new kid?' She looked over at Dawdle but he was busy setting up a telescope by the south window.

'They call him The Prince.' He stared into her eyes, looking for her lie.

'Tell me,' she said drawing on her native training to hold his stare.

'I have little to tell. Rumours from the south. A few of my operatives have vanished.'

'Vanished?'

'Your mother? She has lost no operatives?'

'She has lost no operatives,' Ishbel said, hoping she hid the memory of her mother's recent obsession with the ticker wall.

'Well, good.' Jacques gave a little cough. 'So, tell me Ishbel, how would your mother feel if we joined forces?'

She choked then. 'You want to join forces?' She fought to compose her cough. 'Why? To stop her attacking the Capital?'

Jacques handed her back her drink and almost shrugged, but it was more like a rumbling of his shoulders. 'The State is weak at the moment, you know that. The Land Reclaimists have gone too far with their environmental policies. Getting rid of domestic food animals in one purge was disastrous. The saturated land could not grow the crops fast enough, heavy rains and floods have destroyed vast tranches of the fertile corridor. Even with the diminished populations, greater food shortages are a foregone conclusion. Something is wrong. Things are changing and the appearance of The Prince is part of it.'

'Tell him about the mutant, Ish.'

Jacques whirled on Dawdle.

'It's no secret. The DNA solution.' Jacques tried to hide his interest. 'It has been perfected?'

Dawdle nodded. 'And we have a survivor of the experiment.' Ishbel kicked him. Suddenly Scud sounded like a commodity.

'Do you now?' Jacques could hide his interest no more. 'But if he gets into the wrong hands…'

'He's ill and we need to get him help,' Ishbel said.

'And we'll get him help, Ish.' She didn't miss the look that passed between Jacques and Dawdle. 'Ah'll take him north right after this.'

'Perfected,' Jacques said. 'It is even more important for us to act. We must stop this.' Jacques said. 'If the Purists take power, and that is looking more likely, then we are doomed anyway. My men are mostly natives, as is your mother's army. Yes, we have both worked well to scratch the surface of power but we are a long way from victory.' He took a sip of Mash and gazed back at the reflections in the black glass. He rubbed the dent on his forehead as if it pained. 'There are only a few things outside the law your mother can control. I have many more. Oh, she may have the egg-legs.'

'Egg-heads,' Ishbel corrected him, but she could see by his reflected smile that his mistake was intentional.

'Whatever,' he said. 'But I have men on the ground who can move freely, thanks to the corrupt nature of the State.' He pinged the edge of his glass with his index finger to chime his idea. 'Don't you see how powerful we would be? Your mother's egg-heads and my, what did you call them? Ah yes, my rabble of white van men.'

'And you will attack the Capital together?'

'No one is going to attack the Capital. I know Vanora, I can persuade her of the futility of her plan.'

'And who will rule? I don't see you reporting to Vanora or her to you.'

'Always the power thing with you women, the hierarchy. This is not about power – well, not yet anyway.'

'This is about power. Partnerships don't work.'

His shrug dismissed her doubt.

'And you Ishbel, I need good recruits.' Ishbel felt her mouth blot. 'I need many first lieutenants.'

She remained silent but she could feel Dawdle watch her. Where did he fit in all this?

'Your mother has not always been kind to you.'

'Maybe I have other plans,' Ishbel said at last.

'Ah, and these plans include what? The Prince? Or maybe your brother, your mother's neglected first-born, or maybe they are one and the same.'

'That is a ridiculous suggestion.'

'As you wish.' By the way Jacques jiggled his shoulders she could see he was goading her. 'Maybe we should deal with the other matter in hand before you decide you will contact your mother.' His face was kind, but the steel in his voice cut Ishbel's resolve. 'Come here.'

This man knew so much already, she mustn't let him get the better of her and yet somehow she knew he already had. When she reached him she realised how tall he was. He swung an old-style telescope round and rested the eyepiece end on his chest for a moment. He extracted an old green moulded coin from his pocket and inserted it into the slot on the telescope side before bowing down and sighting it on something. He pressed a button and a light shone from the telescope, casting a beam on the water below.

'Look down.' He pulled Ishbel to stand on a small ribbed platform and held the sight steady until she positioned. It took a moment for her eyes to adjust. She saw a promenade on a pontoon, un-reclaimed metal railings ran along its edge. In a tethered launch two people huddled. They both seemed to be saluting but were probably shielding their eyes against the light. Their other hands held what looked like puffs of cotton on a stick.

'Candy Floss?' Ishbel recognised it from the old movie-casters and vintage postcards she sometimes found in the native jumble sales.

The larger of the two was a woman, she looked about Ishbel's age. The cut of hair and her uniform under a biker's jacket gave her away as being native. The other person was smaller, with a hood pulled up over her head, only just visible from beneath was a flash of brassy hair, a fringe around a pinched white face. Ishbel felt her heart lurch. The last time she had seen hair that colour Sorlie had been with her on their flight from Base Dalriada on their way to Black Rock. She had taken them to where the Dead Man's Ferry docked. She had told Sorlie the reason for their visit was to show him some natives' suffering. The real reason for her visit was to check up on the progress of Tig and Reinya's deportation. Sorlie had thought the red-haired urchin had been a boy, a small strange creature with hateful eyes turned towards them as they sat in their military Jeep.

Ishbel returned her thoughts to the now and the creature below in the boat magnified to the extent where Ishbel could pick out candy floss strands floating in the breeze. As if aware she was being scrutinised from above Reinya raised her face into the light.

'How did you get her?'

Jacques chuckled. 'Easy when you know how.'

She turned to Dawdle. 'I thought he didn't know about Scud.' His faced flushed but he shook his head.

'He didn't know.' She saw a flash of anger pass over Dawdle's face. 'Ah requested her escape tae save time. Ah was just asked tae bring you here. Ah didnae know she'd be held hostage.' This time when he looked towards Jacques the pride he'd shown earlier was replaced with something brittle.

'Sorry, Ish,' Dawdle said. By bringing her here he had played right into the heart of Jacques' plan.

'So,' Jacques brushed the atmosphere away with a rub of his hands. 'Enough squabbling. About this message.'

Ishbel sighed, mentally stored her suicide pill and booted the communicator on her wrist. 'What do you want me to say?'

'Tell Vanora…'

'You don't tell Vanora.'

'Very well. Ask Vanora to reconsider her attack on the Capital. Tell, I mean inform her that I have operations on the ground there. The Capital is the last prize. It can't be rushed. We must not strike until smaller targets have been taken out which will ensure guaranteed success in the Capital. Remind her of the Art of War.'

Ishbel thumbed the comms. 'Why can't you disable her systems yourself? You must have access to her channels.'

'That is where you are wrong, ma chérie. Vanora has some of the finest minds working with her. Each time I get close to breaking into her system they install a more secure version.'

He pointed to Dawdle. 'I have a different type of mind

working for me. Sharp, streetwise, survivors. Different skills, different purpose.'

'Same endgame,' Ishbel said. 'Yes, maybe I can see you two would be better working together.' When Jacques laughed this time it carried genuine mirth. Her comms buzzed.

'She wants to meet.' What Ishbel didn't report from the message was that Vanora had also ordered her home.

Jacque smiled. 'Very well. Ask her to come here. She knows where I am. And I have no doubt she has access to my comms.'

'She won't agree to that.'

Something in Jacques eyes held a long lost secret. 'Yes she will.'

Ishbel shrugged. 'Can I have the girl now?'

Jacques waved his hand vaguely. 'Take her and good luck, I believe she is high maintenance.' He then took Ishbel's hand and kissed it. 'It has been a pleasure doing business with you.'

Ishbel nodded and followed Dawdle into the lift.

'Sorry, Ish,' he said again.

'Stop saying sorry,' clipped from her lips before she could help it. She waved his apology away. 'No matter, we have the girl and we saved ourselves a trip to sector W. Now let's get out of here before Vanora arrives.'

Dawdle manoeuvred his launch towards the pontoon. He nodded to the woman and helped Reinya to switch boats in silence. Reinya glowered at Ishbel, chin up, when she came on board.

'I'm sorry about your mother,' Ishbel began but the girl held her hand up.

'No words.' Reinya scanned Ishbel up and down and hiked her chin further up. 'It's you, from the docks. Saw you there, gawping at us with a Privileged boy.'

Ishbel nodded. 'I'm taking you to your grandfather.'

The irony of this statement was not lost on Ishbel as the words left her mouth. Was this her only role in life, to deliver orphaned children to their grandparents? Except this time, unlike when she took Sorlie to Davie, she knew Reinya would be taken care of.

'What grandfather?'

'Your mother's father.'

The girl flushed a little then shrugged. 'Where?'

'Not far.' Ishbel held out her hand to help the girl settle as Dawdle booted the launch, but Reinya brushed her off and flopped on the wet floor.

'That's it, hen, you get settled. Won't be long, as Ish says. There's someone dyin tae meet ye.'

Ishbel prayed that wasn't prophetic, she was unsure of Scud's health and even more concerned with his state of mind. She had to get him to help.

Scud was exactly as they had left him, curled in a corner but asleep. Ishbel ushered Reinya towards her grandfather and with each step her face turned whiter in horror. She shrank back when she got to within a couple of feet of him.

'What is it?'

'This is Scud, your grandfather, your mother will have told you about him.'

'It's a Privileged and it stinks.'

'He may look that way but he's still your grandfather.'

'No way. You're joshin me, cos that there is a Privileged,' she said.

Ishbel pinched her arm and spoke in lowered tones. 'He's not a real Privileged. He's a mutant. His genes have been tampered with. We're going to get him help and you are going to be nice to him.'

'Never,' she spat.

Ishbel shook her head. And she thought Vanora and Jacques would be a tough pair to reconcile. This girl was going to be a nightmare.

Sorlie

Vanora pursed her lips so tightly the wrinkles around them resembled a fist full of sultanas. Satan's truth, she was old.

'Ishbel,' she whispered as she clacked her reptilian nail on the communicator.

'Where is she?'

Vanora blinked her paper-thin eyelids a couple of times. She heard my question but instead of answering she squinted at Kenneth. Kenneth acted weird with Vanora. It was true he'd been brought up by his grandparents and had admitted to me she wasn't much of a mother, but I assumed there would be some bond. I watched him gather his strength, pull back his shoulders, take a deep breath.

'Aren't you going to answer him, Vanora? Where's Ishbel? We're all dying to know.' Agitation jigged in his newly-shorn features.

'Oh, I suppose I might as well tell you.' Vanora said. 'Your beloved native stormed off in a huff when she discovered she had been stepped over in a promotion. I expected more from her. I assumed her emotional intelligence was stronger. Her behaviour proves I was right in my promotion assessment.'

Kenneth seemed to snap to. 'Merj.'

At the sound of his name I remembered the feel of Merj's blood trickling over my wrist as I plunged my blade into his cheek. The fight on the beach that ended with Merj in a heap, hand blown off.

'You sent Merj to fetch Sorlie.' Kenneth stabbed his finger in the air with each word.

'Don't point, Kenneth, it's rude.'

He stuck his hand in his pocket and paced the room. Vanora watched him.

'Anyway, I didn't send Merj for Sorlie. He acted outwith my orders. My guess is he thought it would be best to move the child out of the way.'

'How can you say that? He was kidnapping me.' I could hear my voice rise. 'You just said you did right not to promote Ishbel. Now you're excusing Merj his insubordination.'

'Thch,' was all she said as she smoothed her hair and rubbed her teeth as if something lodged there; a lie perhaps. 'Anyway, thanks to your skillful fighting I am now one very experienced man down.' No, not a lie, but a platitude.

'Good riddance to bad rubbish,' Kenneth said.

Vanora shrugged off an imaginary weight. 'Come, we must prepare.' She smiled and held out her hand to me. 'Sorlie, I cannot believe you are actually here after all this nonsense of having to watch you grow up from afar through the eyes of Ishbel.' She hugged me to her but the floral aroma I'd at first welcomed clawed at my throat. I wanted to push her off.

'We must train you. We must make you a warrior. '

'I don't want to be a warrior.'

'How so? You've made an excellent start. We were most impressed by the way you dealt with first Ridgeway and then Merj.'

I spotted Ridgeway and Kenneth exchange a look. I'd nearly killed Ridgeway when I pushed him down the cliff, but that was before I knew he was on my side. Before he led the escape of the prisoners he had been guarding for years. He had totally earned the right to be my friend.

Vanora was still speaking. '... and I don't know what you said to that old bastard Davie, but persuading him to blow his brains out was a stroke of genius. Wasn't it, boys?'

The two old lovelies nodded – Tweedle Dee and Tweedle Dum.

'I'd nothing to do with that. All I did was tell him Ishbel was his daughter.' Her face turned grey. She grabbed the desk and sat down behind it.

She wasn't fazed for long and was soon clacking her finger on a comms pad. The ticker wall morphed into a map of Esperaneo. Small digits dotted the wall. In no time I could locate the Capital, blazing bright in the western side of Esperaneo Major. And there, near the middle of this island of Lesser Esperaneo, was Beckham City. The major cities of Stasiland and Oddessa were shining bright in the east, a conglomeration. The coastline of Lesser and Major sprinkled with lights as if a child had thrown beads on the sand and traced their finger around the edge to join the dots. The overall picture showed thousands of lights.

Vanora beamed. 'My kingdom. Every light one of my hidden cells.'

As I took it all in, calculating how many, Kenneth shifted and walked to a solitary light in the middle of the dark ocean. Vanora's smile spread as she watched. When he touched the light it peeped out.

'How could you have been so cruel?' Kenneth said.

'Cruel? Why cruel?'

He wiped his arm across the map. 'Look at all these cells, these conglomerates, the networks, contact, human contact.' His voice wavered. 'Twenty years on that stinking island. Why couldn't I have been here?' He stabbed the wall. 'Or here? Or here? Or here?' He was frantically stabbing now. He would have broken his finger if Ridgeway hadn't grabbed him and pulled him away. But he wasn't finished. 'The fertile land, Ridgeway's home. We could have both gone, where it's warm and dry.'

The benevolent buffoon I'd met on the beach had seemed content in his cave, with his Mash still, his garden and his wall paintings, but now I could see he had made the best of a bad job. Vanora had cast him adrift on an island – detached from a thousand prisoners and totally alone. He was right, it was cruel. He could easily have been one of the many networks visible on the mainland.

'Why?' his voice choked.

Vanora's expression remained fixed. 'You needed protecting.'

'From whom? Not Davie? Even though he knew I was there he never bothered to even swat me like a fly.'

She sighed and gave him the same disappointed look he gave to me the first time we met. 'The State, of course.'

He pointed to the wall again. 'And these operatives? Look at them, millions of them, aren't they protected?'

He whirled round and grabbed me by the wrist, tapping my communicator. 'And what about this contraption?' He was meaning the plug-in provided by Vanora to release the prisoners. 'This was supposed to protect him when you more or less welded him to the control panel during the escape. Did it never occur to you that with this seemingly foolproof protection you put him in danger?'

'Thch.'

'Don't tut me. Davie nearly killed him and he couldn't get away because of your ingenious control devices.'

He turned to me. 'I told you she was a control freak.'

'Don't call me that.' An edge of steel wire threaded her words. But there was a slight flush on her face.

'The prison was too dangerous for him.'

Kenneth dropped my hand.

'The prisoners were under control.'

Vanora batted his words. 'I don't think I like your tone of voice, Kenneth.'

He raked his hands through his hair. 'And I don't think I like your control decisions,' he said as he slammed past Ridgeway and left the room

Vanora clucked her teeth. 'Oh dear, such an impulsive boy. He always was.'

This statement amazed me. Kenneth was a senior, Vanora an oldie. They were both acting like children.

'Ridgeway, go and see he's alright, he might do himself some damage.' She turned from him and hooked her arm through mine.

Ridgeway coughed and his voice croaked as he said, 'Vanora, don't you think you owe him an explanation?'

Her eyes widened. 'There is no explanation. He needed taken out of the equation. His knowledge of the original DNA project was too useful to the DNA experiment. If he had been captured the dilution would have happened sooner.'

Ridgeway opened his mouth to say something but she turned her back on him. Dismissed.

'Now Sorlie, you see here and here.' She pointed to the map.

But I wasn't going to let her away with it. 'Why didn't you give that explanation to Kenneth? Why treat him like a child?'

'Enough! We have work to do.'

She stretched up and patted my shoulders.

'You see on the map how close we are to the Capital? We are almost ready to complete our tests and I want you involved at every stage.' She smoothed her hand down my arm. 'You know I love you very much, Sorlie.'

Whoa, that freaked me somewhat. No one said they loved me. What was love anyway, and what was kin?

'When's Ishbel coming back?'

'Why do you persist in this? Ishbel, Ishbel, always Ishbel.' Vanora sighed and looked at her nails as if the answer was there. 'She will need to be punished, you will not see her when she comes back.'

'Why does she need to be punished?'

'I told you, she disobeyed me.'

'She must have had her reasons.' Based on what I had witnessed so far, I'm sure she had many.

Those lips pursed into dried fruit again. 'I know the reason but it is ignoble. Not to our cause. That girl has a different agenda and you are not to forget that.' She gave me another chummy arm pat. 'We have bigger and better plans. You don't need to bother about her again.'

'You're jealous of her.' I said.

'Don't be silly. Why would I be jealous of her?'

I didn't answer. In her youth she would have been like Ishbel, who had her life ahead of her and was strong and, judging from the fact Ishbel disobeyed her mother to no regard, it seemed Vanora might also be jealous of her courage.

'What if I don't want to be trained as a warrior? I might choose to go along with Ishbel.'

'Now you're being silly. I'll hear no more nonsense. I'm your grandmother and your only guardian now. You do as I say.'

'You may be my grandmother but I owe you nothing and I doubt if you'll go to the authorities to claim legal guardianship.'

'You owe me your freedom.'

'I would have found it eventually. Anyway, this is not freedom. Yes, I want freedom but not your kind.' I expected her to chide me but she was frowning at the ticker wall. Maybe it was my imagination, but I swore a cluster of lights in the southern quadrant had just vanished right before our eyes.

Ishbel

Scud's eyes flickered at the sound of Reinya's voice. He cocked his head her way but it was obvious from the wrinkles on his brow and his innocent gape that he had no idea what he was trying to focus on. Reinya backed away.

'Eugch, make 'im stop gawking at me. What's wrong with 'im?' She held her hand up to her mouth. 'Repulsive or what?'

Ishbel wished the girl's tone would soften. This waif was Scud's granddaughter, why was she so neddish? Scud was an old-educated native, this girl sounded as though she had been brought up in a gutter. Maybe she had. She placed her hand on the girl's back to guide her into the cabin but Reinya pushed her off and stared as if her hand burned.

Ishbel shrugged. 'He's been through an experiment. It isn't his fault he is like this.'

'What you going to do with 'im?'

'We are taking him for help.'

'We?' the girl sneered.

'What would you prefer, Miss? To have been left on the prison ship to hell's future? If it wasn't for him you'd have perished long ago.' The girl slunk into the corner and flounced down. Ishbel almost laughed, it had been many months since she had seen such a stroppy flounce. She clenched her fist and stowed the desire to punch the little brat. Thankfully Dawdle chose that moment to appear with a tray of brew.

'Right, let's be havin ye. Yous lot need tae lighten up. We've a while tae go afore we surface, so chill.' He winked at Reinya. 'A wee cuppa wouldnae go amiss, warm yous up eh?'

The girl glowered at him.

He handed two mugs to Ishbel then hunkered down to help

Scud sit. 'Hand me one o' they brews would ye, hen?' he clicked his fingers at Ishbel. She flinched but obliged.

'Come on wee man, huv a wee sip.' Scud opened his cracked mouth and eased his lips round the rim, he sipped then blushed.

'There,' Dawdle hushed, 'now isn't that just the job?'

The focus in Scud's eyes wavered in and out. 'Where...?' he licked his lips and tried again. 'Where ... girl?'

'She's right here, now dinnae fash. She's huvin a cuppa jist like you.' Dawdle clicked his finger, this time in the direction of the girl. 'Come say hiya tae yer granda.' Reinya shrank, flattened her back to the wall and stared at her feet.

Dawdle snapped his fingers in quick succession. 'Come, come, he disnae bite and naither dae ah.' His voice was light but the clench of his teeth and hard eyes seemed to work on the girl. She began to move towards the crouching pair. 'That's it wee hen, oan ye come.'

He held the cup for Scud and gave him another sip. Then Dawdle sat back on his heels and grabbed the girl's wrist as she loitered near him. He drew her into the circle. 'Ma maw used tae reckon a cup o' brew would put aw the world's wrongs tae rights. If only it were that easy. But it'll sure make ye feel better. No?'

Ishbel sipped her own brew and had to agree.

'Look, Scud,' Dawdle said pointing to the girl. 'She hus your chin and mouth. We'll no mention the eyes and hair, eh? Ah'm sure there wis a resemblance once upon a time.'

A slight puzzle passed Scud's face. 'Ah forgot ah'd been diluted. Ah used tae huv red hair, and green eyes once upon a time.'

Ishbel smiled. Scud's native accent was growing stronger in the company of Dawdle. It was a start.

Dawdle signalled for the girl to crouch down. When she hesitated, he jerked her arm and tugged her down beside him. Scud held out a shaky hand.

'Tig.'

The hard expression on the girl's face fell away, she looked confused. Her eyes darted to Ishbel, to the hatch, back to Dawdle, never once looking at Scud. Tears stood on her lids though her mouth remained tight.

'Goan, speak tae him,' Dawdle coaxed.

She swallowed. ''lo Granda, it's no Tig, it's Reinya.' As she pushed her red hair back from her face Ishbel saw for the first time a softness, a little girl beneath that hard exterior.

'Reinya.' Scud squinted and smiled. 'Ah forgot, what a pretty name.'

Ishbel's communicator buzzed twice. Scud clamped his wrist and shrank into a quivering ball.

'What's wrong, what's 'appening to 'im?'

'He thought he was going to be zapped.'

'S'OK wee man.' Dawdle took the mutant's hands and placed the cup in them. 'No zaps here Scud.'

Reinya's brows pringled so Dawdle filled in the detail. 'Ye see, the prison ships don't have them but at Black Rock that wis a form o' control. Zap.' Dawdle clamped his wrist and started to shake, rattling his head and rolling his eyes into their sockets, he fell to the ground and writhed. Scud looked on horrified.

'Alright, Dawdle, I think she gets the message. You're scaring Scud.' Ishbel pushed her toe at Dawdle and urged him to his feet. Sometimes Noiri ops go so OTT. 'Rather than ham it up, why don't you try to take his command band off?'

'Ah already did, Ish, and disabled his chip, but he's had it on so long he's suffering fae phantom pangs.' He shook his head like an oldie. 'Yep, it's like losing a leg and needing tae scratch the itch in yer toes. It'll take a while.' He pointed to Ishbel's wrist. 'What was the comms that came through anyway?'

'Nothing – Vanora – nothing.' Ishbel was thankful Dawdle let it go at that.

Reinya looked around the sub. Her lips slightly curled then she turned and sat in the corner at the opposite side from Scud. The look was indifferent but Ishbel could see fear in her eyes.

'Reinya.' Ishbel tried to soften her voice but the name still came out hard. 'You're free from that hell now. We'll get you sorted.' Although the Noiri op who rescued Reinya had cleaned her up, a haunted look hung on her, her nails were filthy, scabs crusted on her skin and she constantly scratched at her right leg just below the knee. Even so, the brew continued to have a miraculous effect on Scud and Reinya. They both looked more relaxed than before.

'What did you put in it?' Ishbel asked with narrowed eyes. Dawdle stood back in shock and held out his innocent hands.

'Ish, how could ye even ask?'

Scud's putty colour hung around the edges of his skin. He tried to smile over at Reinya but she found the dirt under her nails more interesting.

'Tell me about Tig?' he asked across the space between them.

She ignored him, turning her shoulder into the wall, placing her grubby thumb in her mouth.

'She was a lovely child, you know,' he said. 'Although ah can't tell whether you resemble her like or not.'

The engine stuttered to life. Dawdle checked the instruments before releasing a lever. A smell of fuel filled the space. Scud held his ears but Dawdle shouted over his shoulder, 'It's OK for a bit, we'll stay above until we are out the bay, and as long as ah safely can. Ah'll knock ye out afore we go under.'

Ishbel hunkered beside Reinya who sidled horrified looks towards Scud. 'What's wrong with 'im? Why does 'e need knocked out?' she said through her teeth.

'It's his ears.' Ishbel looked at the girl. 'Are you OK, your ears, I mean?'

'Yeah,' she said as if Ishbel were a daftie.

'The prisoners of the island penitentiary have part of their brains removed to prevent them swimming, escaping. So you're OK?'

'Said uh was didn't uh?'

'Good. He's about to be in a lot of pain.' Ishbel saw Scud relax slightly with the movement of the sub. His gentle humorous face fell into repose. When he caught her looking at him he winked. Yes, she was right to rescue him, he deserved to have some sort of life, although she had no idea what that life might be, he truly was a mutant.

'Why don't you tell us about Tig, Scud? To pass the time.' His grin took her by surprise. She was definitely glad she rescued him.

'She was a chubby child. Wouldn't stop eating. Always stealing food, packets o' cereal, oats, she loved oats. One day she eats the washing solution,' – Reinya frowned – 'before it's banned,' Scud qualified. 'She blew bubbles for weeks afterwards.' He chuckled. 'Well, maybe that's an exaggeration. It's the story ah've been telling them inside for years.' His eyes filmed over with sadness. 'You start tae believe your own stories after a while.'

Despite her scowl, Ishbel could tell Reinya was listening.

'Of course Tig wasn't her real name. It was Patricia.'

Reinya snuffed. 'What sort o' name's that?'

Scud twinkled at Ishbel and she nodded. 'Ah know, it is a little old fashioned but it was one of her mother's favourite names. As a child she jumped about all over the place, wanting people tae chase her. Man, she was a fast runner, it's a wonder she ever got caught. Anyway, we started calling her Tig and it stuck.'

Silence descended and choked.

'Clever at school she was.' Scud started. 'In the days when natives still went tae school. She was only nine when ah was taken. Just a wee bit thing. They came for me in the evening while she was upstairs doing homework, ah never even had a chance tae say goodbye.' His voice cracked with memory. He shook himself. 'Crimes against the State. Ah was teaching history, for Satan's sake. But it was a history they didn't want taught, not permitted history.' He looked into the past at his own history with the beginnings of tears under the surface of his mutated eyes. 'Your grandmother had just laid the table for dinner, smoked haddock, it's amazing what you remember. The smell o' smoked haddock lingers in the home for days, the smell o' that meal has lingered with me for twenty years. Ah bet you don't get it now.'

'Ah can get some fur ye – at a price,' Dawdle dared break the story. Ishbel batted him to wheesht.

'The news was on the telly.'

'Telly, that's what they had afore games walls,' Dawdle helpfully explained from the control seat.

'The news was on,' Scud continued. 'The Purists had been in power for five years. They had already purged the ethnos, sent them back to their origins. And of course the separation of Privileged and native had happened just the year before. The telly spouted its usual lies and rubbish and ah remember thinking this is getting even worse, and just then the door tae our house flew open. They grabbed me and had me wrapped in shackles before you could say 'hands up'. Your grandmother screamed, tried tae grab me, grabbed my shirt, my trousers, ah could faintly hear Tig crying out for her mother, she'd heard the screaming and shouting, but Jeanie never let go. Eventually one o' the Military kicked her, right in the face. The last time ah saw ma lovely wife she was spitting teeth and blood. Behind her the terrified white face o' ma wee Tig looked on, her little fists clenched. Ah could see she was going tae be a fierce wee warrior.'

'But she didn't,' Reinya said.

'Didn't what?'

'Become a warrior. She was weak.'

Scud shook his head. 'No, not ma Tig.'

Ishbel shifted in her seat, she knew what was coming, she'd scanned Tig's file.

'The drugs, the Mash,' Reinya sniffed back snot, her breath shorter. 'All my life uh've been cleaning up after 'er.'

Scud's thrapple worked hard to stay his tears. 'Sometimes life's too hard tae face.'

'What happened to them after you left?' Ishbel asked.

Scud shook his head and dropped his chin to his chest.

'Right, Scud, ah need tae go down and so dae you.' Dawdle shouted and held up a drug dose.

The journey took aeons because of Peedle's substandard cannibalised components from other crafts. Sometimes they had to stop in isolated bays to allow things to settle and cool and let Dawdle fix the broken bits and pieces.

'This is a heap of junk.'

'Aw, Ish, how can ye say that? She's got ye this far.'

She smiled despite her resolve not to. She knew Dawdle liked her too much and she didn't want to have to remind him this was a business arrangement. He was just so uneducated, he probably couldn't even read and write but Ishbel knew he was very clever. It was rumoured among the female natives at the base that he had riches beyond belief, despite his frugal looks. He was one of the most successful Noiri managers. But still, he was rough as hell.

'We used tae grow sunflowers.' Scud's slurred voice crackled through the throbbing of the engine.

'What?' Reinya's face screwed up with the word as if the mere sound of Scud's voice made her nauseous.

'Sunflowers, before bees disappeared. Me and your mother.' Scud struggled to sit. Ishbel wanted to help him – his granddaughter was nearer, but Reinya stayed put, nose wrinkled as if he'd just walked out of an Alien facility. Which in a way he had.

'We used tae grow sunflowers.'

'What's sunflowers?'

'Gorgeous flowers. Great big heads they had.' He held his hands up as if holding a soccer ball. 'Like the sun, petals and busy inside wi bees. They were always knackered by the time they had pollinated them all.'

Reinya looked towards Ishbel. 'What's 'e havering about?'

Ishbel sighed. 'It's a story from the olden days. A long story.'

'We would watch them grow taller and taller, until they stretched above both Tig and me and we would have tae fetch the ladder tae make sure we tied them securely.' He nodded to his memory, 'before the storms got them and broke their backs.'

'Make 'im stop.'

'We'd have crowning sunbursts aw around us and when they died back the birds showed up and pecked out the centre seeds.'

Reinya covered her ears with her hands and turned her back to the assembly.

'We'd chop the higher heads off and leave them strewn so the ground feeding birds could get a look in.'

'Don't get sunflowers onymair,' Dawdle remarked.

'Who cares,' Reinya mumbled within her arm cocoon and Scud smiled to Ishbel, she'd been listening all along.

'Tell me, granddaughter, what sort o' life have you led tae make you so angry?'

She whirled on him. 'You've no idea.'

'Try me.'

But she cooried her head under her arms again and turned her back on them.

'We're gonnae huv tae go inland fur a bit, folks. Ah'm picking up quite a bit of close activity on the military channel. And it disnae look like simple manoeuvres neither. Something going down.'

He shouted all this over his shoulder while manipulating the controls. 'Ish, you get Scud ready, this might be awful sore.' He turned back. 'They might huv spotted us, but ah cannae be…' The sub thudded sideways then lurched forward. They all sprawled in a heap. Dawdle pushed Reinya off him and bumped back to the seat. The sub rocked violently, almost spinning. Ishbel thumped her head on the side bar, a searing pain ripped through her shoulder blade. Reinya was screaming because Scud had landed on top of her and was now baying like a wolf.

'Get 'im off!'

The commotion lasted only seconds. Dawdle steadied the rocking and tried to help Ishbel into his seat. Blood poured from her nose. When he bent forwards to dab it with a torn rag she winced.

'Leave me. See to the others.'

Reinya had gone quiet while Scud whimpered. 'Water! Water's getting in.'

'Awright, wee man, awright.' Dawdle grabbed some lifejackets from under his seat and threw one to Ishbel.

'I said, see to the others.'

'Look at yer shooder,' he said. 'It looks dislocated.'

She tried to pull the jacket on, but pain surged over her, she saw stars, then spewed on the floor. Dawdle eased it over her head. Ishbel closed her eyes and mind against the searing pain.

'Sorry, sorry.'

Her teeth clamped against her scream. Sweat beaded her brow.

Next he pulled a life jacket over the whimpering Scud. 'Come on wee man – need tae get ye out o' here. Ye won't drown now, wi this on.

'Ah need tae help Ishbel, you get her one on her.' Dawdle pointed to Reinya, who was slumped over rolls of fibre. Scud did as he was told and tried to put the life jacket on her but she sprang to her feet before he put it over her head.

'It's alright, uh can do it.'

'Ah thought…' he stuttered.

'Uh was only winded.'

He tried again to help her.

'Leave me,' she hissed.

'Stop this,' Ishbel shouted then winced. 'We have to get out.' Her words were cut off by her own scream as the sub rocked violently.

'They're going tae kill us if we leave,' Scud shouted.

'Maybe so, but we huv tae get out.' Dawdle manoeuvred the lever and Scud's arms whipped to his ears.

'We're going up, get ready fur the hatch tae open.'

Ishbel set her communicator and pulled Davie's old gun from her belt with her left hand.

'Yeah right, Ish, and that's going tae help how? Yer arm's goosed.'

'Come on, old man, when wis the last time ye were in combat?' he said, handing the old gun to Scud.

'What about me?' Reinya asked.

Ishbel and Dawdle exchanged looks then Dawdle handed her a bandoleer of grenades.

'Do you know how to use them?' Ishbel asked.

She just snorted her affirmative. 'Where've you been? Everyone my age knows 'ow to bomb.'

'Scud, help Ishbel through the hatch and dinnae panic when ye get intae the water, remember ye'll no sink with this,' he said, tapping the life jacket.

'Ready?'

He opened the hatch.

'Ah've launched the escape raft on their blind side. That way,' he signalled left. 'When ah start firing you get in the raft, start the engine and head fur shore, ah'll be right behind ye.'

Sorlie

Vanora studied the ticker wall for aeons. How could she read the rapid text? It wasn't snptxt but a variation, all high value consonants and symbols. Kenneth often moved to interrupt her, then would bottle it, his mouth left open like a drooling daftie.

'What's wrong with you?' She clicked her fingers at him as if he'd just puddled the floor. He slunk away from her, biting his newly manicured nails. Ridgeway was playing one of the VT games she'd instructed us to use to improve our 'Lazy Dexterity', an impediment, according to Vanora, more deadly than the Elepto8 virus. He loved the workout. I could tell by the giggle in his shoulders. Kenneth, who made no bones about his aching joints, couldn't use the dexterity pads so had to content himself trying to decipher Vanora's ticker wall. Unfortunately, his eyesight had never been corrected during his cave years so his squint at the blurred lines fooled no one. Poor Kenneth flitted the room like a useless piece of rubbish blown off the recyk midden before settling in his corner. He began picking flakes of concrete from the wall and crumbling it between his fingers. A puzzle crimped his brow.

'Stop that or you'll have the whole building round our ears,' Vanora snapped.

'Give him a break.' Ridgeway mumbled under the noise of his screaming game.

'Come on Sorlie, we're leaving,' she said, flattening her tone to reasonable.

'What about me?' Kenneth asked. 'Can I come?'

'No,' she nipped. The ka-bam from Ridgeway's game told me he had just made a monumental error. Game Over. Reload.

'I want to go back to work,' Kenneth persisted.

'You need an overhaul first.'

'I've been overhauled.'

'That was a makeover. I mean a proper overhaul.' That frail old woman I met at Black Rock had morphed into a daemon again.

'A proper overhaul?'

'Kenneth you've been under considerable strain while away.'

'Away,' he echoed. 'Am I not your heir?'

She placed a possessing arm on my shoulder.

'In olden terms yes, but we live in a new age. Sorlie is my heir.'

'Me?'

She ignored me. 'You're an old man.' Her voice sounded kindly in a sickening sort of way. 'You can't expect my armies to follow you – it takes aeons to get you moving. No, an overhaul for you my boy, then back to the labs.'

Kenneth looked almost relieved as he stormed from the room. Ridgeway moved to follow. 'Not you, you come with us.'

'He needs me.'

'No he doesn't. He's been alone for years, a few more days won't hurt him.'

'At least let me say goodbye.'

'No! You'll be back before his fizz has settled.'

Ridgeway's face was purple with rage but he was enough of an institutional man to know when to keep schtum. Vanora meanwhile moved into sweetness mode again. 'Now we're going to visit a dear friend of mine. Come, not only will it be beneficial to the cause, it might even be fun.'

Fun? Ridgeway and I looked at each other. Fun?

The last revolutionary Transport I'd travelled on, when Ishbel first took me to Black Rock, had been a heap of junk destined for the Noiri scrappies. Vanora's palatial craft was another story. This one, with the regal insignia, was the same craft that hovered and bowed outside my cell window when I was incarcerated at Black Rock. The plush leather upholstery wrapped a hug around me. The engine purred like a newly serviced gyrocycle. No frayed seat straps here, just sturdy stiff webbing riveted to the bulkhead, securing us for the rapid hurtle from the hillside hangar into the night. Landing lights traced us for a while, then quit, plunging us into the green twilight of the instrument panel. Arkle, the sub-mariner, multi-tasking man, piloted the craft. Could it be Vanora's army was not so well stocked after all? He followed a blackened screen and mumbled into his headgear. We flew for just over an hour then plummeted so steeply my stomach bounced off my diaphragm and I bit my tongue.

A lightening flash jolted us sideways, we bounced then recovered. It was hard to tell in the blue-black of the power curfew hours whether we flew over any Urbans. Tiny flickers sporadically spaced on the ground would be from native camp fires.

The engine changed pitch and we settled down. In the dark my instinct told me there was a mass of something not far to my left. I heard the slosh of water but there was no sensation of rocking.

'Are we on the sea?'

'No.' Arkle spoke before Vanora had a chance. She pruned her mouth. Arkle pushed a lever to open the door. The smell of salty sea air made the sting of memory tear my eyes. A rumble came towards us in the dark, and I had the feeling of being inside the Games Wall super-digie, and waited for the game to eat us whole. A hunter's light shone into the cab and Vanora disembarked first, into the lightbeam.

'Come, Sorlie, these fine gentlemen can't wait about all night.'

A Trac stood below on rippled wet sand. As I stepped out a sea breeze caught my face and turned me back in time to when Pa took me to the ocean, but this was no big ocean. It was a huge bay. Ridgeway unbuckled his seatbelt.

'Not you.'

'What?' We both said.

'Why did you bring Ridgeway then?' I asked.

She sighed as if we were dolts. 'Kenneth needs time to adjust. He has important work to do. Ridgeway is a distraction.'

The cruelty of this woman was staggering, but Ridgeway sat back in his seat, his face working hard to contain his anger and I wondered again at the life of this Bas guard. Exiled from his Lowland home, his family destroyed in the pursuit of the Purists' land grab, forced into the service of the Military. OK, he was higher status than a native, but not much. He still had that air of inevitability about his fate.

I touched his sleeve. 'Don't let her get to you,' I whispered. He nodded which was better than a native shrug.

We'd moved only a few metres when the Transport catapulted off the sand, made off towards the western horizon, leaving only the purr of its retreating engine. My agitation must have shown because Vanora hugged me.

'Don't worry, Arkle will return when we need him.'

The Trac changed key and became amphibious. Ahead a bead of lights rose into the sky. Vanora began to laugh a girlish tinkle.

'Well, I had heard but I didn't believe it. How very quaint, and so very him.'

'Who?' I asked.

'Jacques. Monsieur Jacques to you.'

A tower, at least a hundred metres high, jutting from the sea like a mission ready rocket spacetrain.

Vanora's laugh tinkled. 'Boys and toys eh?'

We were dispatched onto a makeshift jetty and ushered up a gangway by a mousy Noiri man who smelled of stale smoke.

'What on earth is it?'

'It used to be called the Blackpool Tower. It might still be.' That tinkle still rattled her voice. 'It used to be on land before the floods. It should have been dismantled years ago. Goodness knows what he's renamed it.'

Just looking at it made me woozy. 'I'm not going up there.'

'Of course you are.'

We could have argued more but the matter was settled before we had a chance.

The sky exploded. At first I thought it was fireworks from the tower until I saw the falling debris in the western sky and the horror lit on Vanora's face. 'Arkle,' she whispered.

'Ridgeway!' I roared.

Ishbel

'Ew, what's that smell?' Reinya dug her elbow into the wet sand, leaving a bony imprint when she hoisted herself to stand. She sniffed the air like a cub seeking food.

Ishbel breathed deeply. A vague memory flickered.

'Peat smoke,' Scud said. 'Delicious isn't it?'

Reinya wrinkled her nose in disagreement. The sky was turning black. On the beach only a sheen off the sea gave them a glimmer of light.

All four hid behind a huge black boulder poking from the sand, protecting them from the sea and part of the beach. The reef had been close enough to the shore to allow Dawdle to anchor Peedle to the rocks and by a process of coaxing, bullying, ending with a threat of violence he had managed to pull Scud, unscathed and certainly not drowned, onto the beach. Poor Scud. Was there no end to the man-handling of this wretched body? Ishbel tried to lead the party ashore but the pain in her shoulder made her swoon. Little Madam Reinya dropped her act, grabbed Ishbel's tunic and stopped her going under.

The peat reek fought against the overpowering smell of rotting seaware lying in dark patches on the beach a couple of metres from them. Maybe that was the smell Reinya meant.

'Peat,' Scud said again. 'A form o' carbon capture, decayed vegetation. For centuries the fuel o' our ancestors.' He sniffed deeply. 'In the olden days Island natives cut uniform squares from the earth about so big.' He held out his hands to make a rectangle about ten centimetres wide. 'Communities worked together tae cut them, it was hard but willing work.'

Reinya rolled her eyes. 'What's with the 'istory lesson?'

'They dried them then stored them in stacks tae burn on their fires for heat and cooking.' He sniffed again. 'So where have you brought us, Dawdle?'

Ishbel consulted her communicator and pushed it toward Dawdle. 'Why are we so far west? According to the coordinates we're in sector U. Uninhabited. Even the penitentiary was abandoned because it was too difficult to defend on the flat terrain.'

'Shush, listen.' Dawdle placed a hand on her good arm. She shook it off still puzzled with the coordinates, it didn't make sense. They were supposed to be heading north, taking a shorter route through the Minch.

An eerie sound swamped the night air. Singing, lilting, almost a chant in some strange tongue.

'Aliens,' Reinya said. 'Your communicator's porking. You've landed us on another planet.'

'You watch too many movie-casters wee hen,' Dawdle hissed. 'But creepers, what is that?'

'Singing,' Ishbel said.

As the sound moved closer Dawdle pushed them further into the crack between two rocks. Ishbel picked out another sound accompanying the singing; a metallic creeching sound. She cocked her head to get a better look.

Dawdle gently pulled her back. 'Dinnae move and dinnae say onythin until we're sure.'

'Of what?' Reinya asked.

'Ah dinnae ken.'

Light lingered on the horizon but the four were already in darkness. Ishbel crawled forward and batted away Dawdle's restraining arm, she had to be sure. She pulled on her night vision. A dozen or so native men and women traipsed towards their hiding place. Two or three dragged a rusted old trailer along the beach and it was from this that the screeching howled from. The others used longforks to hook and toss the seaware into the cart. The rhythm and movement of the cart and the pitching worked in perfect time to a hypnotic song. Ishbel began to hum along and sway with the rhythm until Dawdle placed his grubby hand over her mouth and pulled her back for the second time. Pain exploded through her shoulder, she spat bile in the sand while the others watched the procession pass and continue along the beach that seemed to stretch for kiloms.

'Ah'm sorry,' Dawdle whispered.

Ishbel raised her head. 'Why did you stop me?'

'Because we need tae suss the set-up.'

'They're just natives collecting seaware.'

'Aye, a shit lot o' seaware.'

'And I suppose you've already worked out the price on it.'

He grinned at her. 'It's the way ah'm wired, Ish, ah cannae help it. Wired fur profit.'

'If we can smell their fires,' Scud said, shivering in his wet clothes, 'they must have dwellings close by.'

'Uh'm starving. Will they huv food?' Reinya asked.

'Possibly,' Scud replied.

'Uh wasn't talking to you.'

He slunk back, stung. Ishbel wanted to slap her. This child, although a native and from a different upbringing, reminded her so much of Sorlie – always starving and hard coded to whine.

She hunted in her pocket and brought out a crumpled and soggy grain bar. A throwback from her domestic days never knowing when her charge would utter those famous two words, 'I'm starving.'

'Here have this. I'm sure we'll find food soon.'

'What if we don't?'

'Shut up,' Ishbel snapped.

Dawdle put his hand on her arm, she winced.

'Sorry, Ish. We'll need tae get that fixed.'

'Stop saying sorry,' she growled. He grinned toward Reinya.

'Dinnae you worry yersel, wee hen. Ah bet ah can find ye something tae eat.'

'Uh'm frozen.'

'S'truth, will you shut it with the whining.' Ishbel said but then she heard Scud's teeth chattering louder than the trailer wheels. She bit her words and said. 'No, Reinya's right, we need to find cover.'

'Aye, it's a bit cauld right enough,' Dawdle placed his hands on the older man's shoulders to stop him shaking. 'Do'ye know what? Ah bet ah can get us somewhere warm and dry right now.'

'How?'

'Noiri code o' practice. And ah reckon it works everywhere even on deserted islands.'

'This island isn't deserted,' Reinya chirped, she was civil to at least one person in the party.

'Even better. Ah'll just nip up here and huv a wee shuftie, there's still enough light. Yous stay right here.' He bounded up the sand dunes and out of sight.

Ishbel blew out a small whistle through her teeth and sat down, conscious of the big gap between Reinya and Scud. She wanted to place her arms around them both, draw them to her but couldn't.

'Huddle into him,' she coaxed. Reiyna made to move away, Ishbel reached out to grab and was swept in agony. She spat again and gulped back pain.

'Steady, Ishbel,' Scud said. 'Look hen,' he said to Reinya, 'we'll be warmer if we stay close. That's simple survival training and you know it.' She yielded then.

It took a while for Ishbel to quell her nausea and the stench both former prisoners effused didn't help. 'One day you'll be warm and dry and clean again,' she said through her own chattering teeth. At least they were free. Well, almost. Although she'd been a domestic all her life she had had a kind of freedom being in the service of her sister and brother-in-law. These two she now huddled next to her had suffered unspeakable horrors. Reinya would have had to live in a vermin-riddled ship, where communal suffering was part of the punishment. She'd watched her mother die. Ishbel needed to remember that.

Dawdle jumped over the rock and landed in the sand throwing it up over the huddled trio.

'Guess what?'

'What?' said Ishbel, humouring.

'Ah wis spot on.' He reached down and dragged Scud to his feet. Reinya was already on his heels.

'What is it?' she asked.

'Come on, wait and see.'

'Just tell us,' Reinya shouted. Ishbel could have sworn she stamped her foot.

'Shush,' Ishbel said. 'We still don't know where they are.'

Dawdle led them, struggling and fighting the shifting sands, over the dune. Ishbel stumbled, put a hand out to save her damaged shoulder. Marram grass cut her like a blade. Something dark lurked out there in the dune. A shape out of place in the landscape, manmade.

'Can ye see it?' Dawdle couldn't contain his excitement. When they got closer Ishbel started to laugh.

'It's a white van.' Except it wasn't white, it was grey and rusted and smeared with age.

'Too true it's a white van.' He beamed with pride. 'And where dae ye think white vans go tae when they eventually die?'

'Eh, the white van cemetery,' now she really was humouring him.

'Naw. They're carted off tae specific places with some provisions for just such a troubled crew as we four are.'

'You're joking.'

'Nut. Ah told ye it's the Noiri code o' practice but only the Noiri ken aboot it. It's a secret.'

In a world of no secrets, Ishbel was stunned. She'd never heard of such things. Everyone knew of her mother's cells around the world, not their whereabouts but their existence, but this was a phenomenon.

Dawdle tugged the door with a flourish but it wouldn't budge. He cleared remaining glass from a panned in side window. The nippy smell of urine wafted through. The windscreen was cracked and the cab sagged on one axle. Dawdle wriggled through the broken window and kicked out the back doors.

'What a mess, what a stink,' Ishbel said, holding her nose. Shredded bedding scattered on a carpet of vermin droppings.

'Oh great, a 'eap o' shit and stuffing,' Reinya complained, but Dawdle ignored them as he kicked the debris out the door with the edge of his boot. From the gold chain he wore round his neck, he produced a small wire and poked it into a tiny hole on the floor. A cover popped up to reveal a hidden compartment. He sat back on his heels to enjoy the marvel on everyone's faces.

'Telt ye? Eh?' He pulled out two sleeping bags and threw them at Scud. Next he produced a small gas canister which he laid by his knee, a few rusty tins and an empty water bottle.

'There's bound tae be a stream nearby.'

'How d'you know?' Reinya asked.

'There always is.'

Scud held a bag out to Reinya but she blanked him. Dawdle took it and gave it to her. 'You need tae wise up young lady. Get in there and get warm.'

'You and me'll need tae cuddle up, Ish,' he grinned. She ignored him as she hugged the gas canister between her knees and assembled the stove one-handed. 'Go get some water then we can have a brew.'

'That's a no then?' He faked a hurt voice. 'And what about a wee "thank you Dawdle for bringing us tae these gifts".'

'Thanks, Dawdle, now get water.'

'First ah'll sling yer arm,' he said, holding up a first aid kit.

'What ah don't get,' Scud said when Dawdle had gone, 'Is why the locals didn't take this stuff.'

Ishbel shrugged. 'Search me, we'll need to ask Dawdle when

he comes back, he seems to know all about this place.' Too much to be a coincidence, but she stored that thought.

He was only minutes away when he came bounding back. 'There's a spring, a nice one, wee bit on the peaty side but braw.' He handed over the bottle, 'Here take a sip, Scud,' but the mutant was already asleep, laid out like an Egyptian mummy.

'When wis the last time he munched, Ish?'

'A while, but let him rest.'

'He's gettin worse.'

'What's wrong with 'im?' Reinya asked Ishbel.

'I'm not sure, he might need a chemical top-up to stabilise his condition. He hasn't had any since he left the prison.'

'So what's going to 'appen to 'im?'

'We need to get him help, to our base, hopefully Kenneth can help.'

'Who's Kenneth?'

'The one who started all this.' Ishbel turned away from the girl. She was too tired to explain that twenty years ago Kenneth had been one of the scientists working on the DNA dilution project. The original architect before the State decided to use the discovery for sinister means, before Kenneth became a native outcast.

After a feast of tinned beans and brew they tried to sleep. Despite the painkillers Dawdle found for Ishbel in the stash, waves of pain continued to wash over her. But she must have slept because she woke to morning light just as Dawdle was climbing back into the van.

'Where have you been?'

He held a finger up to his lips. 'Shhh. Come and have a look at this.' They squeezed past the sleeping pair and left the fusty van into a crisp clean morning. No rain fell but a definite moisture misted the air. Rain wasn't far off. They walked towards the beach. The sun rose behind them, casting a delicate red glow on the machair. The tide returned to wash away the tracks from the seaware harvest and replaced them with more food from the sea. The moist breeze caught Ishbel's hair, washing her face with soft mizzle.

'It's beautiful,' she said and felt a true smile on her lips, not that supplicant native smile that had been trained into her from birth.

'Aye it is,' Dawdle said as he gently turned her injured body round to face him. 'But look the other way.'

She looked over his shoulder. There was a broad opening through the dunes, exposing the inland. The island stretched out flat and green with brown patches, rugged and solid with gut-twisting familiarity. Small lochs shimmered in the distance, puddling the landscape and a couple of hills jutted in defiance of the flatlands.

Dawdle pointed to green mounds a short distance from the beach. Small dunes with more marram grass than the ones closer to the shore.

'What?'

'Look closer,' he urged.

Ishbel narrowed her eyes. She sniffed the peat smoke and then she saw wisps escaping from small black slits in the grass. Smoke puffed from the grass dispersing into the wide open sky.

'What?' She turned wide eyed to Dawdle who nodded like an ancient sage.

'Aye, last night's natives live closer than we thought. We must have practically tripped over them on the way tae the van. That's a Souterrain, an underground dwelling, and so well hidden it can only mean one thing.'

'Outcast natives?' She said. Dawdle nodded.

'What do we do?' Ishbel tasted blood on her bitten lip, wiped it with her finger and cursed her weakness. 'We risk it,' she said answering her own question. Scud needed help, Satan's truth, they all needed help.

Dawdle nodded. 'Agree.'

The temperature was mild now they were sheltered from the shore breeze. The peat smoke seemed to absorb the moisture in the air, turning its normal acrid smell into something sweet and nutty. The fact fires were lit told them the community was up and about although none were visible.

They approached a door in the hillside, an 'Open Sesame' of sorts.

'We'll knock.'

Ishbel nodded, her throat too dry to speak. Dawdle knocked once, paused, knocked twice as he raised his fist a third time Ishbel caught his arm.

'A bit over the top. Yes?' She said. He shook off her hand and held a restraining arm to bar her from the door then knocked once more. Ishbel shoved him.

'What's your game?' It was a signal, she wasn't thick.

The door remained closed. Ishbel felt her anger rise at Dawdle and the door. She was about to suggest they try somewhere else when a hood enveloped her. As her hands and feet bound her like a smokie she screamed in torture.

'Watch…' she heard Dawdle shout before she passed out.

One person carried her but she sensed the presence of others. She felt suddenly sheltered from the wind and her searing pain had disappeared. There was a sound of shuffling, an occasional cough. Her carrier ducked and tipped her body then a warmth suffocated her. They had entered the house; she coughed on the smoke, the dense air.

The rough hood scratched her face, the bindings bit her hand and wrists, her shoulder injury stoonded like a stubbed toe but was nothing to what she had before.

'Dawdle,' she shouted, though her voice was muffled. Something hard dunted her head. A hand?

'Just you wait, Dawdle.' She was hit again, harder this time, so she stayed schtum.

Where was he? She had no fear now, if they'd wanted to kill her they would have by now. She was a native, not worth kidnapping. As long as they didn't know she was Vanora's daughter she should be OK. How could they know that? Then the memory of Dawdle's door knock niggled.

She bum-shuffled to sitting. A cold hard surface chilled her back, a solid wall, ridged and rough but at least it was a lean. She dragged her knees to her chest, waited and listened. There was a hiss and heat from a fire somewhere nearby and a small whispering, a male voice speaking the guttural tone of her native tongue. A language banished from Lesser Esperaneo around the time of her birth, but heard last night in the lyrics of the seaware gatherers. A hard knot lodged in her throat, a great sadness, the mythical cianalas swept through her like a ghost. There was another sound close by, the familiar rhythmic thud, the unmistakable smell of oats, the thud of the spurtle against the porridge pot.

Where the hell was Dawdle? She counted off minutes with the thud of the pot. Every now and again she heard the thump change tone, and a whispered, 'Tapadh leat.'

Her stomach rumbled so loud she was sure the cook must have heard it.

'Ciamar a tha thu?' she whispered. The thumping stopped. She said it again

'Gu math' was the masculine reply.

Result. But she wished she too could say she was 'good'. The thumping did not resume, near silence filled the room. She was sure he had left when she felt the hood loosened and eased from her neck. Ishbel squeezed her eyes tight in preparation for blinding light but she was in semi-darkness. She narrowed her eyes trying to make out shapes. Before her stood a young woman of about her own age. Her hair was black as were her eyes in this gloom.

'Thank you,' Ishbel said in Gaelic.

'You speak our language.'

'Yes, I'm from the exile lands.'

The woman nodded. Behind her a male approaching senior age peered at her. His hair and beard were grey and both were tied in knots. Once he seemed satisfied with her face he returned to thumping his porridge pot, his gummy mouth worked as if in silent protest to the intrusion.

'Where's Dawdle?'

The woman tilted her head to one side as if listening to something, then indicated with her head to a stone pillar, but all Ishbel could make out was dark shadow. She was positioned in the outside edge of a large, stone, circular building with walls separating rooms like spokes in a wheel and the peat fire and the hearth as its nucleus. The swee, an apex frame above the fire, held the cauldron tended to by the knotted man.

'Why am I a prisoner?'

The young woman cut Ishbel's question with the edge of her hand.

Ishbel shifted position, her bum was cold and numb. 'My shoulder?'

'Was dislocated, we relocated it while you were out. It will repair now.'

'Thank you. But…'

'What are you doing here?' The woman asked

'Did Dawdle not explain?'

'I'm asking you.'

'We were shipwrecked.'

'You were not shipwrecked, we found your vessel; there's no damage. It's as well as can be expected given its age and history. So I ask you again.' She clearly had another story in mind.

'This makes no sense.' Ishbel remembered the collision,

Dawdle's insistence they abandoned ship. 'What do you mean no damage?' The woman ignored her. 'We were fired on by a military vessel. We had to escape the water.'

The doubter shook her head. 'And did you see the damage?' Ishbel replayed the incident, Dawdle's handling of the vessel, shouting orders, helping them out. But when they were in the water there was no firing. Dawdle, what was his game?

'Try again.'

'Look, I don't know what game Dawdle's playing but that's my story, I've no other.' Ishbel struggled to get to her feet but was pushed roughly back. 'Look, we have someone who needs help. He has gone through a mutation and is suffering from chemical withdrawal. We need to get him to help.'

'Then why stop here?'

Ishbel wanted to shout but knew that was unprofessional and would get her nowhere. She shook her head. 'Maybe you should ask Dawdle.'

The woman looked angry and pulled the hood back over Ishbel's head, leaving her in the dark with the thumping of the pot and the sucking of the gums. If Dawdle manoeuvred them here intentionally maybe he could negotiate help for Scud – they obviously had healers. Scud and Reinya should be awake by now and not only would they wonder where Ishbel had gone, but they would have to spend time alone together. What if Scud had died? That girl could be alone with a corpse. Ishbel felt her anger fizz. Whatever happened, she was going to kill Dawdle for this.

Her belly still rumbled. 'Can I have some please,' she asked.

The pot stopped.

The hood was lifted but it was the young woman again. She assisted Ishbel to her feet and released her leg bindings.

'Come with me.'

The building was indeed a wheel. Each stone wall, a spoke partitioning quarters. Rough bedding indicated sleeping areas.

In one section a group of about six small children huddled in bedrolls, staring bug-eyed at the intruder. Another room was filled with buckets of grain and crates of vegetables. In another women and small boys stacked bolts of cloth. Ishbel paused to get a better look but the girl prodded her between her shoulder blades, as if to test her injury.

'Keep moving.'

A clattering banging sounded nearby, the noise growing louder. A fist of nostalgia gripped Ishbel's heart; she knew, she hoped. And there it was in the next room. An ancient and wooded complicated contraption threaded with hundreds of fibres. At the other end new made cloth folded onto the paved floor. A hand loom for making cloth, primitive and yet surviving. The man who clattered and rocked with the shuttle looked as though he too had survived the last century. In her birthland of the North West Territories every community had a loom and here it was again, something familiar from the home she and her mother left when she was young.

She was led round the exterior, the outside rim, where people bizzied, mostly, from what she could see, in food preparation. She was ushered under a stone lintel into a smaller passage leading to the chamber of another wheel, an annex of the main wheel. In this chamber sat four men and four women all dressed in rough plaid, woven in colours and patterns of the landscape, mottled auburns and greens.

And there in the centre of the group, eye to the floor was Dawdle, untethered and unharmed. If Ishbel's arms had been free he would have felt more than her glare.

A female oldie with grey hair knotted in the same style as the cook nodded to the young guard and Ishbel felt her bindings fall free. She wrung out and rubbed her wrists. There was no need to stand on tiptoe, even though they were sitting she could see she was taller than all in the room.

'Well?' was all she had to say to the room, but her eyes stayed on Dawdle's face. He had some explaining to do.

The older women nodded now to Dawdle, who took his cue and stepped forward.

'It's like this Ish.'

'Don't you Ish me,' she gritted even though she was calm, kept her voice low.

Dawdle squared his shoulders and cleared his throat.

'Ishbel,' he began, 'These kind people huv agreed tae look after Scud.'

'How can they? We need to get him to Kenneth, he'll know what to do.' Ishbel swept her arm round the assembly. 'No disrespect but he needs specialised care.'

Dawdle nodded his head. 'Ah've explained that but they're sure they can help. They huv healers.'

'Healers, but not geneticists.' Two of the elders stood, the girl closed in, breathing on her neck. 'Look, I don't want to be disrespectful,' Ishbel said, addressing the elders directly. 'I just don't understand how you can help him.'

'Ancient arts – you don't need tae understand,' Dawdle said. 'Need tae know basis only.'

She pointed a finger at Dawdle. 'You planned this?' She swung her finger round to the girl. 'She told me there's no damage to Peedle.'

'Ah'll explain th…'

'No.' she hissed. 'You want him out the way.'

'Enough,' said the old knotted lady. 'Take your squabbles outside. We can help your friend, take the offer or not, but you must leave us soon. We do not want the State searching for you here.' She clicked her fingers and the girl stepped forward. 'Take Dawdle to see the quartermaster to arrange the seaware contract and take payment for the bolts of cloth.'

If Ishbel had been closer she would have slapped Dawdle. The seaware contract? Cloth?

'Wired for profit.' Ishbel spat at Dawdle as he passed, head still bowed.

The woman nodded in agreement. 'This community has hidden from the State for twelve years. We grow each year but will soon be unable to support ourselves. Your friend Dawdle helps us trade.'

'He's no friend of mine.'

'That's as maybe, but we are indebted to him and we will help this friend, Scud. Now go and bring him here.'

'Did you fix my shoulder?'

The woman nodded once. 'It was not difficult. Exercise the joint and it will heal.'

Ishbel was led from the room, into the open air where she blinked at the dull daylight. Dawdle stood waiting for her. She punched him square in the face. His neck snapped back with the impact. But he'd been waiting for it, she was sure.

He held his hand up to his nose. 'OK, ah deserved that, but if you'd known you'd huv held a gun tae ma heid and set the controls fur Freedom.'

She walked from him back to the van. 'They can help him, Ish.' He stumbled after her. 'Ishbel these folk need me and they're harvesting everything this coastline gives them.' He was gaining on her. 'We're sitting on a profit gold mine.'

She stopped suddenly, birled and punched him again. He pulled a rag to wipe the blood that now dripped from his nose. Then held the bloody rag to her. The fabric was the same as the plaids worn by the islanders.

'You saw. Ah supply the fibre from another community, they make the cloth here. They have industry. Ah'm only a facilitator.'

Ishbel whirled on him again, he stepped back from the punch.

'Do you have any other surprises you want to spring on me?'

Dawdle stood his ground. 'That's how Noiri works, Ish, keeping a constant eye open fur the main chance. It's a win-win.'

'Any more surprises?'

'No, no, Ishbel.'

Sorlie

The numbness was complete. I wanted to scream, I wanted to punch Vanora, who stood panting, her body as rigid as my own. Instead I could only gape at the dying embers of our Transport, breathing its last before sinking into the fringes of the bay.

'Poor Kenneth,' I whispered. He had been alone for so long and had only just found his soul-mate.

'Never mind Kenneth, Arkle was one of the best.' Vanora's words were harsh but I could see by the colour on her cheeks and the shake of her hand that she was bluffing.

'No time to gape – move!' The Noiri man grabbed me, propelling me towards the van.

'What happened?' I tried to push off his urgent hand.

'How the snaf should I know?'

'Vanora?' But she was already in the passenger seat, face pinched, and staring straight ahead as if I too had disappeared in the wreck. I started towards her but was held back.

'No time for that now, we 'ave to get you out of 'ere.'

The driver had a permanent drip on his nose threatening to plash but hanging on with a vengeance as he opened the back doors. The van was stuffed full of bio crates, FRAGILE stencilled on the sides.

'Sorry, man,' he said. He pushed the crates with both hands, sweating and swearing at the bulk.

'There, you'll just about fit,' he pointed to the space the size of a boot box.

'I…'

'Move!' he roared. Even thought he was a smowt, he scooped me up, wedged me into the space like a size ten foot stuffed in an eight boot and pushed the door to. Pressure popped the small of my back when the door clicked, my chest crushed. It was pitch black, the windows had been tarred out. My chest was glued to the door and crate corners spiked my shoulder blades. Travelling in style. I heard the cab door slam then we were off. I set my breathing to shallow and waited for the short trip to the tower to be over.

After about five minutes I heard another engine roar behind us. The driver swore, the van weaved, braked. The crate pressure released, then whammed me into the door with the velocity of a bullet. I felt a rib snap. A shot fired outside, Vanora roared in anger or pain. More shots. Then silence. I shoved at the door, it didn't budge. Was it Pirates, the Military, the same beings who shot Ridgeway from the sky? I checked my comms for a signal - dead. No, not dead, blocked, I could see the signal with the cross through it. It had been aeons since I heard Vanora roar.

My belly turned to water, I felt in my pocket for my knife. I pressed an ear to the window and heard scuffling. Putting my back against the door I pushed, I eased a hand free but didn't want to punch in case they heard. I might be able to make a run for it. The door didn't budge. If they wanted the cargo why didn't they come? I heard a door slam, another engine rev then drive off, leaving the only sound, the thudding of my heart.

The door inner mechanism felt gritty, rusted. I hooked my finger through it and pulled it up. The force almost broke my finger and the door stayed firm. I pushed it down. Nothing. I levered back into the crates, but there was no room to manoeuvre. Sweat trickled my spine, I leaned into the door again, a panic fluttered on my belly. I couldn't breathe, it was like the time the power failed in the prison and I nearly suffocated. I balled my fist to punch, then something stopped me. A sound from outside. Giggling? Shouts, laughing. Doors closed, the van engine fired, filthy fumes filled my small space. The van shuddered forward, kangarooed, stalled, laughs, fired again, began to move. I yanked the door, a dread filled me. I kicked, breath short, my ribs ached. The van jounced from side to side, bounced. Somehow I managed to twist my foot up to the tarred window, I kicked, my knee locked. The van bucked. Curdling screams rang from the cab. The crates fell, rumbled, the world rocked, my head under heels and a box on my chest, rolling, rolling and I knew I was done for.

There were lights, blinding lights. Rough hands held my neck, clamped my throat, throttling me. I struggled as something rigid replaced the hands. I was banded in a collar like a slave.

'It's OK, son, it's OK, son,' a voice said over and over.

Something soft and warm swaddled me, like Ma's embrace, floating me to another place. A searing pain burned my lungs and somewhere lower down. My legs. Screaming bled my ears. My screams.

'It's OK, son, it's OK, son.' A sharp pain stabbed the back of my hand and, and…

Purple and orange swirled in my eyes, like a mushie trip gone bad, but my eyelids were open and I was looking at a ceiling, solid and painted in a hideous manner. I heard breathing. Someone was close.

'Who?' The word blotted the top of my mouth.

My body jarred, spasmed and screamed - I couldn't move even if I wanted to because I was strapped to a bed. Memory dripped back; the tower, the van, the crash.

'Vanora?' my voice croaked, I licked my lips. There was a movement, a draft of air, the purple and orange swirled, the ceiling moved, like fabric. I was in a tent. A hand laid gently on my arm.

'Where?' I looked up into the face of a young girl. Her bark brown eyes were curious. Her tight black hair corkscrewed around her broad brow like a mad hat, her exotic looks scared me for no reason other than instinct. My ancestors warning me.

'Shh, lie still,' she said.

'How long have I been here?'

'A while, your injuries were severe. We kept you suspended while you healed.'

'Where am I?' My voice was misty and frail. The pressure of her hand on my arm increased. I tried again.

'Where am I?'

'Steadie.'

'Steady what?'

'No, Steadie, it's the name of our reservation.' There was a slight huff in her voice, like I'd offended.

I licked my lips again. 'A reservation?' The girl nodded. 'A native reservation?'

There were hundreds of reservations dotted around the northern lands of Esperaneo. Domestic natives lived with their owners, but the non-domestic natives, the ones who worked in Urban factories, fields and service industry either lived in purpose-built dorms on site or in the reservations. I struggled to move.

'Why?' I said as I wrestled with the bindings.

'For your own good. We were worried about your neck, back,' she said, making no move to release me.

I looked around my gaudy surroundings. 'It's a tent.'

Her laugh was more a croak, as if she didn't use it much. 'Sort of, hideous isn't it?'

'Can you let me go?'

'We say 'please' and 'thank you' here.' She shrugged a native shrug. 'But I suppose you're Privileged so don't know how,' she said as she undid the bindings and eased me up to sitting. She smelled of earth and moss. The hair on my neck tingled at her closeness. She'd called me Privileged but I was too sore to argue. I still wore my black overalls but a small badge like a bar had been attached to the pocket.

'Do you need to keep me under surveillance?'

She ignored my question and I let it drop because she too

wore a bar badge. She placed a beaker with a straw to my lips and I almost cried with the blissful taste of the cool sweet juice it contained.

'What happened? We were on our way to a tower. Our Transport destroyed. There were shots. My grandmother. Vanora.'

She looked quickly to the door, her expression native set, emotionless.

'There was an accident, your van crashed, came off the road and was rolling towards the lake but it stopped just before it plunged. You were lucky. Unlike the driver.' She ran a slice of her hand across her throat. 'Stupid boy racers.'

'My grandmother was kidnapped.'

She shook her head.

'They took her,' I persisted.

'That was someone else,' she said it as if she knew who.

'Who?'

'Don't ask me. We just wanted the van. We saved the van,' she said as if that should matter to me. 'We couldn't let a Noiri van disappear into the water – too valuable.'

'More valuable than my grandmother?'

She shrugged.

'It was Vanora.' I said waiting for a reaction.

The girl looked blank.

'You know Vanora, the revolutionary leader.'

'Never heard of her.'

'All natives know her. She's the great saviour of the native race. She organised a break out of a thousand prisoners from Black Rock, to save them from DNA dilution.'

Those dark eyes looked at me with – what? Pity? How dare she?

'She's building her army. You should be ready to mobilise as soon as she gives the signal.'

'Mobilise for what.'

'Are you joshin me?' My head hurt bad.

'You better get some rest.' She turned to leave.

'No, wait. The revolution, you must know. We have to get rid of the Purists, fight the State, free the natives.'

'Haven't a clue what you're talking about, mate.'

'Wait, where am I?'

'I told you, Steadie reservation,' she threw back. But we both knew that wasn't what I meant.

I had to get out of here and find Vanora. I clenched my wrist. My communicator was gone.

'Where is it?' But my fight disappeared as my eyelids gummed.

'You'll get it back,' she said. 'Now get some rest.'

It was dark when I woke. My head was louping. Lights flickered in from outside and danced on the tent wall, morphing into cartoonville. Sounds of the camp filtered through to my fogged brain. Music – slow, mournful. Someone sang, bolstering the beat, laughter and joyous shouts rang out. The girl returned minutes after I stirred, as if I were movement monitored. As soon as she pulled the tent door back the warmth of the celebration flooded in.

'Do you have it?' I asked. I shucked to sitting, trying to hide how weak I felt, but I caught her looking. 'Where is it?'

'Where's what?'

I tapped my wrist, my communicator. 'I want it back.'

'I don't have it.'

'Well, who does?'

She shrugged, a discernible little lift of the shoulders but the eyes were to the floor.

'Liar.'

'Stop harpin on. I told you you'll get it back.'

The girl lifted her head and stared me down with those wise dark eyes that made her appear older. She might even have been older than me.

She held my stare then turned to leave. 'I'll bring some food. Stay here. It's not yet safe for you to show yourself in the camp. We don't normally have Privileged guests.'

'I'm not Privileged,' I shouted out. There, the truth was out my mouth. Only a few months ago I would have baulked at such a statement. The truth. How much had changed. A few months ago I would have demanded better treatment from these natives. A few months ago I was a spoiled military kid. Ishbel attended to my beck and call. But Black Rock had changed all that. The discovery I was part native, a discovery that changed my future forever. There was no choice any more, there was no going back.

My true DNA passport, the one showing my native heritage, the holograph of Vanora, the secret documents that revealed Ishbel as my aunt, was safe in the keep at the rebel base. My tainted family. My sweet mother, Kathleen, sold to the Military as a child, given her life for the State as Hero in Death, blown apart with her victims. Now, with the passport safe and my communicator gone, I had no identification, no way to prove who I was. I had to either escape or trust my captors.

So far they had shown me only kindness, no sign of hostility and yet the girl said it was not safe to venture into the camp.

She came back carrying a steaming bowl. I expected only grain, but the grain was coated in a film which gave away the fact it contained the banned substance meat.

She met my questioning gaze with the answer.

'It's forbidden,' I said.

She said nothing. I knew the Noiri dealt in meat. Ishbel had provided me my first taste of it on the way to Black Rock.

'What was in the van? Meat?' I asked.

'Boxes.'

I touched my bruised back. Too true! 'But what was in the boxes?'

'Noiri contraband.'

'You kept it.'

'What's it to you? You know the Noiri? You part of the gang?' She squared her shoulders, trying to look tough, it didn't work. 'Looks to me like you were a captive of them, jammed in a space no bigger than a rat cage.'

I was tempted to boast I'd been on my way to visit the big boss but the girl's hostility towards the Noiri stayed my tongue.

'What's your name?' I asked.

'Harkin.'

'Harkin?' I never intended to sound sharp, it just came out like that.

When she narrowed her eyes she resembled a wild cat. 'It was the name my mother gave me,' she said.

'Harkin back to the past?' A wave of pain passed over her face. She jumped up and made to leave. I grabbed her arm. 'Sorry.' The word felt weird. When was the last time I'd said that – if ever. 'It was meant to be a joke.'

'Anyway, Sorlie is just as odd,' she said brushing my hand off her arm. So they knew my name.

'It's the anglicised version of Somhairle.' Harkin laughed so hard she rocked back on her heels, but remnants of pain remained.

'It's Sorlie Mayben,' I stumbled on to stop her laugh. 'I'm from Camp Dalriada.'

'You were born in a camp, like me?'

'It's a Military Base, not a reservation.'

She nodded.

'How long have you been here?' I asked.

'I just said, I was born here.'

'In a tent?'

'So?'

I looked around at the space, one big room separated by curtains to partition off different sections. There was no heating, no place to cook, no privacy, nowhere to hide. Cold crept through every corner. It was bleak, even with its many gaudy colours.

'Why aren't you at work?' All natives, male and female, were required to work from the age of twelve. She didn't answer the question, as if weighing the consequences of the answer.

'What's your work?'

'I'm studying. My examination is soon.'

'Studying what? Do you have text?' There was a belief among the Privileged that some form of informal education was given in the reservations but as long as it stayed there the Privileged weren't too fussed.

'You've a lot of stupid questions, don't you, eh?'

'When can I go? Or is that another stupid question?'

'No, no, it isn't. The healer wants you kept subdued for a while longer.'

'Healer? Subdued?' I looked to the empty bowl and felt the soup I had just devoured swirling in my gut.

'Yes, Privileged, natives have healers too, you know, we get sick.'

'But how..?'

'Sake's but you're dumb.'

'Can I see this healer?'

'No, he's busy. He has a much more serious case to deal with.'

'Well, can I see the person in charge? I need my communicator, I can send a message. Someone will be in the area searching for me and my grandmother. They don't know I'm alive. I need to find Vanora.'

'Don't know nuthin bout that.'

'Can I at least go outside with you?'

The music had stopped, a woman sang a slow melody in words I didn't understand. There was a pattering on the roof. We both looked up.

'Rain,' she said. 'Maybe when you're better. Tomorrow.'

She tidied the room the way all natives did and cleared

imaginary crumbs into my bowl. I watched her slim hips sway in time to the music; the way she moved reminded me of Ishbel and Scud, tidying and fussing. School of natives, the phrase made me giggle and put me to sleep.

A young boy of about twelve with a broad face and flattened nose brought me some kind of stinky soup. It looked as though it was made out of wood ash and smelled of rotting sea. When I screwed my nose at it he said it was 'airtight' whatever that meant. He said loads of things I didn't understand, like he spoke in some secret code. My shoes had disappeared and my socks had been removed. When I asked him where they were he put his hand up as if to push me away, even though I was nowhere near him and said, 'Kibble, Sor, I'll swipe you some hicks later.' He sang the words like he'd been on some hash binge.

According to him the soup was 'sound'.

'Sound of what?' I asked. He laughed and called me a bunny. This behaviour was a worry. A bunny what? Bunnies were the short name for the State-diseased vermin set out in the countryside to poison natives.

He looked at me with a fatherly expression. 'We can split some corn later,' he said.

'What are you talking about?'

Even though I think he had assured me the soup was good, when I tasted it the warmth it gave me almost brought tears to my eyes. It was warm and comforting, like being wrapped in a big fluffy blanket. Something I hadn't experienced since Ishbel and I fled the base. My stomach grumbled when the soup hit the decks but soon settled. I wondered if this food was drugged like the last, who cared? After a couple of minutes my head became swampy and dense.

I tried to stand then flopped onto my cot. 'Why do you keep drugging me?'

Harkin watched from the tent door. 'It's for your own health.' She said as she scooted the boy out with a friendly pat.

*

I opened my eyes to a crack of daylight squeezing through the tent walls, the smoky air blurred with the remainder of celebration night. Somewhere nearby I heard a rustling like an animal rooting about just outside. Someone coughed in the distance, a rough, hard to clear cough, deep down and deadly. When I moved my legs a pain in my ribs jabbed like an eager boxer. I gasped out.

Close by someone turned in their sleep. Farts and bad breath fogged from a mass of humanity I sensed just beyond the thin tent door. When I exhaled clouds of vapour escaped my lips into the cold. I huddled under the ugg blanket and bulleted a few facts.

Ridgeway's dead (best not to think about that)

Vanora's missing, might be dead. Do I care?

Joy riders crashed the van

I'm in a place called Steadie

Held captive by natives

Friendly? They haven't beaten me

They're feeding me food and drugs - could be pirates, holding me to ransom

I told them I'm Vanora's grandson – that was pretty dumb, Sorlie

They've taken my communicator

Am I really being kept against my will? Sure, I was being drugged, but I was in a tent, how hard is it to escape a tent? I pushed up to sitting, ribs flared as I swung my legs off the bed. Woah. My head swam like a turd in a puddle. What the snaf were they giving me?

Daybreak sounds filtered from outside. The rich smell of burning wood elbowed the body smells into yesterday. My legs wobbled as I teetered to the door. I pulled across the tent flap expecting a guard to push me back. Instead I was knocked back by the sight before me. A city of green and white boxes arranged in a grid, with streets narrow and intersections so precise they would make any urban planner swell with pride. I looked up at my tent and saw the same green and white exterior.

'Freight containers,' I said out loud, not quite believing I was awake. But not all were solid. Many like the one I recovered in were heavy plastic tarps.

The grid was not as uniform as I first thought. Many streets led to an open area where a statue of a man stood. His features weren't clear but he looked neither Privileged nor native.

Some of the containers had ripple tin roofs, pierced through with crooked metal pipes that belched grey plumes of smoke, clearly defying the Clean Air Directive. A few small kids aged about four or five chased what looked like a wolf cub. It yelped and jumped and seemed almost to be smiling.

I didn't notice her until she and her smell were right by my side; a sweet smell of sweat and smoke but not stinky, pleasant like the smell of the island's peat bogs after torrential rain. She was small and old with a wrinkled face and a deepset mouth that turned up at the side in a perpetual smile. And although she was old her chipped yellow teeth were strong, as if they could tear knots from driftwood. Her eyes were rayed with wrinkles of mirth. She was an oldie who should have been sectioned or released years ago. So why was she still living among the useful? I waited for her to speak, but she remained silent and smiling.

'What is this place?' I asked at last. A reservation, Harkin said, but the containers stretched for kiloms until they reached a conglomeration of buildings in the distance. An Urban? I always believed reservations were erected far from main Urbans. This scene had no resemblance to the clean, ordered housing and happy smiling natives I had witnessed on Academy cultural fields trips.

'What's that Urban called?' I asked the woman. She followed my gaze to the horizon and chuckled.

'Is no Urban, boy.'

'What is it then?'

She reached to touch my hair, I backed off so she dropped her hand and looked at it.

'They say you're Privileged.' The burr in her voice scratched my hackles. 'I see...' She pulled her rough jacket round her shoulders. 'Celt,' she whispered. Could she hear my heart thundering?

If she could see, who else could?

'I'll let Harkin know you're about.' She stumbled towards the silent crowd that gathered to stare at me.

She weaved her way through the now six-deep mass (and growing) and pushed out the other side. Children mobbed her, the wolf pup yapped at her heels, she dug into her pocket and threw something to the animal and it snapped, catching the morsel mid-air. If that woman had been at Base Dalriada, she would have been removed as a 'past date' long ago.

A rock landed at my feet.

'Who threw that?' I tried to roughen my voice against thudding heart. Blank faces with brows arched over wide eyes turned in my direction. Men, women, oldies, seniors, kids. Not one smiled. They all wore tan overcoats with the familiar bar badge stuck to the pocket. A couple of oldies opened pained grins, like the old hags and dafties who cleaned the latrines at the Base. I could smell their hostility. I tried to find the woman with the smiling face but she'd gone. Fear bile bubbled in my stomach. I backed into the tent. They moved en masse, keeping step with my step while maintaining the native distance of a metre length, bred into their genes and fixed for life. Stones however can cross where no native can and with that thought I failed to dodge the one that belted me in the arm.

'Stop this,' I shouted in true Privileged voice. Even though my mouth was filled with fear, my weak words still held clout. 'Go about your business, I'll not harm you.' I pulled the tent hap closed to shut them out, aware of how flimsy it was. If they chose to step over their class line they could rip me apart limb from limb. A scan of the tent gave me nothing else to arm myself with but soft pillows and blankets, even my eating utensils had been cleared away. This was a rest tent. My knife had gone the way of the communicator. I grabbed a blanket and twisted it in a loop, knotting it several times, it would do some damage but not much. There was a scuffling and murmurings from the tent door, I wound the blanket round my wrist, knotted end ready to strike. The tent flap flew open and Harkin stepped in. She stopped short when she saw me with the blanket and blinked.

'What you gonna do? Smother them to death?' She took the blanket from me and prized the knots open. 'They won't hurt you, they're only curious.'

'They threw rocks at me.'

'Just to see if you were real. They thought you were a holo.'

'Why aren't they at work?'

'Didn't you see? They must remain here where no Privileged can see them. They are the specials.'

'What's a special?'

'Don't you know?'

'No.'

'They were born special. Their kind before them were the first to go during the initial purges. No use to the Purist economy they said, but they keep being born. The Privileged have tests, see, kill them before they're born, but not for natives. Our tests come during the chipping. Killed after birth.

In this reservation we believe everyone has a use so we hide them. They're given special status, a safe haven. When the State carries out its annual census, they're not declared.' Harkin shakes her head. 'Not that an annual census is carried out here. They hardly ever come here. The same with the seniors. I hear you met Bug-Eyed Betty.'

'The smiling woman, is that her name?'

'No, just what I call her. Her real name is Mary Eliza. She's a senior.'

'A senior? More like an oldie.'

She gave a grave head shake. 'Natives have no oldies, only seniors. Everyone stays senior. Once they reach a certain age we un-declare them from the census, deactivate their chips. The State never checks.'

'So you keep saying, but why don't they check?' My mind was louping. What's she banging on about?

'You haven't worked out where you are yet, have you? Come on, I'll show you. You seem well enough today.'

We walked out into dull light, drizzle dewed our clothes but Harkin didn't seem worried. The specials had disbursed, some sat in a circle, matting what looked like grass. They seemed oblivious to the rain. She led me along duckboards made of hard plastic. A few tent doors twitched as we passed. The green and white container walls swamped us. Close up I could see they were old, cracked and faded, patched in places.

'During the native purge they put our families here, thinking the land was spoiled. At first our families worried. Some got sick but now...' She stopped to give way to a tall special man carrying sheets of that ubiquitous green and white plastic.

'Hey, Harkin.' His voice was slurred but his smile was wide.

'Hiya Joel,' she said as he passed. 'House maintenance,' she explained before continuing. 'We adapted to our poisoned environment. I'm nexgen, you know, next generation, and we are stronger. Stronger than most natives in other reservations. We grow good food and they leave us alone.'

'But why?'

'The land is contaminated by radiation. There was a big scandal many decades ago.'

'That's not taught history.' But even as I said it I knew her word was gen. Hadn't I had enough history debunked at Black Rock? Nuclear was banned over the world in 2030, everyone knew that, but that doesn't prove anything. I touched the bar badge on my pocket.

'This isn't surveillance, is it?'

She shook her head. 'This place was a processing plant for the spent fuel. They put my ancestors here. I'm positive the State banked on mass death. They thrived instead. The ground isn't as poisoned as everyone was told, food grows well.'

I almost gagged as I remembered the soup I'd eaten, how delicious it was.

'We've nothing to lose. And we have beachware. There's a beach on the other side of the plant. Come I'll show you.'

'The containers – where are they from?'

'At first lastgen were put in makeshift tents, inadequate against storms, flood and such. Conditions were monstrous, not even refugees from the floodlands would come here.' She banged the side of one ringing it loudly.

'Oi!' someone shouted from inside.

She almost smiled. 'Some are solid. When transport was banned and the Local Produce law was passed, these things became obsolete.' She nodded towards the male statue I spotted earlier. 'Yer man there gave us these to build our city. His life here was over and he fled to goodness knows where.'

As we walked through the camp many specials lifted a hand in greeting to Harkin. One boy with intense eyes hugged and kissed her but shied from me. She gave him a cuddle and I wondered what that would feel like.

'Where're you're from, was there a gate? Was there a fence, guards?' she asked.

I thought about the past months I had spent on Black Rock, in my grandfather's penitentiary but decided that was a story too far.

'In a Military Base? Yes, of course.'

'So you were a prisoner.'

'No,' I said a little too loudly, many of the specials raised their heads. 'It was for our own protection.'

'Protection from whom?'

'Well, natives, I suppose,' I felt my face pink. 'And insurgents.'

'So you think you're safe from insurgents here?' She swept an arm around the area. There was no fence in sight and I knew where this was going.

'No, but you're not troubled because of fear of the land.'

'And have you been to any other reservation?'

'Yes.'

'And no fence.'

I remembered the clean neat buildings, the happy natives of those other reservations, I now see it was a scam to keep Privileged kids deluded. 'No, no fence.'

I looked at this strange girl with chocolate eyes and I realised she was wise.

'But in all reservations, fence or no fence, if you don't attend to your work placement you will be terminated and replaced.' There speaks a Privileged.

'Do you know there's more radiation in your communicator than in the soil?'

'Where is it? My communicator, where is it?'

She frowned. 'I think it will be returned soon. But now I will show you around. Just try not to look so Privileged, you are freaking out the specials.'

She pointed to the Urban that Bug Eye said wasn't an Urban. 'We're luckier than most reservations who have no materials except recyk. We can strip the material from the plant buildings we do not need.' She was like a tutor giving a lecture and I wondered what her game was.

'How old are you?' I asked her.

'Seventeen.'

'You're older than me.'

'If you say so.' There was no pride in this statement, it was a matter of fact. At Academy it was a boast to be older. In charge of the younger ones. Show good examples. But I suppose Harkin still believed I was Privileged so age gave no advantage.

Before we reached the workshops we passed what looked like a recyk midden. A couple of dozen people dressed in heavy coats, with scarves wrapped round their faces, were sifting through the rubbish, throwing bits and pieces of flimsy plastic into multi-coloured hods lined up along the edge of the field. Each sifter had a straw bag strapped to their backs.

'You have a recyk midden?'

'No, this is where the raw material is dumped before being sorted. We collect what we can from the beaches and the tracksides. We discovered a rich seam of old landfill just over there.' She pointed towards the coast, to where rows of broken and jagged turbine posts stuck out of the seabed like a mouth of rotting teeth.

'The work is hard and dangerous. What we can't get there we raid from the official recyks. But that is also risky. If we had a moorlogger we could drag more from the ocean.'

'What's landfill?'

'Ginormous buried middens.'

'Buried? Why?'

'Because in olden days no one recyked.'

'That's madness.'

'Yep.'

We seemed to be walking towards the coast. Breeze increased and I could smell the salt air. We passed increasingly larger crates, made from what looked like bio-pulp sheets. In these was stored a varying array of materials the majority of which was plastics.

She stopped between the midden and a small tent. The young boy who spoke the nonsense words leaned against the door. He lifted a hand in greeting but he didn't move.

'The plastic is reduced, remoulded and reused.'

I looked for any sign of a furnace.

'How?'

She signalled to the largest building on the plant site. But said nothing. Before I had a chance to ask, a hand grasped us both by the shoulder and a bear of a man steered us away from the midden and past a low building made up of higgledy sheets of planks plastered over with mud.

'Right,' he said. 'We have to get this young man back to his people.'

Harkin blinked but didn't look disappointed. She looked back at the boy in the doorway and I think I saw him signal an OK with thumb and index. What was going on?

'But I was going to show him the workshops, but...'

'He'll have no interest in that.' The bear scowled over his significant eyebrows. 'He's already seen enough.'

'But Con—'

The man's eyes widened and she seemed to step back.

'No buts, I said he's seen enough.'

'Do you know where my grandmother is, sir?' It was worth a try.

The man scratched his stubble and looked somewhere into the distance but he remained silent.

'Vanora?'

Something changed in his expression at the sound of her name, subtle, no more than a flutter like a baby's breath.

'Do you know who that is?' I persisted.

'No,' but he'd already given himself away. He was lying. 'We have no need for such knowledge here. We've a good life, see? Settled, steady. We want left alone.'

'But not every native has a good life. There are experiments. They're going to kill you all. DNA dilution.'

The man laughed then in much the same way as the girl did.

'I'd like to see them try,' he said.

As the man handed over my communicator and knife, he tapped the knife. 'You'll have no need of that here.' There was a warning in his voice.

Ishbel

'Come on!' Ishbel huckled Dawdle along the beach but he was intent on his comms.

'Official sources say Purists are fighting a fair campaign tae regain power in the next election.'

'Fair and Purists don't work in the same sentence.'

'Ma sources say voting has awready been rigged. Purist activists are intimidating Privileged in the Capital and Beckham City.'

'Fake news! How do you know that's true?' Dawdle raised an eyebrow in response. 'I wonder if Vanora knows, she could use this to try and pull some Privileged on her side.' Ishbel knew she should report Dawdle's intel. But not yet, she would do it once they checked on Scud.

'Things are hotting up Ish. Just sayin.'

They arrived back to find Reinya sat outside in sullen silence. She squatted on hunkers, a waif in her tattered prison uniform, her head slung low between shoulders as if asleep, but when Ishbel spoke her name she lifted a tear-streaked face to meet her gaze.

"e's dead.' The words choked her throat and barely made it passed her lips before she dropped her head again.

Dawdle jumped past the girl and into the van. Ishbel followed. Scud lay where they'd left him but Reinya's sleeping bag had been placed over his own, its blue colour highlighting his deathly grey pallor. His head twisted towards the side panel, his eyes closed. Ishbel touched his forehead. It was stone cold. Dawdle checked his pulse.

'There's something, faint but something. We need tae get him tae the settlement healer.'

'We can't move him.' Ishbel rearranged the cover over him. Dawdle scratched his head.

'Well, get in beside him an ah'll go get help.'

'No, you get in, I'll go, I'll be faster.'

Dawdle looked horrified. 'No way, dae ye no ken the penalty for man on man?'

'Get a grip, Dawdle, it's an emergency. And you owe me one.'

He shot her a glance, he knew what she meant. He was cute enough to know if the debt was paid now she couldn't recall it later.

'Quick, man, before he goes or you'll be done for necrophilia.' She didn't mean to joke, it just happened sometimes.

Outside Reinya hadn't moved. Ishbel grabbed her by the uniform front and yanked her to her feet.

'You were supposed to keep him warm, I told you, body heat.'

The girl shivered. 'Uh give 'im ma covers.'

'That was big of you.' But Ishbel's anger fizzled and died when she saw the girl's hurt.

'What do you know? Nuthin', that's what.' She shrugged off Ishbel's grasp. 'Uh couldn't do more. There's paedos everywhere,' Reinya whispered.

The words slapped Ishbel hard. 'He's your grandfather.'

'He's a stranger,' she hissed.

'Sorry,' Ishbel said and moved to smooth the girl's hair.

'Piss off.' The girl sprang back like a wild cat.

'Look, Reinya, get yourself a brew then crawl into the other bag. You'll be safe with Dawdle.'

'Another man!' The girl stayed where she was.

'But you trust Dawdle, I've seen that.'

Reinya growled like an animal.

'Go on, before you make yourself ill. I need to get help.' Ishbel handed Reinya her gun. 'Take it. Try to keep close to them even without touching, the more heat the better.'

She left her without waiting for the girl to do as she was told. Ishbel had wasted enough time.

Sprinting the beach was quicker than negotiating the dunes. There could be boats out in the Minch, or air reconnaissance, but the cloud was low so she risked it.

A rusty old post she remembered from before told her where to cut through the dunes to the wheelhouse.

She rapped with what she remembered of Dawdle's secret chap. She heard the lock scraping, the door opened a crack. The darkness inside hid the host.

'Well, well, well, this is a surprise.'

Her legs turned to water at the sound of the familiar voice. The door opened fully and there he stood. A patch over the left side of his face and the tunic sleeve pinned on that side, empty.

'Hello, Merj.' Ishbel only just managed to keep the composure in her voice.

'The lovely Ishbel.'

The last time she saw him he lay bleeding, presumed dead, on the Black Rock beach hours after both she and Merj had accompanied Vanora to Black Rock.

Merj had been so charming to both Ishbel and Vanora, basking still in his new promotion to Vanora's first lieutenant. Immediately after the meeting Merj had requested leave to visit his sick mother. What Vanora didn't know was of his intention to kidnap Sorlie, but Ishbel guessed. She had watched the way Merj studied Sorlie during the meeting, she could almost smell greed on his breath as they travelled back to base on the Transport. Ishbel deserted her post and followed Merj, stowing away on the small boat he used to return to Black Rock. He'd held a gun on Kenneth, Ridgeway and Sorlie until he had Sorlie in his grasp. That was when Sorlie surprised Ishbel and pulled a knife on Merj, puncturing his face. They'd wrestled; Ishbel had forgotten what a fine wrestler Sorlie was, he used to spend all his days in the Games Room wrestling with his virtual friends, nagging Ishbel to keep the room dust-free. But good as he was she had thought Sorlie was beat so she intervened by throwing a butterfly bomb in Merj's path. He reached out a hand to hoist to his feet and it blew his arm off. He'd been left for dead but somehow managed to get back onto the boat and get help. She was a fool to have pushed the suspicion of his survival from her mind when she found the boat missing. That was an admission of her own stupidity at not finishing off the creep when she had the chance.

Now he held his good hand out to her and stroked her cheek. Once they had been lovers, something Ishbel couldn't even contemplate now. Another life. Vanora had thrown them together, had almost orchestrated the perverse arrangement, despite her jealousy. Ishbel jerked her face away.

'I need to speak with the healer.' She took a step to enter but Merj blocked her way.

'Get out my way.' Sorlie's blade had scarred his perfect good looks and Ishbel clawed her hand ready to inflict more when a figure appeared at the door, the young woman who had hooded Ishbel before. She placed a protective arm on Merj before she snipped, 'What d'you want?'

'I need help, your healer for our friend, he's dying.'

The girl let go of Merj's arm. 'Wait here,' and returned in to the wheelhouse.

'Looks like you've been in the wars, Merj. What happened to you?'

'Hadn't you heard? You're losing your touch. Or have you lost the boy already.'

'I never found the boy.'

'Oh? And where have you been?'

Ishbel knew she had walked into a verbal trap so kept it shut.

'Went running back to Vanora, did you? She's short of a lieutenant.'

Ishbel shoved her bunched hand in her pocket. 'What are you doing here?'

'Same as you, seeking a healer.' He moved to stroke her cheek again and Ishbel pulled away. 'We will finish our business later perhaps,' Merj said and disappeared behind the door.

'Creep,' she said under her breath. Even though she wanted to shout it, her native training prevented that.

Ishbel expected an old healer, instead the girl returned with a felt bag.

'Come,' she said. 'There is a short cut to your van.'

When they arrived Dawdle hadn't moved, he had Scud in a huddle but his face looked grave.

'Where've you been?' he snapped.

'Tell you later.'

He opened his mouth to say more then noticed the girl and smiled. 'Glad you could come, Shasta.'

Shasta nodded and moved to Scud's side. She removed the cover and Dawdle crawled into the corner of the van. 'His pulse is still weak.'

The girl dug into her bag for an ancient-style syringe and vial, the types only found in run-down non-Military hospitals. She pulled the liquid into the vial and plunged it into Scud's stomach. Reinya yelped in sympathy.

The girl clocked the van. 'He can't stay here. We'll carry him to the wheel. We must make a stretcher.'

'What did you give him?' Ishbel asked.

'Something to deepen sleep. Give his body a chance to fight the withdrawal, keep him alive till we get expert help.'

Scud's colour seemed to have greyed even more, if that were possible. Shasta grabbed the other sleeping bag from Reinya. She sat back on her heels. 'Do you have any rope?'

Dawdle hauled a tow rope from under the front seat. It was frayed in parts and duck-tape mended.

'Thread it through the bags.'

She slashed the bottom of each bag and eased Scud into both, the rope threaded on either side of him. He looked like a shish balanced on two skewers.

'Ish, you take the front, ah'll take the back.' Dawdle helped Ishbel get her rope ends wrapped round her wrists before moving to the back. 'Right, lift.'

Ishbel pulled on the ropes, which burned her wounded shoulder but they soon had Scud hammocked between them.

'Watch out,' Reinya shouted. Scud had begun to slide out of the bag. Ishbel was taller than Dawdle so let out more slack to level the field.

'Reinya, you follow us, watch he doesn't slip again,' Ishbel said.

The early mizzle had turned to a downpour. Shasta grabbed a tarp from the van and flung it over Scud and Ishbel pushed the image of a body bag from her mind.

This time the healer headed for the beach. 'I know it's longer but it's level terrain, better for the patient.'

By the time they reached the wheelhouse Ishbel's shoulders seared and she was soaked to saturation.

Merj stood in the doorway and watched their approach, his hand rubbing his damaged cheek. He nodded to them as they passed and Ishbel had a queasy feeling; the look passed between him and Dawdle was not that of stranger to stranger.

Shasta led them through the wheel into a cramped corridor. Ishbel had to crouch to enter a small room with only a slit opening to the sky, giving a concentrated intense light beamed onto a stone table in the centre where Shasta instructed them to lay Scud.

'I'll get Llao,' she said.

The room had bottles and trays of instruments arranged on shelves. The pins and needles in Ishbel's arms were excruciating and as she swung her arms round to try and relieve it she collided with Dawdle doing the same.

'Maybe your Shasta can give you something for that.' Ishbel saw from Dawdle's step back she had hit her mark.

Scud's breathing seemed non-existent, but when Ishbel leant down towards him she felt a faint current like a butterfly's wing on her cheek.

The old lady with the knots in her hair entered and examined Scud while they looked on. Reinya shuddered a sigh. Ishbel had almost forgotten her and moved towards her but the girl shoved her off and scuttled ninety degrees round the room.

'Where's Shasta?' Ishbel asked. 'We need a healer.'

'I am a healer as well as an elder, young lady.' It was always difficult to tell with seniors but Ishbel detected Privileged genes in this elder. 'My name is Llao, Shasta is my apprentice and is preparing some medicine.'

'Can you help him? We can contact our base, see if we can get some remote help,' Ishbel said, clutching at straws, she wasn't even sure if she could get reception on this coast.

The old woman ignored her and set to her task. Ishbel noticed her small hands and neat, clipped nails. The hands of a Privileged.

'How is he?' The hands waved Ishbel's question away.

'Sit and be quiet.' Her tone held no room for argument.

Ishbel felt her anger rise but contained it. She hated the idea of Dawdle seeing her on a back foot. She fiddled with her dead communicator and tried to find a signal in the room. After what seemed like an epoch the old woman straightened, she groaned and rolled her shoulders and creaked her neck muscles.

She beckoned them all from the room into the narrow corridor. The older woman's knees crackled and popped as she moved and Ishbel was so busy working out the elder's age she forgot to hunker down and clattered her forehead on the stone. They all gasped but no one stopped to see if she was injured. When they were assembled by the main door the woman stopped. 'It looks bleak, I know.' They waited for the pronouncement. Ishbel's mouth was dry. 'We can try a few things but we have not seen this type of mutation before.'

'It's a DNA dilution.'

The woman gave her a sharp look. 'I know what it is. What I mean is we've never had to treat it before. We knew of the experiments. We've been expecting it, preparing for it.' It seemed impossible that this woman was calmly explaining in these primitive conditions that they had been preparing to deal with mutation created by the State to turn natives into Privileged. She scratched her forehead with her fingernail. 'You mentioned remote help.'

'Yes, I can call, but I can't get a signal.'

The woman pointed. 'Just outside and to the left. But once you've established a link you must leave your comms here. You can return home, and we will contact Dawdle with our results.'

'No, I'm staying with him.'

Dawdle stepped up. 'Look, Ish, we need to go.'

'No. Anyway I can't leave my communicator behind.'

The woman's face raged. 'What do you need more, young lady, constant communication with your friends or the mutant's life?'

Ishbel booted the communicator again and supressed the urge to chuck it at this elitist hag.

'They will trace you if you use your normal frequency,' the woman said.

'They haven't before.'

'But that was in places where there is lots of frequency noise. Look around you, child. There's nothing here. Any signal from this island will alert them to our presence.'

'Then how will I contact our base?'

'You must use the neo-frequency.'

The old woman took a small key from her belt and inserted it into Ishbel's communicator.

The communicator fired up and almost immediately Ishbel saw the worried but scrambled face of Kenneth. She backed from the stone walls until his image cleared.

'Ishbel, at last! Where are you?' he asked.

'I can't tell you that.'

'Are you with Vanora and co?'

'No, why do you ask? Isn't she with you?'

'She left with Arkle, Ridgeway and Sorlie aeons ago to visit an old friend. They've disappeared.'

'What do you mean disappeared?'

'We've no contact with them.'

'Is this a trick?' Ishbel didn't mean to say this out loud.

'What do you mean?'

No, Kenneth sounded genuinely worried

'What about their chips? Sorlie had a long-range inserted, didn't he?'

'Yes but there's nothing. They've disappeared into thin air. We haven't even received a ransom demand.'

Ishbel rested her back against the stone wall and dragged her hand through her hair.

'Ishb..l, wha..' Kenneth was breaking up. Something in this stone deflected the signal. She pushed off the wall.

'Sorry Kenneth, repeat.'

'I said what did you want from me? You didn't know about the missing.'

'It's Scud.'

'Scud?' Kenneth's voice sounded wary. 'He was left on Black Rock.'

'I rescued him.'

'Why? He's a danger to the cause.'

Ishbel felt her anger return. 'He shouldn't have been left behind.'

'He refused to come. He wanted his few days of glory as a newly mutated Privileged.'

'He's an historian.' Kenneth of all people should understand the value of such a person. 'No matter, I have him now but he's very ill.'

'Well, he would be.' There was a pause. 'I wonder what Vanora will say.'

'Who cares?' Ishbel said with as much calm as she could muster. She wondered what came first. Vanora's ambivalence to her eldest, only son, or the wittering boy seeking approval.

'Let him die.'

'No! Kenneth, we are where we are.'

'And where are you, Ishbel?' He asked. The old lady nudged Ishbel and shook her head.

'I don't know, but you need to talk to the healer, they have suspended him. Can you advise her what to do next?'

'If they have suspended him, they can keep him alive until I get there. OK, let me speak to the healer?'

Ishbel passed the communicator to the healer and walked towards the sound of the sea.

How could it be so peaceful here? They had said the beach was dangerous but there seemed no other sign of life. By the way the natives had harvested the seaware, there seemed to be no mines. They had their own food, their own source of income, an industry, no predators. It reminded Ishbel of her home in the North Western Territory. No, she should not think of home – it was past. But the memory persisted like a cloud of midges, nibbling at her. Her first memory was of collecting berries in the deep pine woods, those ground-hugging berries that only grew well in that area. She remembers eating the sour fruit and her mother laughing at her, saying 'Don't eat them raw, child, we need to cook them in pies and jams and juice to freeze the sunshine in for the dark days.'

'How can you freeze sunshine?' Ishbel had asked. She had a vision of catching a sunbeam in her hand and placing it in the freezer. But in the days when even the hair on her head snapped with the cold and the nights lasted more than twenty hours, Vanora would dig around in the big chest freezer she took everywhere with her, except that last move across the ocean, and pull out little blue plastic covers and would hand Ishbel a frozen stick of bright red berry. 'A frozen stick of sunshine' she would tell her with a great rollicking laugh. Her mother had seemed gentle then, it was only later that Ishbel realised Vanora carried a bitterness that could survive the coldest winter and the longest nights. There were no freezers now. They were banned in the first timetable of power shutdowns. She looked around, there weren't even electric supplies here, wherever here was. She had no idea whether they were on an island or the mainland, but she saw no evidence of the natives leaving each day to serve their Privileged masters. They seemed to stand alone with no masters other than the elders.

Ishbel had a pull in her gut to stay with these people but now she'd have to go to find her mother and Sorlie whether she wanted to or not. But before she went she had to pick an old scab. She still didn't trust Vanora and had to make certain Merj was no threat, wounded or not.

The old woman touched Ishbel's arm. 'He's coming.'

'I thought you didn't want him to know where you were?'

'That was before he pointed out our limitations. He can teach us and if more DNA dilution victims arrive here, he can make us ready.'

Ishbel wasn't too convinced of that, after all Kenneth had spent the last twenty years in a cave, he had no opportunity to study recent developments even though he was the architect of the process.

'Let's hope so,' Ishbel said. 'Will you be able to keep Scud alive?'

'Yes, he's very ill but stable.'

'He's a great historian you know.'

The woman arched her brows. 'Is he now? We have great need of historians here.' Her brow pringled. 'And a survivor.'

A nail of doubt raked the back of Ishbel's neck. Scud the survivor, Kenneth the architect, a valuable pair. Dangerous in the wrong hands.

The woman passed her the communicator. 'You have to search for your mother, I believe.'

Ishbel tried to hide the anger she felt for Kenneth. He was a stupid old fool to tell the woman about Vanora.

She saw Merj in the distance, scraping round the corners of a wooden post with a chisel-like tool he seemed born to use.

'Tell me about that man with the missing hand.'

'Merj? My son.' Llao's voice softened.

'Your son?'

Llao blinked at the sharpness in Ishbel's voice. 'Why yes, why do you ask?'

'Nothing, I thought I knew him. I must have been mistaken. How did he become injured?'

'He was training for the Military. An accident, friendly fire.'

Friendly fire indeed. 'Military?' This time she kept her voice even. The Military Base where Ishbel had served Sorlie and his parents had been for Privileged officers, she forgot the lower ranks were made up of natives. She looked at the woman again. Or maybe he was Privileged after all.

'Yes, he had such a promising career.'

Ishbel wondered why Merj did not tell his mother the truth. Why hide from her the fact he was the highest ranking officer in the revolutionary army of Vanora?

Sorlie

I punched coordinates for Freedom into my communicator. Nada. All I got back was the time of day. I couldn't even be sure that was correct. It felt like afternoon, but the sky remained in perpetual grey mood so it could have been daytime, anytime. Next I tried to access my library. Wiped, the whole snaffing lot.

'What? Even my SnapLib's gone. I'd some real classics in there.' Con, the bear, looked over my head as if waiting for something.

I searched some more. 'Oh, I can't believe you wiped the Wresto-match Plus.' I'd dumped it from Vanora's system and had almost cracked Ultimate Showdown Level. I looked at the silent bear. 'Why'd you have to wipe it? It took years to build that Snap collection.' He shrugged. He might be a southern native but he had that north native shrug down to a tee.

'Calm down, your folks will've backed you up. You can retrieve them when you get home.'

There was that word, it had been a while since I thought of home. It was best forgotten.

He runnelled his beard. 'That's if you want to of course, some of the content was pretty juvenile.'

I bristled but didn't rise to that bait. 'How am I going to find my grandmother without a working communicator?'

The man grinned and for the first time I noticed the gleaming white teeth, strong, with no sign of akceli rot.

'We'll take you back to the spot your Transport dropped you.'

'What good would that do?'

'Even if your folks aren't looking for you, the Noiri will be searching for clues.' He glowered at me. 'No one messes with them and gets away with it.' He tapped my useless communicator. 'We'll wait for darkness then head off.'

The man steered me away from Harkin who'd lingered silently by my side during the whole exchange, and when we moved I felt her, trailing us. She seemed distracted, always turning to where the nonsense boy stood. Up ahead I could see the van I'd been squeezed into before the accident. The roof stoved in and the front bumper hung like a torn fingernail.

'That's not going anywhere,' I said, pointing to the van.

'No, we go on foot.'

'What about the cargo, won't the Noiri want it back?'

'If they want it they know where to find it.'

'How do they know?'

He laughed. 'Because we told them.'

'And did you tell them about me?'

'No.'

'Why not?'

He didn't answer. He thumped the back door with the heel of his hand and it popped but didn't open fully, he dug his huge paws in the gap and yanked it open a crack. There was the smell of biocrates and pine freshener but that was diluted by something familiar, ancient. I must have been too scared to notice before. I knew what the boxes held even before the bear cranked the door fully. But the hold was empty.

'Who moved them?' he asked Harkin. She shrugged.

They walked me to a low building on the plant site. Here, tall wire fences had long ago been breached and damaged with no care for a repair. Men and women stomped around without protective clothing, only regulation uniforms.

'Why no protection?' I hovered on the periphery. Years of scare stories stayed my feet. My bowels began to flutter.

'Come, it's OK,' Harkin whispered. She put her hand out to me and I almost took it. But a tiny smile on the corner of her mouth spelled 'coward' to me, so I shoved my hand in my pocket and pulled in the fear.

'Why no protection?' I asked again.

She tapped her bar badge. 'These are all the protection we need. There's a protected area inside, highly radioactive, but in these outer buildings there's no need. We've had hardly any incidents.'

'Hardly.'

'The Privileged run a mile from the stuff but in the right hands it can be tamed.'

'You treat the spent fuel to create more, don't you?'

Con nodded. 'Smart lad. It's all very simple when you know how. There are native engineers here who developed a safe process to recyk the waste. A small reactor feeds the smelter where we recyk the plastic.'

'Into what?'

'Fibre mostly, for barter with the Noiri, but we hope to make our own cloth soon.'

Con held out his arm, the workwear looked like fine linen.

'Feel that,' he said with pride. 'It's made from plastic, recyk ocean waste. Small scale compared to the State's operations but we've access to good recyk. The Noiri can't get enough.'

'What do they do with it?'

He shrugged again. 'Who cares? Sell it to the State probably.'

'Is that what you're studying?' I asked Harkin.

She nodded. 'Alchemy, the best profession we have here.'

Con slapped her back. 'The most talented alchemist we've had in years.'

'You should join forces with my grandmother. She needs good techies.'

'What…?' Harkin began but stopped. And then I heard it. A motor. Not a Transport, a boat.

Con steered me to a door. He unlocked a rusting old padlock and crunched open the door. As I watched him shoo Harkin away and pull it closed behind, I felt a flare of fear. It must have shown on my face because when he turned he burst out laughing.

'Look at you. There's no harm found here. She has work to do is all.'

Despite his words I felt for the hilt of my knife in my pocket and thanked the ancestors that these people had given it back to me.

There was that familiar ancient smell again.

'They'll need to come for these soon, we don't have the space or the climate control to store such a precious cargo correctly.'

'They're books aren't they?'

'Well done, lad. How did you guess?'

'My grandfather had a library.' I walked over to one of the crates and tried to open it but it was hammered shut. 'Where did they get them?'

'Search me but if they don't come soon we will have to burn them before they get too damp and turn to pulp.

'You can't do that! When will they come?' I stood in front of a case.

'Soon I hope. The Noiri normally only come round here after every full moon, and we are only just into the third quarter. But for these they'll come.

'Can I look?'

Con nodded. He pulled a crow bar from a graith belt and popped the crate. The books were carefully packed. I lifted one and cracked open the pages and smelled it in exactly the same way I had when I first entered my grandfather's library.

I spotted some familiar titles. The History of Black Rock, the first native text I read while in my grandfather's library. I had nearly spoiled the whole deal by falling asleep and folding back the pages to a crease. I opened this book in the middle, the back section creased over, and my mouth began to dry in anticipation.

I picked up a copy of Brighton Rock. And turned to the back page. Sure enough there was the ragged remains of a torn page, the blank piece of paper I tore from the book and passed to

Scud. He'd risked his life writing the message to me about the DNA experiments in the prison.

'I know these books.'

'Oh really, that's a bit of a fluke is it not?' he said with misplaced mirth.

'This is my grandfather's library. From Black Rock.'

'Never heard of Black Rock.'

I held out the history book.

'Look at this.' He blanked the book, and began tidying up the shed as if we had all the time in the world.

'How did the Noiri come by these?' I said more to myself.

'Search me, lad, you'll need to ask them.'

'Can I take one?'

'I don't think so. The Noiri'll have catalogued this little lot, see, they'll want it back in one piece.'

'But this belonged to my grandfather. Doesn't it now belong to me?'

He laughed so hard I thought he was going to croak. 'You don't understand, do you? These belong to the Noiri now, whether you like it or not.'

'You make it sound like the Noiri are more powerful than the State.'

Con flashed me a stiff smile. 'And you're just realising that, son.' I heard his comms buzz and his smile eased. He placed a hand on my back and steered me away from the books. 'Come on, let's catch the brew run before it all goes. The domestics are always hungry when they return from the Privileged tasks.'

We stepped from the shed into dull afternoon light and I felt myself being propelled along as if I had a bit part in a movie-caster and everyone around me were players acting out their parts before the curtain fell on evening darkness.

Children, women and men natives of working age trudged into the camp from the north. Some carried bundles, most were ill-clad and ragged, all looked exhausted. They were welcomed at the camp entrance by the specials who silently handed out mugs of brew and cake before the workers disappeared into their trailer shacks.

The specials gathered their brew-ware and disappeared into a huge circular tent erected at a junction between streets. Guy ropes stretched from a domed roof, tugging the faded striped canvas, anchoring the monstrosity to the ground with metal pegs. Harkin ran up behind us, out of breath and sweating.

'Come on, there's loads of time before nightfall. You must be hungry again,' she said, with no words of her absence. When she pulled back the tent door a wave of warmth and rich cooking smells hit me. Plastic trestle tables were laid out in long rows, I counted twenty rows before I gave up, there must have been space to sit over a thousand, but no one sat. Some men and women wandered the rows eating from plastic bowls. Small children played round their feet, occasionally jumping to graze on some titbit the adult held out for them. Teenagers openly prowled the tables, picking up pieces of food with their fingers from plates arranged in the middle. To the right of the door specials served food to those waiting in line. Bug-Eyed Betty spotted us and nudged the girl next to her, but the girl stared out to the room while mechanically slopping soup into a bowl. When we drew to her level she handed one to me and Harkin without a word. Next to her, an oldie in a chair with wheels smiled a gummy as she balanced a piece of damper bread on top of our mugs.

As I perched on the edge of the table to eat it seemed the whole room stopped and stared.

'What are you doing?' Harkin hissed.

'Hate grazing, I sit to eat.'

She turned to the crowd and shouted, 'Privileged, hey? What are they like?' There was a mass relaxation in the tent as folk went back to their grazing.

I tried to remember the last time I tasted something so

delicious, but the thought was yanked from me by the ear-piercing klaxon wahhing warning, red lights pulsed above the main entrance. Many specials sank to their knees, hands over ears. Natives rushed to them, grabbed them, pulled them. The specials screamed resistance.

'Stop it,' I shouted, but Harkin hauled me towards the door.

'Quick,' she shouted.

'They're hurting them.' The screaming rose as the klaxon ceased.

Many door flaps opened around the tent. Natives dragged specials with them as they ran.

Con appeared at our side, picked me up, slung me over his shoulder and ran with the crowd.

'What the snaf...?' We were heading for the grey building that sat alone at the plant side. I was bounced on Con's shoulder, but no matter how hard I pummelled his back, his grip viced.

Seconds before Con dumped me at the doorway I saw military trucks pour through the northern gate, each carrying a load of what looked like white-suited monsters. They all wore bio-suits. The gummy oldie on wheels scrabbled to get out their way, the truck swerved towards her and knocked her to the side, the chair toppled, began to roll, arms wild, scrabbling to get away. The truck behind, served, a suit raised a gun and zapped her.

'Get in there with the rest and don't make a sound.' Con roared before slamming the door, shutting me inside with a couple of hundred specials and oldies.

I didn't realise where I was until Betty clipped a flashing device onto my collar.

'Let me out of here.'

'I can't,' she said.

'But it's radioactive.'

She nodded. 'Which is why they won't come here.'

The special girl I saw staring and dishing out soup took my

hand and led me into the ravaged huge hall, yellow lines and circles painted on the floor meant something to someone once but now acted as invisible borders.

They were huddled, behind that border, hands and bodies pressed by their sides as if trying to petrify, their screams had turned to hooping sobs, harsh rasps of breath. Oldies were hirpling round the huddle, soothing, brushing hair, rubbing the backs of hands, giving sips of water from canteens they carried with them, easing the specials to move in a particular way, it didn't matter if their legs went over the line, they told the specials, as long as they kept moving, as they'd been taught. Shushing them, like mothers with new-borns. There was an overwhelming smell of piss. They grew silent again. Harkin took my hand and moved me into the huddle.

'Move with them,' she said, then let me go.

The specials kept a certain distance, each giving just enough room to move. Heat and pisshap and oat breath began to build in the orchestrated dance step we were in. I felt my stomach flutter, my pulse race and fear fill me.

Over a shoulder I saw Harkin, crouched, cuddling a little boy with too wide eyes. She had been watching me but when I spotted her she put her head down and buried it in the child's hair, as if by avoiding my eyes she would disappear. And then I realised what this was. We were creating a barrier against the radiation. Those on the outside, after exposure, moved inside, the constant movement meant we could minimise the amount of exposure. I remembered the Snap TV clips of the long extinct emperor penguins, those funny little birds that once lived on ice. They huddled to keep warm, those on the outside were coldest, whereas here those on the outside caught the most heat.

'Sorlie,' Betty whispered. She was struggling with an oldie who looked so old she could pass for her own mother. I helped get the old lady seated on a three-wheeled buggie that doubled as a seat.

'What...?' my voice boomed in the chamber. The specials shrank, broke rhythm.

'Ssh,' Betty said

'What's going on?' I whispered. 'We can't keep this up.'

'Raid. It happens sometimes.'

'Is it because I'm here?'

She shrugged. 'Could be.'

A groan came from an oldie male who sank to the ground as if he'd been tipped from a cart. I put my hands under his withered arms and hoiked him up.

'Thanks son,' he said, showering me in his powdery breath. 'It's not your fault. We've been due one.' He pointed to Betty. 'She likes to dole the guilt, that one.' He settled against my arm. 'What you doing here anyway, son?'

'I don't know.' I looked along at Harkin her head still buried in the small child's cuddle. What's she doing here?

Betty handed me a bag of hard green candy. 'Help yourself and pass them on.' She lifted her head. 'Only one each, mind,' she said to the huddle.

Each special did the same thing; took one candy, popped it in their mouth, closed their eyes to suck, while still shifting position. A ritual they seemed to have performed many times before. An old lady with straggly hair and a hand full of worry beads handed the poke back to me.

'It's OK, take one,' I said.

'I should have stayed. I shouldn't have left him.'

'Who?'

She lifted her weak watery eyes to meet mine. 'My son, he's too old to walk.'

'It'll be OK, you'll see him when you get out.'

She shook her head. 'No, I won't.' And I knew she was right.

When the sweets reached Harkin she took two, popped one

in the child's mouth before taking her own and closed her eyes like the specials had done.

Betty took my elbow. 'You take one too. I know you don't need it but...' She shrugged.

'Is it a drug?'

'No, nothing like that, just simple old fashioned psychology.'

I almost spat it out again it was so sour. Betty chuckled. 'Your face,' she said. 'Soor Plooms, horrible I know but it keeps them from fretting.'

The doors eventually opened to a twilight sky. Mizzle slashed through the weak beams of the native's hunter's lights. We walked out into a clean-up operation. Slashed canvas container sides were being repaired, strewn bedding, collected. Some of the oldies hobbled forward to help but a row of men halted them and steered then towards the western field. Over the men's shoulders I saw limp bodies being carried out of trailers and towards the main gates a row of body bags were arranged with respect.

'They got what they came for.' Betty sighed.

'Why do they do it?'

'Purge. They see us as a waste of resources.'

'But you don't take any State resources.'

'We take the energy of the useful natives.' She pointed towards the native men and women who were now systematically dealing with their dead. Their white, tear-stained faces told me they didn't see it as a waste. They were in pain.

'It's not so bad for us oldies. We've had our lives and to be honest I've had enough. The next raid I think I'll stay outside. They can put me out my misery.' Her grim expression told me she wasn't joshin. 'But the specials are different. They're young and deserve a life.'

'What about the radiation?' I remembered the clip she gave me, not wanting to look at the damage done.

'They're used to it. There are plenty other things will kill them first.'

'You can't live like this.'

'Maybe we won't have to for much longer. When The Prince returns we'll be saved.' She looked around the devastation. 'If we can wait that long.'

'Who's The Prince?'

'Our saviour,' she said and scuttled into the crowd of helpers.

It was fully dark when Con found me in the big tent, drying out after my 'decontamination shower'.

'You have to leave. I'll take you south to look for your people.'

I had tried searching for Harkin, but she'd disappeared after we were released from the hall. One of the oldies led me to a shed, handed me a bar of strange-smelling soap and a bristle brush, told me to strip and scrub every part of my body. When I left the shower my old clothes had gone and a new set waited for me. The old gentlemen handed me my communicator. 'We should get rid of this too but I suppose you'll need it'. I began to feel sick the minute I clipped it round my wrist.

Of course we walked.

'Why can't we take the boat?'

'What boat?' Con said. 'I see no boat.'

'I heard one, before the raid.'

'You're mistaken, there is no boat. Now shut up and let's go before I change my mind and hand you over to the State.'

Con led me out onto the path the natives trod to and from their work placements each day. Then we turned south and joined a track that hugged the coast. In my mind I imagined the strong sea breeze scouring the last of the radiation from my body. After sixteen years spent in a landlocked base it seemed my life was now destined to be with the sea and that thought put a smile on my face.

'We'll take the back road till curfew then we can travel on the main road. We should spot military lights well before they see us.'

'How far is it?'

'A ways, but not far. You were lucky we were so close-by when you had your little accident. Of course, they did drive you a good many kiloms before that. If we push on and stick to the good roads we should reach your drop-off point in a day or so.

'Will I get radiation sickness?'

He turned his low res torch on me and studied my face in the way my grandfather had, looking for my native genes, but this was a different type of scrutiny.

'You'll be fine. The dose was small.' Subject closed. 'You look like a good strong walker with fine sturdy Privileged legs.'

It was easy travelling with Con. He didn't say much. I wanted to ask about the massacre at the site but every time I asked a question he batted it away. 'The less you know the better.'

'Why can't they speak?' I asked.

Con grunted.

'The specials? They don't speak. The only one I heard speaking was Harkin.'

'Who said Harkin was special?'

I felt my face warm. 'Sorry, sometimes it's hard to tell, but she was in the radiation hall with the others.'

Con grunted again. 'They can speak, but they choose not to. I can remember when it started. I was a teenager, the camp wasn't long established. Some of the elders saved a couple of specials destined to be destroyed. I think they spoke at first but some of the normal natives laughed at their ways, their voices. It only took one or two to remain silent and they all followed.'

'Do they speak among themselves?'

'Not that I know of.'

'How do they communicate?'

'They have their ways.'

I remembered Ma and Pa, their speech ban after Ma was

given Hero in Death status. They communicated with their eyes, their gestures, sometimes I think telepathy too.

After a couple hours walking the road moved inland, into a valley of nestling tarns crowded by high mountains.

The only sign of other reservations in the area was when Con led me onto a stony path that zigged upward through a narrow pass. Below I saw the flickering lights of a dozen or so fires puncturing the blackness of night. Con stopped and I heard what he heard, a faint waft of sorrowful music travelling on the breeze.

'What is it?'

'Nothing for you to concern yourself about.'

'A reservation.'

Con shrugged. 'If you say so.'

'The music is so sad. Ceòl a' chianalais, the music of longing Ishbel used to call it.'

Con coughed. 'Come on, the rain's stopped, the midges'll be after us if we don't move.'

The path followed a high ridge before dropping into another valley. A small lane edged on both sides with a dry-stone dyke wound for kiloms before opening out to a wide lake.

We only ever saw one convoy of military trucks and as Con had predicted we saw them in plenty time to hop over the wall and hide.

A short skirt round the lake brought us back onto the coast road. After the confines of the valley and hills it was good to follow the open aspect of the sea again. The moon fought with low cloud to give us some light. I lifted my face to the wind and drank in the salty spray. We rounded the headlands. Before us lay a huge bay, but I couldn't be sure it was the bay where Arkle had dropped us. There was no sign of the tower. The sea was out there somewhere but the tide had taken it so far out it was only a shimmering notion, as if the ocean had been sucked out and a tsunami would crash through any minute. The urge to run inland was strong but Con put his hand on my shoulder and pushed me south. The sight of the mud flat was unnerving considering all the flooding reported in this area last year and it wasn't empty. On the runnelled expanse I spotted a couple of Tracs and further out groups of natives bent, harvesting something from the mud.

'Are they from your reservation?'

'No, they're refugees from the wetlands over the Minch. A sorry bunch of reffos, no Privileged wanted them for domestic or service work so they end up with the worst jobs, digging, or this. Men, women, children alike.' He looked towards them. 'If you're looking for recruits for your revolution, they're your best bet.' He scratched his beard in thought. 'Looks like they're heavily guarded though.'

Sure enough one of the Tracs had mounted machine guns and there were armed guards patrolling the thirty or so workers.

'Maybe word got out you or someone else were recruiting.'

'What do you mean someone else?'

He watched them for a while but remained silent.

'How do we get past them?' I asked.

'We don't, we sit here and wait for the tide to shift them.' He pointed across the bay. 'Look to the other side, the boatshed. If someone was here looking for you, that's where they'd be.'

'It looks deserted.'

'Yep,' Con said while digging in his sack. He handed me a grainer bar to eat. We crouched to watch while trying to chew on chuck regulation food.

'What a miserable life. Why can't they come to your reservation? They could work on the recyk.'

'No chance. We took a few of this mob once, but they couldn't take to the specials.' I watched his jaw chew his anger. 'Mistreated them they did. We have to look after our own, see.'

'Did you send them off?'

'No, they would have betrayed us.'

'What then?'

He was silent again.

'You killed them?'

'We have to keep our specials safe.'

A lump stuck in my gullet. The grainer choked.

'So when will you kill me?' I couldn't believe how calm my voice sounded.

'You'll not betray us.'

'How do you know?'

'Because...' He lifted his head and seemed to listen for something. 'Because you're Vanora's grandson.'

'So your tribe do know her.'

'Some do, most don't. As I said, we lead a peaceful life and want no problems with Vanora.' His face was resigned, this was the way it was and he knew his place in the scheme of things.

'Tell me what you know about her.'

'I know she needs an army.' He pointed to the refugees. 'And there are some of it there. If she wants them. They say she'll only take educated.' He shook his head. 'Good luck to her. She'll need it, what with all the enemies she's made over the years.'

'She's been kidnapped.'

'So I heard.'

'Who's The Prince?'

He whipped his head round to me. 'What do you know of The Prince?'

'Nothing, Betty mentioned him. Said he is your saviour.' Con stared out to sea. 'Do you know if The Prince is Vanora's enemy?'

His face clouded. 'Rumours, only rumours.'

'Do you think he kidnapped Vanora?'

The Trac bumped over the sand followed by a trailer that rattled, scooping up workers as they made their way back to the shore.

'Could have been anyone got her. We live in a lawless State.'

He took my grainer wrapper and tucked it in his side pocket for recyk. 'Tide's coming in, let's see what we can see.'

'What if there's nothing there?'

'We go on until we find one of your own.'

'One of my own?' But of course he meant Vanora's coverts. I tried to visualise Vanora's map, the conglomerate of cells on her ticker wall. The ones that blacked out. Were there any on this part of the coast?

'She had covert people dotted around the coast.'

He nodded. 'So I heard.'

'Well, do you know where they are?'

His chin got a right old scratch at that question.

'They normally live in caves and bothies,' I said.

'No caves around here. The sea's been invading the land since the '20s. There are some bothies though. Some signs of life but they're not doing much of a job if they are supposed to be recruiting an army. Of course they'll be further south too. There are some deserted coastal towns on the way to the tower.'

'So you know about the tower? That's where I thought we were going.'

Con's eyebrows shot up. 'Could be but we don't want to be hanging about there.'

'Have you heard of Monsieur Jacques?' The words were hardly out my mouth when he grabbed my collar.

'You don't want to be mentioning that to no one. It's dangerous, that's what it is.'

'Why?'

'The less you know the better, just stay away.'

He released my collar. 'Now let's find these coverts of yours.'

But by then it was too late, I knew I had to go back to the tower. That was my only chance of finding Vanora.

Ishbel

Dawdle left the wheelhouse, his body buckled with the weight of the bolts of cloth he carried; Reinya followed, similarly laden. When she saw Ishbel she put her head down, avoiding eye contact.

Ishbel stuck out a hand to take the cloth, ease the burden, but the girl jooked past almost tripping in her haste.

'Wait, give me that, you'll need to stay with your grandfather.'

'No, uh'm coming with you.'

Ishbel made another grab and the cloth landed on the ground.

'Heh, heh, watch the merchandise, Ish.' Dawdle shouted. She ignored him.

'We'll come back for you.'

'Uh'm not staying with that mutant. What if 'e dies? Them, there're strangers, anything could 'appen to me.'

'Kenneth'll be here soon, he'll look after you.'

'Another stranger'

'He's safe.'

'Nobudy's safe.'

Ishbel shook her head. 'He is.'

'Let her come, Ish. She terrified o' strangers. She can stay in the sub while we look fur yer ma.'

'How did you know about Vanora?' There was a pinkness to his usually pasty cheeks.

'That bloke Merj telt me.'

'How does he know?' Ishbel said not expecting an answer. 'You know him, don't you?'

Dawdle shifted his bundles dropping one on the sand. He cursed. 'Never met him before today.'

'Meeting is different from knowing.' She tugged a bundle from Reinya. 'OK you can come, but go say goodbye to him.'

'No chance.'

Ishbel could see by the hard set of the girl jaw she was wasting her breath. 'Well, wait for me, I'm going to say goodbye.'

Scud lay on his back in a small alcove, part of the outer wheel. Shasta, the young healer, tended the sores that blistered his mouth, applying ointment and rubbing moisture sticks on his lips. His eyes were open.

'I thought you were putting him in suspension?' Ishbel whispered.

'We are, but he's waiting for you.' Ishbel made a silent prayer of thanks to her ancestors for sending her back.

She took Scud's translucent hand, she could almost see the blood struggling through his veins and arteries.

'We're leaving now, but Kenneth will be here soon.'

He nodded wearily. 'Look after her for me.'

'You can do that yourself when you're well.'

'You should have left me there.'

'No, never.'

'Ah'm a burden tae the cause. Let me be. Ah've done my time, ah've served your dynasty well.'

Dynasty, was that what they were?

'Some dynasty. Now rest, you must get well.'

He swallowed. 'Ah'm that tired, Ishbel. My Jeanie's crying out tae me, let me go tae her.'

Ishbel squeezed his hand. 'Listen to me Scud, you are a great historian, we need you to teach us the lessons we can't afford to repeat. You know it all, you must teach the young, the next generation. So much was lost when the Net disappeared.'

'The Net wis warped, needed tae go. Loaded wi lies, it was.'

'Which is why we need a credible source.'

A croaky laugh rattled his lips. 'Oh Ishbel, you don't know how ridiculous that is. What could ah dae that other historians failed tae dae in the past. We are where we are. Start wi a clean page.'

'Promise me you'll get well.'

'We are where we are,' he whispered.

Ishbel bit her lip on the words she wanted to speak. She knew her mother had bloodshed planned, but there were more people involved now, things would change.

'We must build a better, more peaceful world.'

Scud nodded, but Ishbel wasn't sure if he understood. Shasta came up behind her and said, 'We'll suspend him now.'

'If not for the world, then for Reinya,' Ishbel whispered. It was a cheap shot.

Scud squeezed her hand and this was all she needed to assure her that he would at least try.

'Look after her for me, Ishbel.'

They drank a bitter brew Con carried in a thermos. The beach operation packed and left.

'Right, let's get going. There's a boatshed on the far shore, I'm guessing that there's your drop off.'

'This isn't the place.'

Con stood with glass to eye and searched behind us.

'What?'

'Nout. Let's go.'

Even though darkness fell through the clouds of sea mist, I could see there was no tower nearby.

Con shrugged. 'We'll have a look anyway. It's there for a reason.' The boatshed was deserted.

Con grunted a couple of times as he searched for clues to its purpose. Rain began to staccato on the tin roof. We both looked up, amazed the Military hadn't commandeered the material for a greater use or the Noiri stripped it for profit. It was a big empty shell, with hooks imbedded into the walls and gaping holes where other fittings had been roughly pillaged. I wondered why Vanora had never installed one of her coverts in here. Con read my thoughts.

'Too exposed,' he said. 'Too open for pillage, nothing secret about this place. Nothing full stop,' he said as he slung his bag over his shoulder. 'Let's go.'

'Where?'

'South.'

'To the tower?'

'Where else?'

He led me to a huge muddy estuary surrounded by waterlogged fields. The rain pattered and puddled and ran from our hoods. The land churned into grasping mud until we were wading shin high in the stuff and each step began with a wrench of our boots from the sucking earth. Dampness crept across my shoulders where the overcoat had been patched. At least the rain was growing warmer as the days moved into the third quarter.

To the south I could make out the mass of an Urban draped round a hill, a crumbling castle rampart perched on top. In ancient days this would have guarded its citizens from invaders, now it looked deserted. We trudged along an overgrown wide track.

'Once the main rail link to Original Beckham City, before it was dismantled,' Con told me. Railways, like helicopters were history lessons.

Two bridges crossed a river; one with a road, cracked and potholed, the other bore the impression of long-recyked railway sleepers. Both were blocked off with concrete blocks the size of double decker trucks. Some parts had been chipped off in an attempt to make steps but the whole barricade was coated in something slick, there was no way we could climb over. Graffiti had been daubed on in danger red. N.F.F. Con began to laugh.

'What's so funny?'

He pointed to the graffiti. 'That.'

'What does it mean?'

'You don't know?' He shook head. 'Native Freedom Fighters. But we call them NAFF, because that's what they are, they do naff-all for natives.'

I'm sure Con could feel the heat pulsing from my face, but I was beginning to see his point. So far I'd seen no evidence of Vanora's freedom fighters. Everyone was laughing at her. 'If it's so naff then why kidnap the leader?'

'Search me.' The joke was still in his voice so I dropped the subject. Vanora was an embarrassment.

'What do we do?' I said, slapping the block instead of his stupid, laughing face. 'Can we get round it?' This seemed impossible. 'Is there another road?'

'Yeah but it's too heavily guarded, see. Only the Noiri can travel freely on that road.' He climbed onto a rusty overturned car that hadn't yet been collected for recyk. From his pocket he pulled the scope and surveyed the scene.

'The Urban looks deserted, probably abandoned during the great sea surge.'

'Where did they go?'

'The Privileged? To newly constructed Bases in the North. Their natives? Probably to refugee camps or if they were lucky, new reservations built near the Bases.'

From what I could remember from the taught history it was around this time that Beckham City was moved further north and re-established as the administrative hub for Lesser Esperaneo. This island had always been cut off from Mainland Esperaneo and the Capital, separated by the North Sea. Coastlines had been changing for decades, rising sea water became unmanageable. After the great flood surges of the thirties, many sea defences failed, the larger islands of Lesser Esperaneo became an archipelago of many small islands. Control became tricky. There had once been a tunnel connecting Lesser with Major Esperaneo but that was sabotaged long ago, some say for the best.

Con offered a hand and hauled me up beside him. It felt good to get my feet out of the mud if only for a little while. He clocked 360° with his glass. His jaw clenched for a moment then relaxed.

'What is it?'

'Nothing. You said your grandmother had operatives around the coast.'

'Yes, her operation is vast. There's a huge map at her base showing their positions.'

160

He scrutinised his fingernails for a nano then said, 'There was one lad came to the camp, some years back – just a youngster, not much older than you. He asked to be taken in. He looked pretty emaciated. Had the most horrific skin condition, warts and sores, crawling with beasties.' Con sat down on the car, I joined him. We had a good view of the surrounding land.

'He seemed unsure of his history, first he had deserted the army, but when we cleaned him up we found he hadn't been chipped so he changed his story and said he had fled the mass ID tagging, said it was a violation against his human rights.' Con looked to me. 'The elders accepted this, there had been quite a battle went on around that time, see, many did protest against chipping, but as always, in the end the State won. Anyway, he persuaded us he was two minutes short of being a special so we put him to work with them but it soon became apparent that he had other ideas.'

Con looked though his glass as if searching for this history. 'I can't believe I'd forgotten all this. It was quite disruptive to the camp dynamics at the time. The stranger turned minds, bent the ears of the leaders, then tried to radicalise us younger ones. Promised us something called Freedom.'

I gulped at that word. Freedom, the place Pa promised that day on the beach before everything changed.

'Our leaders were seniors,' Con said. 'The recyk production was still new, they were unsure of how the camp would work out. We were all scared then. Weren't so comfortable with radiation. I could feel a change in the way the camp was being organised. The leaders wanted to move fast, form a fighting force to protect us. A fighting force? Against whom? They had forgotten no one came near us through fear.'

'I was a young man then and worked outside with a few others from the camp for a big sporting estate. The owners lived in a huge house surrounded by a guarded fence. I saw what they had but didn't feel the resentment the others did. They became unsettled. It was subtle at first; this lad – the freedom fighter he called himself – told stories of Privileged in the north, how they beat their natives. Did we want that? Although we knew our positive plans for the future, many wanted it now. Oh, he was good – got us fired up with the talk of change see, even I fell under his spell. He was the same age as us and yet seemed to have so much more experience.

'He told us we would need to prepare and in a few months, if we were ready to fight, change would come. He wanted some of us to go with him into the wilds and create havoc against the Privileged.'

'What happened? He must have been one of the coverts,' I said. 'Did he mention Vanora? Is that how you know her?'

'No, he didn't mention Vanora, I hear of her from Noiri men.'

'So why didn't you go with him?'

'Because just before he left, he showed his true colours. He only wanted young men. No women, no seniors and especially no specials. I saw how he treated the specials, kindness on the surface but there was a disgust hidden in his eyes, we'd seen it before. It came to a head when one of the special females grew attached to him and wanted to leave. He mistreated her and beat her. She died of her wounds. He thought he'd done enough, charmed us into blindness. He was wrong. We banished him. Should have killed him. His younger followers were forbidden to join him. It seems what he had planned was no better than the State policy.

'But that can't be right. Vanora would never sanction that treatment.'

Con bristled. 'I still wanted to go with him, I couldn't believe what the elders were telling us so I asked him straight out. "What about the specials, the oldies?" He said, "We need strong people for this fight. We can leave some caretakers to mind them if it's important." Con became silent. 'It was that phrase that did it. "If it's important."'

'Word got round that he was trying to take the young with him. There was enough elders with enough clout to stop them. But the damage was done, divides were made. Some refused to believe their saviour was tainted. Many of the young were entrenched in their belief of a better future and even though they were too scared to follow him you can still feel the unrest sometimes. Only one young couple went with him in the end. Everyone else was persuaded that our plans were more feasible. We followed the deserters and this is where they came.'

'I thought no one could leave in case of betrayal?'

'Oh, that was before our operations were fully established, nothing to betray except dreams.'

'What's the name of this freedom fighter?'

'Merj.'

'Merj?'

Con looked at me. 'You know him?'

'Tall, white hair, pale grey eyes.' Con nodded. 'I fought him.' I tried to keep the boast from my voice but failed. 'On Black Rock. He tried to kidnap me. I think he's dead.'

'Well if he is, I wonder who that boat belongs to?' Con said pointing to the river.

I looked to the far bank, there was nothing there except mud. Con nudged me, 'Not there, look this side.'

And sure enough a short distance along the bank a small boat was tied to a post.

'So let's use it.'

'But if it's on this side so is he or they.'

'So what do we do?'

'Wait.'

The thought of waiting out in the open for Merj's ghost to arrive did not fill me with joy but it seems I had no option.

Ishbel

Ishbel wanted to kill Dawdle all over again when they reached Peedle. There was not a scratch on it. He watched her, wary of her punch, waiting for the accusation, no doubt forming his lie before she asked. But she stayed silent. No more lies.

Reinya however was not so reserved.

'What? Uh thought this was scrapped. There's no a scratch on it.'

'Dawdle scuppered his boat,' Ishbel said with as much cut as she could slice.

Reinya whirled on him and thumped his shoulder. 'Why did you? 'e could have died in the water.'

Dawdle flapped her fist away as if she were a hoard of midges. 'What dae you care?'

"ow dare you,' she spat.

But Dawdle wasn't moved.

'Look, ah've a business tae run. Loads o' folks depend on me. These people need me tae collect thir supplies. Things don't just stop because o' a prison break, you know. Ah wis a'ready late, because ah had tae go get them off Black Rock.'

"e should have been taken straight to Freedom,' Reinya said.

'We had to get you,' Ishbel wished it didn't sound like she was backing Dawdle.

'Ah should huv left the lot o' ye,' Dawdle said.

Reinya gasped at his words.

'Look, they'll care fur him here, he probably wouldnae huv survived the trip tae Freedom anyway. And Kenneth's coming tae help. It'll be good fur the old boy.'

Ishbel noticed the subject had neatly moved on from the non-injured boat.

'How do you know Kenneth?' Ishbel asked, beginning to wish Dawdle had never involved himself in her affairs.

'How d'ye think he got the pickles ah collected fae you every month?'

Ishbel had always known of Kenneth the hermit, even before she began supplying him with pickled and preserved food in all her years in the base. She'd always assumed it was a family secret and the Noiri just made one anonymous drop. She didn't realise Kenneth's situation was common knowledge among the Noiri, but then she supposed he may have had dealings with the Noiri for other supplies. What did she know?

'So where are you taking us now?' Ishbel asked.

'Tae the tower.' Dawdle's chin was to his throat but he looked at Ishbel with raised eyes. 'That's what ye want, isn't it? Go look fur Vanora?'

'And no other stopping points?'

'No, not this time.'

When the engine sparked first time Dawdle patted the panel. 'Good girl.' They glided into the Minch to the sound of the engine purr. Reinya sulked in her corner, Ishbel sat beside Dawdle and stared at the murk. After too many minutes of strained silence she said, 'What I don't understand is why I needed to be hooded?'

'Och that?' He chuckled but there was no mirth in it. 'That's just overzealousness. They weren't sure about ye. They didn't want ye to see the wheelhouse set up. Ah had tae persuade them you were kosher. '

'Don't make it sound like you did me a favour.' Her stillness hid her anger but this time she wanted him to see.

'Ye huv tae admit, Ish, these souterrains are pretty impressive eh? This land had been cleared fur use as a prison but it was so remote, even though it's no longer an island. The cleared families bided their time in a flood refugee reservation. Then in dribs and drabs made their way back and built their home based on ancient designs. And with the materials from the abandoned prison.'

'What about their chips?'

'Their healers removed them. Only a few at a time. You know how the State didnae bother when a few dribs and drabs fall off the wall, but this dribble has now turned into a puddle of over a few hundred souls.'

'Not many.'

'Ah, but how many other communities are there like this?'

She studied him. Yes, he knew of others but wouldn't tell.

'Why doesn't this area flood then?'

'Because they know the best bits, they'll be good fur a few decades yet, if they remain undetected. And they keep a constant eye on the terrain and conditions.'

This time when they surfaced it was daylight. They were south of the tower underneath the old rotting pier that should have been demolished long ago for recyk and firewood.

'Saving it fur a raining day.' Dawdle said with a chuckle.

'What makes you think she'll be here?' Ishbel asked.

'Ah don't, but this wis the last place she was seen. Ah've been in touch with ma men…'

'How many men do you have?'

'Never you mind,' he said. 'Anyway, Monsieur Jacques's driver wis found with a bullet through his head with no sign of Vanora, or the boy or the consignment. We're not sure which they were after, but ah've had a report that the consignment turned up a bit further north in the Steadie reservation. One o' my men is headed up tae collect.'

'Haven't you even looked for Sorlie and Vanora? It seems the consignment is the most important thing for you.'

'Don't start, Ishbel. Ah never ask them tae come down here.' He quit the engine. 'Right, let's get this done.'

He put his hand out to Reinya. 'Come oan, wee hen.' But she

shrugged off his offer of help. He opened the hatch and Ishbel gulped in the sea air.

'Do you think Sorlie's with Vanora?'

'Nut. We've had a sighting of a boy.'

'What? Where?'

'Hold yer jets, Ish. It's just a stray sighting, it could be any boy. And the place is further south from the native camp. The Steadie natives didnae give us any info, they dinnae trust naebudy, that lot. But we think he might be with one of them.'

'How do you know all this?'

'Ah told ye, ma men. Anyway this leads me tae believe they've been taken separately. No word of Vanora, so we start here. Monsieur Jacques might know more. Let's hope he's calmed down about losing the consignment.'

'And his man?'

'Come again?'

'He's not furious about losing his man?'

Dawdle deafened to that comment.

They climbed from the sub into an early morning haze, with just a promise of some weak sunshine. The calm water in the bay swayed the sub gently. Reinya was reluctant to get out. Ishbel tugged her arm but the girl jerked it back and slumped onto the deck and huddled near the conning tower.

Dawdle secured the pod they had been towing to the pier. 'The seaweed harvest,' he said unabashed. Ishbel stowed her fist in her pocket. Before the day was out she would punch him again.

Out of nowhere it seemed, a van pulled up on a causeway close to the pontoon and two men lowered a hook to relieve Dawdle of his burden.

'Look, Ish, you're goin tae huv tae dae somethin about that girl. Ah cannae stand aw that mopin.'

Reinya hardly lifted her head from her picking at a line of scabs on her right hand.

'What happened to your arm?' Ishbel asked. Reinya glowered.

She looked as if she would enjoy slamming her hand into a brick wall just for the feel of it. The skin was trying to heal but the girl was intent on opening old wounds and breaking off ripe scabs. Ishbel wanted to ignore Dawdle and his operation. She had foolishly believed he had helped her as a friend but all the latest evidence proved profit was his primary concern. Each time she thought of the indignity of the hood she could feel her blood foam. How could he have allowed it to go on so long unless he had another reason? He must have witnessed her capture. He was right beside her when she was taken.

'Hey, Ish, can ye at least stop her clawin. It's pure givin me the boak.'

And now that he had what he wanted; being shot of Scud and his collection of seaware and cloth secure he was acting as if nothing had happened. And if he called her Ish one more time she'd throttle him.

Ishbel ducked back into the cockpit and hunted around for a first aid kit. There was bound to be one, even in a heap like this. It was under the pilot seat. As she pulled it from its place a badge the size of a large button fashioned into the shape of a Celtic knot dropped out too. Its silver body had tarnished with age but locked in its centre was a blue pearl, the ancient emblem of her ancestors. Not a real pearl but an enamelled imitation that shone as bright as new and stung Ishbel with its significance. It was hidden, Dawdle could have worn it but didn't. She could hear Dawdle's steps back on the hull, so stowed the badge back in its place.

She carried the first aid kit to the girl and, prepared for a fight, was amazed when the girl sat back, her eyes closed ready to accept her fate. Ishbel found some antiseptic cream, the old style that hadn't been around for years. It contained banned chemicals, deemed harmful to the skin by the Land Reclaimists. There were also chemical wipes. They would be out of date but no matter. She took Reinya's bleeding hand and dabbed while the girl tried to pull away.

'It's OK, I'm not going to hurt you.'

'You already are.'

'Don't be such a baby, you'll end up with an infection.'

Reinya yielded. Her hands were grubby and Ishbel realised hers were too, it had been a while since anyone had even managed a top and tail. Although they'd all had a duck in the sea their clothes were soiled and the girl looked as though she had been raking through a landfill. At least they all stank with the same vintage of ripeness so it didn't matter.

Ishbel used one of the wipes, first to clean the girl's hand; another fresh one to clean the wound.

'Hey, easy on the wipes, Ish, they dinnae grow on trees.'

'Shut the snaf up.' Ishbel found that since she left the Base she could at last open a rung or two on her emotions. She would need to remind herself not to let too much go. But she could see by the pink neck of Dawdle that she had hit him bang on the mark.

'How did this happen?' she said to Reinya, trying to soften her voice.

'Uh told you.'

'What?'

'That ship, wasn't safe.' Tears stood close.

'So you fought?'

'Of course uh fought, what do you think uh um?'

'Yes, of course you fought.'

Reinya turned her face and stuffed her fist in her mouth.

'Did they get you?' The question had to be asked and Ishbel had no idea why it was so hard. The horrors of the natives were everywhere, especially those inflicted on young fresh girls.

She remained quiet. 'Reinya, tell me, you're safe now.'

She sniffed noisily like an oldie. 'Yeah, uh was got. Uh was safe when Mum was alive but when she went uh was easy pickings, just like some of the others.' She faced Ishbel, hatred shone in her eyes. 'Can we go rescue them?'

'What do you mean?'

'My grandfather, Scud, 'e was on Black Rock. Now 'e's free. Can we go to sector W, to the ship, set them free?'

'No we can't.'

'Why not? You got them out that Black Rock place, why not sum more?'

'The prison ships are for addicts, what would we do with them?'

She actually seemed to think about this. 'You got me out.'

'You're not an addict.' Ishbel raised an eyebrow. 'Are you?'

The girl shook her head. 'There were other non-addicts on the ship, children who smuggled on to be with their parents, like me.' The heat of her stare burned Ishbel's conscience.

'We can't go in for anyone else.' Ishbel used another wipe to clear the girl's snot. 'I'm sorry for what happened to you but we are where we are. We have a reconditioning programme in the north. You just need to hang on 'til we get you there and fix you up.'

'Listen to you. "Fix me up." Who the snaf do you people think you are?' she said.

Ishbel sat back on her heels. Yes, who did we think we were? she thought. We, the oppressed, trying to help the oppressed. It needed more.

They remained silent for a while. Then Reinya whispered something so ludicrous that Ishbel thought she had misheard.

'What?'

Reinya lifted her face to Ishbel and for the first time since they had taken possession of the girl did Ishbel see that spark of fight she had first witnessed on the dock in Ulapul, all those months ago when she was delivering Sorlie to Black Rock.

'Uh said, put them out o' their misery. Kill them, blow the

boat up, drop gas on it, poison the food, uh don't know, but put the tortured out o' their long-drawn-out misery.'

'Are you mad? Think of the horrors they would endure before they succumbed.'

'No more than what they are going through now.'

'It's genocide.'

'Well, why don't the State do it? They do for oldies and specials.'

'Oldies are sent to preparation homes.'

'No they're not and you know it. 'Ave you ever seen a prep home?' Ishbel remained silent. 'No, because they don't exist. Everybody knows oldies are destroyed, so why not addicts?'

'Because o' the lesson,' Dawdle decided to chip in from the front. 'Privileged and natives alike need tae learn that excess is bad. The State takes a perverse pleasure in keepin them as a deterrent against excess. After aw it isnae fur long. Life expectancy in those ships is – what? Eight to ten months?'

'Then destroy them,' Reinya persisted like a rat in maze.

'Not our priority, hen.'

'Well if you don't, uh will.'

Dawdle shrugged. 'Go ahead,' he said gesturing to the door. Ishbel decided to let this ride, she could stop the girl if she made a bolt. But she didn't. She stood with her hands bunched.

'Anyway, you have a nerve. Where do addicts get all the drugs and Mash?' Reinya spat out, swaying to her feet. Dawdle ignored her. 'The Noiri, that's where, the benevolent Noiri.'

'Just servin a need, hen, that's aw,' Dawdle said, probably well used to this accusation. 'Simple supply and demand. Now, can we get off and get on?'

But she wasn't ready to stop, she tore at her wrists springing fresh blood, she squared at Dawdle. Ishbel was sure she would have swung for him again so she stepped in and injected a tranquiliser to shut Reinya up.

'Jeez thanks, Ish. Right, time tae move, we cannae hang

around waitin for dark. Leave her here, she's just a pain in the butt.'

'You were the one who said she could come.'

'Aye, well, ah thought she might come in useful, but ma heid's nippin wi her moans. How wis ah tae ken she'd go radge and stert aw that genocide gum bumpin.'

'We can't leave her, I promised to look after her.'

'We can't take her like this.'

Reinya moaned and struggled to her knees. 'It was just a stun, she'll be fine in a minute.'

Sorlie

'What if Merj doesn't come?' I asked Con.

'We wait till near day break and if still no show we'll cross.'

The wind funnelled up the estuary. The tide turned and light leeched into the sky. It was nearly time.

'What's your real name?'

Con squinted at me. 'Con.'

'What's it short for.'

'Nothing, that's my name.'

'Funny sort of name.'

'And Sorlie isn't?'

A pass of déjà vu whooshed me, I'd had this conversation with Harkin.

Con dumped his sack and pulled from it a small mat, placed it on the damp ground then sat on it cross-legged. He patted the sack. 'Here, sit on this, keep the damp out.'

So I did. He handed me a flask. As soon as it was in sniffing distance I knew it held Mash. It burned and curled my toes in the same way Kenneth's Mash had done when I tasted for the first time in his island cave, but this brew was cruder, not so strong. I wondered if Kenneth knew of my disappearance, of Ridgeway's death. Poor Kenneth. I tapped my communicator, still nothing.

After only a short while we heard the rattle and drag of chains. We crouched behind a bush, my knees soaked by kneeling on the boggy moss-sprung ground. Two men dressed in heavy, hooded jackets dragged a crate. By the look of the effort and the ruts left behind in the mud it weighed a ton.

'Here's your man,' said Con.

I felt my mouth blot dry. Merj was dead, we left him for dead on the beach. He couldn't have survived the blood loss of his arm blown off by a butterfly bomb.

'Wait here.' Con said. He crawled from under the bush and circled behind the man at the rear end of the crate. Quick as a viper Con put his hand across the man's face and yanked him back. The sudden change to the crate's progress caused the front man to stagger and fall. I sighed in relief to see neither man was Merj. The front bearer was female. She reached her hand out but said nothing.

Con faced her with a knife to the man's throat. She began to shake her head.

'What do you want?' The captured one said, struggling in Con's grip. 'We've nothin' worth taking.'

Con loosened his grip and laughed like a daftie. He kicked the box. 'What about this?' The box rocked with the kick then seemed to rock on its own momentum. Con was grinning.

'Nothing. Take it, leave us alone.'

The woman backed way, shaking her head, wide-eyed with fear. The other was scrabbling his feet trying to get purchase on the mud, free of Con's grip.

'Come out, Sorlie, they're harmless,' Con shouted.

As I emerged from the bush the woman backed off even further. Their heavy grey waterproof suits showed no sign of Privileged nor native. They were anonymous.

'What do you want from us?'

'What's going on?' The man glowered at me as Con draped his arm over my shoulder

'Do you know who this is?' Con asked him.

'No, why should we?'

'This here is Sorlie, Vanora's grandson.'

The woman gasped, she stepped forward and peered at me. She was older than I first thought, thirty winters maybe.

'No way. He's Privileged,' the man said after he took a good shuftie in my face, his rank breath invaded my space, native, definitely native. The manner was familiar, Con knew them.

'Yes way, and now you can take care of him.'

'No, wait,' I said, 'you can't hand me over to these. How do you know it is safe?'

Con prodded the man with his finger. 'Because this here's my brother. These are the two who left with Merj all that time ago.'

'Your brother?' When the man squared against Con the bear resemblance was obvious.

'I ought to kill you for this,' he shrugged his clothes straight.

Con laughed, 'Yes but you won't. I've brought you the grandson of Vanora. She's been kidnapped, and you'll help him get to the tower. This is your chance of glory, boy, your fifteen minutes of fame. How long have you devoted to the cause?' The pair looked to each other.

'Well, now's your chance. Sorlie has been to the tower, take him back and find your god.'

They stood immobile.

Con tapped his ear. 'Go on then, what are you waiting for? Tympan your base, check if you like, and tell them you have Sorlie, we need someone to come and take him back.'

'The tympan broke about three years ago. We asked for replacements when we sent our supply order but they never came. Then the food got less and less. We're fed up with Vanora and her false promises. We started fending for ourselves.'

'Fair enough.' Con said.

'Where's Merj?' I had to know.

'Gone, a long time ago,' the man said. 'He set us up in this deserted Urban and told us to wait, but we got tired of waiting. We're on our own. Our own bosses, answerable to no one, see!'

'Then why didn't you come back to us?' Con asked.

He man nodded to the woman. 'Would've killed her.'

Con nodded. 'She belonged to another man,' he told me.

'Are there any other operatives in the area?' I asked.

'No, they all cleared out too – to the north or the east, away from the floods. As far as we're concerned Vanora deserted us. We tried to find the revolutionaries but the whole thing is one big shambles. We'll wait for word of The Prince, but if he's not here by next quarter we head north.'

'Who's this Prince?'

'No one, a myth,' Con said too quickly. 'If you take Sorlie to the tower I'll guarantee your safe return to the reservation.'

The man shrugged and pointed to the crate. 'Why can't you take him? It isn't far. We've this to take care of.'

'What is it?' Con knelt down and sniffed. 'Animal?'

'Give us a hand getting it across and we'll show you. We'll feed you before you go on your journey.' He looked to his brother. 'Although you don't deserve it after that assault on me.'

Con held his hand out for his brother to take, the other man shook it off. 'Hey, come on, Al, what was I supposed to do?'

Al bristled. 'You could have walked up to me and said, "How's it going, bro?"' He brushed down his clothes. 'Look at the state of me.'

Even though they were of Vanora's clandestine clan, they were in a better state than the caveman Kenneth had been when I first came across him. Both were clean and Al was shaven with only the finest line of a vanity moustache.

'Get the crate onto the raft, we'll tow it.' The crate juddered, causing the occupant to grunt.

'You haven't kidnapped Vanora, have you?' Con asked.

'Very funny. Come on, let's get going.' Al said. He nodded to Con. 'It's fortunate that you turned up – we could do with a hand with the load. You can control the crate on the raft, the boy will fit in with us.'

The water was murky and the swell rocked the boat. When the rope tightened on the tow we rocked even more fiercely. I clutched the sides as Al struggled with paddles to keep us afloat. When I looked back the raft was pitching madly. Con tried to hold the crate steady while struggling to stay on the raft. When we arrived at the other shore, the woman carefully stepped waist high into the water and guided the boat onto the shore. Al joined Con and they both eased the raft through the shallower water.

Most of the bank was flat on this shore so we all dragged the raft with the crate until it was safely on land, then secured it to a large rusting metal ring that was riveted to the jutting sea wall.

'OK, we can carry them from here.' Al prised open the crate. Inside was a brute of an animal suckling four wriggling pink creatures with small bead eyes and snuffling snouts. Con laughed so loudly one of the young jumped in fright. 'Where did you get them?'

'Noiri,' Al said.

'What are they?' I asked.

'Piglets,' Con said

'And sow,' Al followed.

The woman picked up a piglet and snuggled it. It squirmed a bit then settled into her arms. She held it out to me.

'Take it,' Al said, 'don't let it go or we'll never catch it.' He pulled a rope from his waist and tied it round the neck of the stinking lump he called a sow.

Ishbel

Ishbel knew what the Blue Pearl badge signified but nibbled at that knowledge like a skelf in her thumb. She didn't want to admit that Dawdle could somehow be mixed up with it, even though she knew Dawdle must have for years had access to Vanora's group and therefore Vanora's fanatics. But what did Ishbel have to fear of the knowledge?

The Blue Pearl adored – no – they venerated Vanora. They had tried for many years to have Vanora come to their secret meetings, preach to her disciples, let their doubters learn from the great leader that they were right to follow her, make her their mortal goddess. But Vanora, unknown to the Blue Pearl, had scorned them. She'd been respectful of their requests in public but privately she called them kooks, 'up-the-close weirdos', whatever that meant.

Ishbel knew she had two choices, confront Dawdle or keep schtum. They were at the base of the tower and he was the only one could take them up. What business was it of hers anyway?

But wasn't it a dangerous faction of her mother's organisation? They were fanatics whose fundamental ideas wiped out all rational thought as to the sanctity of human life. They lived in the dark ages where the value of life was negligible. It wasn't much different now but it was better. But it was still part of her mother's organisation so what harm would it do to ask?

'Why do you have a Blue Pearl badge?' she asked Dawdle's turned back. It was out before she thought. She watched colour flush his neck. Such a well-groomed neck, trimmed hair, she'd not noticed before. Noiri men were always scruffy, the women no better, no matter what their rank. Their hair in tangles, their clothes, though clean, were scuffed in some sort of uniform of grungy honour. All looked as though they lived and slept in their clothes, curled in a corner of their vans, which she supposed some of them did. Dawdle was scruffy but now she noticed that it was designer scruff. His nails were clean, even though hers were filthy. But it was the nape of his neck, the colour of which was now calming in his silence, which surprised her and betrayed the fact that he took a pride in his appearance. When he still refused to answer she moved to sit beside him.

'It's just that if you know the Blue Pearl they might know where she is.' Why was she trying to appease him? She had a right to know. 'They might be able to help.'

'Ah don't know any Blue Pearl.'

A lie. She knew it and he knew she knew.

'Nutters,' Ishbel said. Was that another flash of pink on that clean shaven neck? His jaw definitely tightened. Good, thought Ishbel, let him be bothered. 'Vanora finds them hilarious.' She sneaked a look at Dawdle but his feelings were stowed.

'Aye well, they're nae concern ae mine. Let's get crackin.'

'Uh'm hungry,' Reinya mumbled.

'There's food in the bag,' Dawdle gruffed, motioning to the canvas bag stowed under the steps. Ishbel rooted in it.

'Just make sure ye find only food.'

She had him riled all right. She found some grainer bars and handed them out.

He led them up the metal rung ladder attached to the tower base. It was late afternoon and the sky was metal grey but a fresh wind blew in from the sea. For once there was no rain but that wouldn't last. They all breathed audibly in gulps, as if they had been incarcerated for years.

The tower loomed upwards, disappearing into low cloud.

'It looks stupid, doesn't it?' Reinya said. 'What a waste o' metal and effort.'

Dawdle and Ishbel looked at each other. 'It's true though,' Ishbel said.

This State, so oppressed, so short of resources, filled with follies of rich men who could buy their way through reams of red tape and thumb their nose in the face of poverty. The fact that this belonged to a criminal overlord made it seem even worse, as if he should have known better.

Rising water encroached the base of the tower and they had to stumble over broken railings and twisted, crumbling concrete to reach the eroded steps to the door.

There was no guard. The electric door gaped open.

'What the...?' When Dawdle punched his finger into the lift control, nothing happened. 'The generator's out. Ah'll nip up the stairs and see what's what. You stay here.'

'No, we all go.'

Dawdle narrowed his eyes but Ishbel was past caring. Her trust had left her with the memory of the bag over her head.

It took them longer than it should because Reinya was still groggy and dragged her feet.

'Told ye we should've ditched her.'

'I'm not leaving her.' She dug Reinya in the back. 'And you, Miss, don't want left, in case a predator's about.' That got her moving. But Ishbel wasn't joking, something in the crawl at her neck told her they weren't alone.

'Come on, you'll enjoy the view from the top,' Ishbel jollied.

'View,' the girl grumbled.

They found the main room clear of some of the heavy items but a few scraps of smaller artefacts remained. The Mash was gone.

'They haven't left in a hurry, took their time tae clear up. Ah wonder where Jacques is?'

'Look for something, anything,' Ishbel said. 'If Vanora was held here she'd have left a clue.' Ishbel also looked for clues of Sorlie. Where was he? She tried her communicator again, maybe he'd be in range now. She'd got a good signal from here last time, she'd risk it. Nothing, only interception of the regular airwaves.

'What the snaf, Ish? They'll pick that up.' Dawdle roared. He grabbed Reinya's arm and propelled her to the door. 'We need tae go. Now!'

'Calm down. It's Vanora's frequency. It'll take them at least an hour to unscramble it to pin down our coordinates.'

An abandoned chess set lay out on one of the tables, stour covered the board. Ishbel was tempted to wipe it but her love of chess forbade her to walk past it without making a move at the very least. Something wasn't right. It was a valuable set and yet it had been left. But that wasn't it. The white queen and the black king had swapped places; the white king was missing from the board, leaving a dust-free square showing its recent abdication. What did it mean? Was it a signal to her from Vanora? But did Vanora even know she could play chess? Sorlie's father, Dougie, had taught her to play so she could challenge Sorlie. At first she'd always confused the king and the queen and placed them in the wrong squares. Had Sorlie been here? Ishbel lifted the white queen. It was one of the Lewis Men but like the one that was lost from their set at the Base home years ago. She remembered Sorlie's father had to find a replacement but it wasn't quite right, the eye was wrong. This one had a distorted eye. Ishbel's mouth drained dry, it was the same one. Jacques' set was similar but this one was out of place, as if it never belonged anywhere.

She rubbed the face of the queen, asking for a sign, but the distorted eye blanked her so she put it in her pocket. If it was a signal Sorlie would know she'd taken it.

Reinya stood by the window peering through the widening mist at the ramshackle buildings that had once been an Urban, the broken-down pleasure beach now under water and reinstalled on a pontoon. The tsunami had covered it all and had toppled the tower but the mad, much younger, Monsieur Jacques had rebuilt the promontory before the river systems had failed and the waters rose for good and settled around the base. And now he was old and he too was missing.

'What do we do now?' Reinya asked.

'We leave, hit higher ground, try tae make contact wi Freedom.'

"ow can we get 'igher than 'ere?' Reinya asked.

Ishbel shrugged. 'We have to try. Here we're sitting ducks.'

Sorlie

'Someone's following us, aren't they?'

Con sighed and put down the spy glass. 'Yes,' he said and handed the glass to me.

A solitary figure walked over the marsh we had crossed just hours before.

'The roads are scattered with solitary displaced people trying to secret a way outside the system,' Con said as he followed my gaze. But he was lying, there was nothing secret here. This person wore a white hat, they wanted to be seen.

As we pulled the boat out of the river and looked back across the waterway there they stood, quite blatantly waiting for us to see. A small, lone figure in a white hat, legs slightly apart as if they had trouble keeping balance, hands swinging in a pendulum as if revving up for some mad dash and splash across the strait. There was something familiar in the arm swing.

'It's...'

'Ignore her.'

'But...'

'She's been with us since we left the reservation.'

He looked back across the river and pursed his lips, then turned back to help his brother with the crate.

The silent woman stood by the shore side and shooed Harkin away with a flapping of her hands.

'You can't just leave her, she's too far from home,' I said.

'She shouldn't have come then, should she?'

'You knew she was there, why didn't you turn her away before?'

'She doesn't normally come so far.'

'You can't send her back, it's dangerous. If the Military get her they'll kill her or worse.'

Con sighed and look back across the strait.

'You should have sent her back before,' I said again.

He whirled on me. 'Look, I've told you she never normally comes this far, see. To the crossroads and then she goes back. We've tried to keep her in but she's a stravaiger, wanders, see. She knows the score, she's been warned enough times. She's not such a special that she can't pass as normal, if they tested her, they'd know. She'd be sent back.'

'Back where?'

'Her ancestors' homeland. The Desert States. She's special but also ethno-tainted. None of her colour shows much – it's been diluted.'

The word 'diluted' sent a shiver down me as I remembered Scud and how he suffered during the prisoner experiments. The patched skin of the other prisoners as we sprung them from the prison. The reversal process Kenneth worked on in Freedom to return the prisoners to pure native. But the ethno gene was different. The State didn't bother with DNA manipulation; they tested and if there was a hint of ethno, back they went, back to their ancestors' homelands, whether a war zone, a desert zone or underwater. Neither Purists nor Land Reclaimists cared about the outcome as long as Esperaneo was kept pure and the sparse resources went to the deserving few. Harkin's dilution was a natural one occurring through years of mixed breeding. She was a mongrel like me.

'She's not moving,' I said.

Con sighed again then pushed the boat back into the water. 'I'll get her just now. She can come back with me when we're rested and fed.'

I didn't realise I was smiling until it was wiped from my face the moment Con reached the other side and whacked a slap across Harkin's face so hard she fell to the bank. She held a hand up to her face but he grabbed it away, hauled her to her feet and shoved her into the boat as if she were a piece of recyk.

As he rowed back, Harkin sat with her head down, her hand cradling her face.

She didn't look at me as I helped land the boat. The woman waded into the water and put her arm around the girl. Con said something to her but the silent woman spat in his face.

'Why'd you slap her?' I spat too.

'She's to learn she can't go traipsing round the countryside. Could put all the specials at risk.'

I grabbed Con's arm. 'You had no right to strike her.'

'Give it a rest, Mr Privileged. I should have throttled her.' He brushed my fist off his arm.

'She's not your property.'

'She's as good as.' As he squared to me his anger flared, but I'd felled bigger than him in wrestling bouts so stood my ground. He dropped his gaze first.

As Con passed her she stuck her tongue out at him. It was so sudden in this violent scene that I sputtered a laugh. Harkin's features didn't budge but I'm sure a smile touched her chocolate eyes. Con turned and stared us both down.

The woman gestured to Al to take care of the boat and led Harkin away. Two days on the road and she was as scruffy as a fox, her hair in tangles, her face and bare feet clarty. She looked as though she'd enjoyed a dinner of mud.

As they left, I noticed Con's gaze follow Harkin, his expression soft.

'You care,' I said.

'She was dumped at the gate as a week-old baby.' His voice was hoarse with memory. 'She didn't even look special, but we suspected one of her parents was Privileged, the other an ethno mongrel.

'She'd have been tested before chipping. She lived in my sister's home because they had no offspring. We all loved her the minute she came through the gate. I was the one who spotted her differences. She never spoke for the first six years of her life.'

Just then a light burst around us. The whole sky lit up with tracker flares.

'Come on, let's get under cover before the trackers come over,' Al said, as he ushered us through a stone archway.

They lived in the castle. It was ancient, medieval even, and looked as though it was the only structure not affected by the wave that hit the area thirty years before. All the other houses in the Urban were derelict, broken-down and stripped like midden shacks.

'Almost everything ripped off when the wave hit. What wasn't destroyed in the wave was reclaimed later and taken to the recyk for barter.'

Con noticed me looking. 'They say some people tried to return and rebuild the bones of their homes but the Noiri were in before them and anything left was picked clean and resold, refabricated or recyked. They stayed in tents on the fringes, they stayed in the castle but the sanitary conditions were appalling, cholera broke out, there was no medical care and no medicine so those who didn't die cleared out to the High Lands. And now they're scared to return because of the rising water levels.'

The castle was solid rock and where tapestries had once hung there was hand paint daubed on the stone in the same way Kenneth had decorated his cave.

And just as Kenneth had done, the bedding was animal skins. Pig skins.

They now herded the pigs into what I guessed had once been a sentry house. Dried vegetation lay ready for their manger. Al explained how they collected poverty grass and weeds from the waysides and dried them for months. 'Pigs will eat just about anything,' he said. 'But we want them to have dry bedding too.

186

We can't have them outside because the Military Transports might spot them.'

Once the animals were settled into their new home Al led us up the cobbled ramparts, chipped and broken where someone, probably the Noiri, had tried to steal the stone. I smelt it first then saw a whisper of smoke curl up through the stone work and disappear into the vaporous sky. In the kitchen the woman was fussing over Harkin: drawing a cup of water from an urn that stood in a dank corner and holding it to her mouth as if she were a child. Harkin looked pale even with her dark skin. Her hand shook as she lifted it to the cup. Her fingers were filthy. The woman handed her a biscuit and she wolfed it down.

'What you staring at?' Harkin asked.

'Wasn't staring.'

Her chocolate eyes flashed. When I saw her with Con in the reservation she was just another special, but I still couldn't work out what was special about her. She seemed perfectly normal, just a little weird.

I opened my mouth to ask why she came but my communicator buzzed.

Con spun on me. 'What are you doing leaving that on? The Military'll pick up the wavelength.'

'It's Vanora's wavelength, I thought they couldn't get through that. Anyway I thought you guys disabled it.' The signal was weak. 'It's Ishbel.' Ishbel.

'Who's Ishbel?'

I shook the comm as if that would help.

'Come on, come on.' But the signal died, along with my hope.

Ishbel

The spotlights went out.

'What..?' Reinya said.

Dawdle drew his gun and stood in the corner facing the lift.

'Over to the window, Ish,' he hissed.

Ishbel pulled her father's relic gun from her belt.

'Reinya, do you still have..?' but Reinya already had her gun primed. She might blow her foot off, but one more gun could shorten the odds.

The lift started to run with the heavy clank of the rusty mechanism. Ishbel took a knee, steadying her hand.

The lift slowed. The door opened.

'Nothing, nada,' Dawdle called.

A hot flash erupted around them.

Ishbel was flung into Reinya. Glass showered like rain. Someone screamed.

The world lifted, tilted. Black smoke poured from the lift shaft, sparks buzzed from the floor lighting. The whole tower screamed around them like a wounded dragon.

'Get out quick!' Ishbel shouted.

She crawled to where Dawdle lay pushing debris off his legs. She helped him up, then turned to find Reinya.

Fire whooshed from the shaft into the room. Ishbel's face seared, she smelled her singed hair.

'Stairs.' Dawdle grabbed Reinya's arm. 'Help me, Ish.'

Blood trickled down Reinya's forehead. 'Uh'm good,' she gasped through coughs.

Ishbel took her other arm and the trio stumbled toward a door, grabbing parts of the wall to stop them falling back on the listing floor and into the lift shaft.

188

'What if there's fire on the stairs?' Reinya asked.

'We have to risk it.'

The tower listed to the jetty side. The stairs opposite led to the sea side. The screaming tower quietened as it settled on its broken leg.

'We'll need to swim for it,' Ishbel shouted behind her as they clattered down the stairs.

Near the bottom she heard Dawdle by her ear. 'Ah cannae.'

'What?'

'Ah cannae swim.'

'You've been a prisoner? Had the operation?'

'Dinnae ask.'

'OK. Later, though.' More secrets but not now.

Ishbel shot at the door lock, it flew open to the twisted foundations of the wrecked leg of the tower.

'I'll help you.' She began to unbuckle her belt and thread it through his.

'No, not strong enough. Yer shooder.'

Ishbel had no need to reply. Smoke bellowed around them. As they stepped out of the tower a hunter light caught them in its beam.

'Drop your weapons,' a voice roared.

Ishbel arched her face from the light and saw two military Transports bobbing in the bay. A RIB sat below them. There was no way out. Ishbel took a deep breath and got ready to bite her pill but before she had a chance Dawdle yanked open her mouth and stuck his fingers in. She bit him hard but he fought harder. He had it, threw it in the sea. Her communicator followed.

'I'll kill you for that,' she said as two men jumped onto the founds and grabbed her.

'Had tae be done, Ish.'

A man with a tree-trunk neck held out his hand to Ishbel and helped her into the RIB.

Two other crew manoeuvred Dawdle and Reinya.

'Snaf's going on, Zane?' Dawdle asked neck man.

'Sorry, Dawd. Orders, see.'

Dawdle pointed to the tower. 'Jacques'll no be happy.'

'Jacques' gone.'

'Gone where?'

'That's what we want to know.'

Ishbel dug her tooth into her tongue and hated Dawdle even more.

'Who told ye we were here?' Dawdle said, too familiar with this group.

'A tip-off.'

Dawdle didn't react. 'Look, Zane, let's call this quits. Give us a break an' yous keep the scrap.' Dawdle swept a hand towards the tower and it obliged with a shift and scream, giving another notch to its demise.

'No can do, mate.'

'Mate!' Ishbel couldn't believe she had trusted Dawdle.

'What dae ye want wi a Noiri Don and his mare?' Dawdle asked. Ishbel fought to freeze her expression at this description of her.

Zane smirked. 'Your mare? Aye? No bad son,' he said, letching Ishbel up and down as if ogling a pile of porn cards. His teeth almost watered with greed.

Another man stepped behind Ishbel and dragged her to her feet.

'Watch it, pal,' Dawdle said.

Ishbel, used to such treatment being a native, had a face for every occasion and if needed she could take whatever came her way. Zane swiped a hand at her, she didn't flinch. Amateurs. He jabbed at her uniform and ripped the badge off her lapel.

'What's this tat? Part of the revolutionary army, are we?'

'Got it at a jumble,' she almost sang. They didn't know who

she was. This was the first time she spoke out and all the men turned at her words.

'Ooh, an island native. Not had one of those for a while, have we boys?'

Dawdle moved beside Ishbel as the boat began to swing landward. He still had one hand on Reinya who was huddled into his back trying to be invisible.

'Step back, Dawd,' Zane bellowed.

From this angle the explosion damage to the tower was more obvious. A hole the size of a Jeep was blown from one leg causing it to list dangerously.

The Transports stayed well out in the bay. On the causeway behind the pontoon an army of white vans strung out in unregimented chaos.

'Looks like you have a welcome committee,' Zane said.

'They're never far away,' Dawdle said.

'Tell them to get back, we're heavily armed and armoured. There's nothing they can do.' He slapped Dawdle on the shoulder, chummy. 'In fact, my boys might fancy a little shooting practice. You don't want them picked off like rusty tin cans on a fence, do you?'

Ishbel could see Dawdle chew his anger in his cheek. He signalled the vans back with a semaphore arm wave.

Zane spun round to his men who looked equally puzzled. 'What did you say to them?' He snarled at Dawdle.

'Whit? Call yersel a Military man. D'ye no ken?'

'Don't get smart,' he said, hooking his gun from his holster. Ishbel's head spun as the butt hit her cheek. She thought she heard Dawdle swear, but it might have been her ear ringing.

'OK, OK,' she heard him say through the buzz. 'I telt thum tae move back.'

'So why aren't they?'

'Mebbes they're disobeying orders.'

The gun slammed into Ishbel's stomach, she sank to her knees and she retched.

'Stop it,' she heard Reinya's voice. 'Dawdle, stop them!'

From where Ishbel knelt she saw him signal again, this time the van lights sparked and they reversed back a few hundred metres.

'Where ye taking us?' Dawdle asked.

'We're not taking you or that rag tag anywhere.' He hauled Ishbel up to her feet by the collar, giving it a deliberate choking twist on the way. 'We're after only one prize.'

'Where're ye taking her?'

'Never you mind, we're just dropping you off and following orders, see. Told not to harm you, we were. Know you can't swim so you're getting a lifeline.' The man grinned at Dawdle. 'Now isn't that nice of us? You can pay me back later. Maybe a cut of that next grain consignment when we get back here next week?'

The boat slowed. Ishbel's gut throbbed. Her face stounded with pain. She knew they wouldn't kill her right away but they could do other horrors before they handed her over. As the boat approached the shore they hobbled her hands and feet as if she were an addict, destined for Dead Man's Ferry.

'Don't!' Reinya rushed forward, but Dawdle stopped her and shoved her behind his back again. His men were out of Ishbel's sight. The fact they were just after her made her feel more in control. If only Dawdle hadn't taken her pill. She might betray the NFF. Vanora had never subjected her to extreme torture before.

'Look after the girl and the old folk,' was all she said before the gun butt smashed her face again. She hoped Dawdle understood.

The boat berthed at the pontoon and Dawdle held out his hand for his gun.

'Don't be soft, run along to your white vans and don't forget the extra grain.'

As they swung the boat round and headed for the Transport, the tower gave an almighty groan as if in support of Ishbel's plan.

'Let's get out of here,' Zane said to the boatman. Ishbel looked over the side. 'Don't even think about it,' he said.

But she didn't have to.

The night behind them exploded in fireworks, not far from the tower. The hills above the pontoon erupted.

'What the…?' The lights of the Transports shifted.

Ishbel threw herself off the speeding boat. She only just heard the roar of Zane's voice above the whoosh of the water in her ears. The wake and water forced her under. Swirling and tumbling, lungs bursting, she touched something solid, the bottom, hard concrete. She somersaulted and brought her feet to touch. Above the pounding of her lungs she could hear the boat circling, the water was not too deep. Air. As a child she could stay under for over four minutes. The water was dark, grit scratched her eyes. Her stomach hit a bar, she grabbed it in her free fingers, a hand rail. Which way? Her instincts took her right. She shuffled along, the boat sound grew less, the water bubbled, another explosion. Her ancestors led her the right way, to a larger object. The rotting pier, she let go of the bar and floated up, surfacing to grab gulps of air. Fire replaced the boat. This time there was no Dawdle to help her. In the south stood a Trac, a rocket launcher trained at the Transports in the bay. Two rockets fired in quick succession, hitting one then the other Transport clean out of existence. They hadn't stood a chance.

Sorlie

Vibrant reds lit up the sky far off to the south. Something was going down.

'What the snaf...?' I asked.

'It's the spirits of our ancestors come to save us,' Harkin whispered.

Con lifted his hand to strike her. I grabbed it.

'Leave her alone, she's not doing any harm.'

'Needs to learn to stop talk like that.'

Harkin was mesmerised at the lights in the sky.

'I hope it isn't what I think it is,' Con said.

'What?'

'The tower.'

My stomach lurched. If the tower went, how would I find Vanora?

'Who would attack the tower?'

'Don't know but it must be someone pretty powerful. It's the symbol of Noiri dominance.'

An alarm barked in the distance. 'Is there a Base nearby?'

'No, the sound's moving. Let go.'

'How long will it take us to get there?'

'Many hours on foot. Maybe we could hitch a lift from the Noiri?'

'What about the Military?'

'We take a chance. We don't want to arrive just in time to see the wreckers leaving with a heap of twisted metal, and the big old ocean the only thing left to answer your questions.'

As we walked along the river southbank, I checked my communicator again. It had been Ishbel. Where was she? The bridge north had been taken down, all that was left was stumps like a junkie's teeth, rotting where supports had once been. We joined a road at a junction where many tracks met. The alarm grew louder and had multiplied.

'This is serious, hear those sirens.'

It reminded me of the warnings before the Purist insurgent air raids on my home Base. 'What is it?'

'Noiri.' Harkin volunteered.

'She's right. Some of the Noiri vehicles used to be used for something called 'Emergency Services', they sounded sirens to alert other road users to shift.' He louped up a banking and scouted. 'Maybe we could cadge a lift.'

Con grabbed hold of Harkin and started to run. 'Come on, Sorlie, I hear one coming.'

Just then a white and orange van rounded the corner. Harkin shook Con free and made a dash across the road. Halfway across she halted with her arms held high as if in surrender.

'Harkin!' We both yelled but it was too late. The van veered towards Con and I. We jumped clear. The van bumped off the verge and shuddered to a stop with its nose in a ditch, siren killed.

The female driver staggered out the cab, clinging to the side of the van as she made her way to the back door. Her male passenger held a palm to his bleeding forehead, but his spitting face showed more fury than hurt.

Con had already sprinted after the driver and I found them both at the back of the van helping Harkin to her feet. She seemed unharmed other than grazed hands.

'Can't you keep your mutt under control?' the woman shouted. 'Look.' She pointed back at the crashed van.

'We'll help you get out if you give us a lift,' Con cheeked.

'A lift?' she spat.

Con held his hand up. 'How you going to get out of this then?'

'Somebudy'll come along.' But sirens persisted to the south, all heading away from us.

We turned towards the sounds. She shrugged. The wounded man appeared and moved to kick Harkin. I stepped in the way.

'It was an accident,' I shouted. 'Let's get this van moving before the Military stumble upon us.'

The man growled and pointed. 'Privileged!'

'Yes, Privileged!' I said with as much force as I could muster. And it worked. With a grumble they all reverted to type. I helped shoulder the van out the ditch despite their sudden aversion to my status. It was even easier than it at first looked.

'What's going on in the south anyway?' Con asked as he rubbed his grubby hands on the back of his overalls.

'The tower, we got a signal. It's under attack. We've all been summoned.'

'All?' I asked. 'Isn't that dangerous? What if it's a trap?'

The man looked at me as if I were stupid then the puzzlement passed. 'Why would the Military trap us? They depend on us to keep vital supply lines open.'

'Maybe we should be cautious,' Con warned.

'You don't think it's Military?' the woman asked us as if we were in on the plan.

The puzzle remained as the man studied my face. 'I think they should come with us,' he nodded my way. 'Bargaining power.'

Just as well they didn't know I was Vanora's grandson. As the siren fired Harkin sank to the roadside, hands over ears. She rocked back and forth.

'Kill the siren,' I roared.

'Ooh, ever the gentleman,' the woman sneered but she killed the siren just the same.

We weren't that far from the tower after all. We breached the brow of a small hill into the throes of chaos below.

Two amphibious military Transports floated on the bay. The tower still stood but only just. One of its corners had been blown and it listed precariously towards the illuminated pontoon where lights sparkled in the dull daylight. It should have been pretty but slapped incongruous and grotesque amongst all the chaos that ranged, it was a bit like a jester performing at a wake.

Con held his spyglass to his eye. The driver had one too.

'Let me see,' I asked, but they ignored me.

'Looks like someone's taken prisoner,' Con said. 'A native woman, strange uniform.'

The driver let out a stifled cry. 'Dawdle's negotiating. Arguing.'

'Dawdle?' The name familiar. The sharp Noiri guy that hung about Base.

I grabbed the spyglass from Con. 'Let me see.'

At first all I could see was the gaudy garish lights, then I focused on the group.

'Ishbel.' She squatted in the bow of a RIB. Her hands and feet were tied.

'Who's Ishbel?' The woman asked.

'My native, a revolutionary in Vanora's army.'

'Well, they have her now.'

'We have to help.'

'Looks like Dawdle's working to get her released.'

'And who's Dawdle when he's at home?' Con asked.

'Are you mad? He's the High Heid of the Noiri. The Military know how powerful he is. If he can't get her released, no one can.'

It looked hopeless. The boat was beginning to rev. One of the Military on the pontoon was holding Dawdle back. Along the edge of the causeway rows of vans were lined up but remained a good distance from the action.

'This can't be happening. First Vanora, now Ishbel.' I thought no one was listening until Harkin put her hand in mine and squeezed a reassurance.

'We have to do something, they're leaving with her,' I said.

Con looked back at the sight. 'I've an idea.' He turned to the woman. 'Can you look after the girl?'

'I'm coming.' She let go my hand and squared to Con.

'No!' we all said. But her face was set. She had already proved tricky so we let her be.

Con handed me the spyglass. 'Let's go, then.'

I took one last look. There was no sign of Monsieur Jacques but a girl with red hair held on to Dawdle's sleeve. I focused in on her face. It was the kid I saw on the dock at Dead Man's Ferry waiting to be transported to the prison ship.

As if she knew I was looking she turned her face to me and I could see those hateful eyes again. Just then an almighty explosion threw me off my feet.

'We're gubbed, that's what we are,' the driver said. Her deep voice had the burr of a Northern Celt.

'What d'you mean?' I couldn't believe how calm Con sounded after what we'd witnessed.

I lay on poverty grass with Harkin huddled into my side. We'd been like that since the explosions. A few white vans screamed past us heading into the northern wilderness. The rest remained at the pontoon. The damaged tower lay like a dead soldier, Noiri crawling over it like maggots on a carcass.

I put my arm around Harkin, we needed to go, but she was shaking so much I'd no choice. She wasn't crying, but she shivered like a jellyfish. My ears were still ringing from her scream. It's a wonder she wasn't hoarse.

'What was it?' I asked when the noise died down. One minute the Transports were in the bay, the next they were bits strewn over the water.

'Snaf knows. It wasn't us and I don't think it was them.' Con pointed to the chaos of the Noiri wreckers. 'So it must have happened internally.'

'Na, there was a rocket,' the driver said. 'Didn't you see it?' We all looked at her as if she were mad. 'Suit yerself. I saw it and now it's vanished. But it wasn't one of ours. Look.'

The RIB Ishbel had jumped from minutes before headed back

to the pontoons where Dawdle's men helped the three military crew from the boat.

'Ishbel?'

'The woman?' Con pointed further south to the broken pier. 'There.'

'Where?' I saw nothing but damaged wood and rotten spars.

'Under, in the water.'

A head bobbed like a curious seal, but with long strands of hair fanned out. She struggled to stay afloat with tied hands.

'Come on! We have to help her.'

'No,' the driver said. 'The place'll be swarming with Military soon.'

Con grabbed her by the lapels and propelled her to the cab. 'Then we better hurry.'

'The place is crawling with your men. How can it not be safe?' I helped Harkin to her feet. The woman looked grim, her mouth downturned with the sour taste of my words.

Con came to relieve me of the quivering Harkin but she wouldn't let me go.

'What's wrong with her?'

'Don' know, something in her memory maybe.' He touched her arm. 'Come Harkin, it's over, gonna have to move.' For once his voice was tender.

I wiped her face with the cuff of my jacket. 'Go with Con,' I tried to match Con's gentle words. 'You're OK.' Her face blanked me, but she allowed Con to take her hand.

'M'on then.' The driver twitched.

As we drove down the hill towards the pontoon I saw white vans changing position. More left for the north, some moved forwards. A couple of Noiri operatives took the RIB back out to the bay and began salvaging. Bodies floated in the water. It was horrible.

'These guys are the pits,' I heard Con say at my shoulder.

'What d'you mean?' The driver bristled.

'Look at them. Your Noiri pals.'

They watched as the Noiri hooked bodies into the RIB like a catch. They rifled their clothes, digging fingers into the corpse's mouths.

'What are they doing?'

'Looting the bodies, even checking for gold teeth.' Con said. 'Vermin.'

'Only doin a job,' the driver said. 'Trying to find cause.' But I noticed she didn't look.

I had no words.

'Know what I think?' Con suddenly said.

'What?'

'This was a Hero in Death job.'

My mind melted at these words. Hero in Death. The status my own mother was given. Ordered to strap bombs to herself and detonate within range of her target, killing herself in the process.

'A suicide mission, has to be.'

'How? On both Transports?' This seemed incredible.

'What about the rocket launcher?' the driver insisted. Con ignored her and I couldn't understand why.

'But who?' I asked. 'Hero in Death is State policy.'

The driver flicked her gaze between the road and the Noiri who still worked their way through the bodies, pulling other materials onto the boat, salvaging what equipment they could.

The main man, Dawdle, stood on the pontoon also watching them while the girl with the rust hair rushed up and down the pontoon shouting into the water.

'She's looking for the woman.' Con had noticed her too. 'Move it!' he roared.

The driver booted her engine, heading for Dawdle's men.

'No! Head for Ishbel.'

She swung the wheel and miraculously for once did as I asked.

'Who did it then?' I asked the driver who I suspected was not as clueless as I'd thought.

She chewed her cheek. 'I reckon it was The Prince.'

The Prince – again. It was like some myth they had created to relieve their stupid lives. But that was what Vanora was too; a myth and she was real enough even if what she stood for was not exactly as everyone believed of her.

'Who is he?'

'Dunno but they say he's all over the place. They say he's working his way north. Collecting an army of water reffos as he goes. Seems he's reached here now.'

'What about the Noiri in the south?' I asked. 'Why don't they work with him?'

The woman skewed her mouth in thought. 'Maybe they do. Dunno. Not much down there now. Too much water. Too much pollution. We have one water operation but it's hard to operate without vans, see. Everything is moving north, chased by the rising water. Lots of water reffos.'

'How do they feed?'

The driver shrugged. 'Dunno. Mebbes someone helps thum. The Prince, maybe. The State maybe.'

As we raced past the last of the white vans, Con roared, 'Good pickings, boys.'

Men secured ropes and pulleys to the tower. Heavy duty saws sparked. Noiri operatives swarmed over the base of the tower like flies on a turd.

'They're bringing it down.' The driver confirmed my suspicions.

As soon as the van stopped I jumped out. 'Give me a rope.'

The driver threw me the tow rope. I tied one end in a bowline around my waist and the other to a board on the pontoon, then launched myself into the freezing water before I had time to think. Breath was whipped from me. I touched something hard on the bottom, any shallower would have broken me. I surfaced, the water was filthy. I tried not to swallow. Ishbel was only metres from me, still struggling to keep her head above water. She watched me breenge towards her. When I almost reached her she smiled. Her cheek was busted and her left eye was starting to swell closed.

'Come to rescue a damsel in distress?'

If that had come from anyone else I would have thought she was being smart and left her to get on with it. But she genuinely wanted saved and everyone else had failed her.

'They've all been prisoners at one point, I guess.' Meaning they couldn't go into the water without sinking like stones.

'And they couldn't have thrown a rope?'

Her arms and feet were tightly bound. My penknife sliced through the rope on her wrists. I took a breath and ducked back into the filthy swill to slice the rope from her ankles.

As soon as she was free she struck out for the pontoon.

The girl with the rusty hair waited. I saw her eyes widen as she recognised me.

'Dawdle, it's Ishbel,' she shouted and he came running.

'Ish.' Was relief there? Or was salvage still on his mind?

They both hauled her out and then me. 'Where the snaf did you come from?' Dawdle said, grabbing my sleeve with more force than was needed to get me on dry land. My clothes were soaked and stinking. I shrugged him off and pushed him aside.

'Doing what you failed to do.'

He glared at me as he shook a blanket one of his men handed to him and draped it round Ishbel.

'Come on Ish, let's get ye dry.'

She coughed and spat.

'Where can we get dry?'

Dawdle whirled on me. 'Not you.'

'Dawdle,' Ishbel crackled. 'He's just saved me and in case you forgot, we were looking for him. You remember Sorlie.'

Dawdle peered at me. True, he'd only seen me once or twice.

My encounters with him at the Base had been brief. Times when he delivered mysterious packages to Ishbel.

'Ah thought it was a child.'

'I'm not a child.'

She put her arm around me. 'We found you.'

'Eh no, I found you.' I expected a smile but she went limp and I only just managed to stop her hitting the deck before Dawdle stepped in and lifted her in his arms and carried her to a van.

'Get a move on, we need tae get out o' here,' he called behind him.

*

I banged on the cab wall. Dawdle opened a small sliding door. 'What now?' he shouted.

'Where's Con and Harkin? I need to say goodbye.'

'No need, they're up here wi me.'

'Where are we going?'

'We need tae get out o' here, the Military'll be crawling all over soon. Only one place they won't go, and your Con and Harkin are takin us there.' He slammed the sliding door, plunging us back into semi darkness. I leaned back on the cab wall. Of course: Steadie. We were headed for Steadie.

Rusty handed me a blanket without looking. Even though I recognised her as the one from Dead Man's Ferry dock, there was something else familiar about her. She knelt beside the unconscious Ishbel, untangling her wet hair, combing it dry with her fingers. Ishbel wasn't out for long; her eyes flickered after a couple of minutes. She took the girl's hand, unravelling her fingers from her hair.

'Help me up,' she croaked. It was a gentle request and unnecessary because she seemed more than able. She'd always been more than able.

'I can't believe I've found you.' I knew I was grinning like a daftie, but so what?

Once sitting, Ishbel took a drink of the puri-water the girl handed her. A touch of colour rushed to Ishbel's pale cheeks. She held a hand to her bruising.

'I wonder how long that putrid water will take to work out of my system.'

'And mine,' I said. And she smiled at my bigging up.

'What happened?' Ishbel asked me. 'How'd you get here?'

'I could ask you the same.' When she stayed silent I said, 'Do you know where Vanora is?'

'No, I got word to find her. Tell me.'

'I've no idea where she is. She's been kidnapped.' I couldn't believe it. Ishbel was here. 'It's good to see you, Ishbel.' I should have said more. I should have hugged her, told her what I'd been through and how much I'd missed her but I didn't. The Rusty girl glowered at us.

'You were on Black Rock, Ishbel. I saw you.'

She nodded. 'I know you did. I went to help you – and to bring Scud back.' Did I imagine Rusty bristle at Scud's name?

'Scud? Is he OK?' I'd hated to leave him behind, he'd been such a good native, so brave.

The girl stiffened again and this time Ishbel put a hand on her arm, the girl pulled away and hugged herself tight.

'Reinya is Scud's granddaughter.'

'Granddaughter?' But of course I saw the resemblance, the fierceness in the eyes even with Scud's altered state. I wanted to ask more but Ishbel turned her back on the girl and closed the subject of Reinya.

'Scud's safe but in a bad way with chemical withdrawal. Kenneth should be with him now. He'll save him, I'm sure he will.'

The mention of Kenneth forced me to tell. 'Ridgeway's dead.'

'Oh no. Oh, poor Kenneth, I don't think he knows.' I'd forgotten how emotionless Ishbel could be.

'No.'

She looked worried.

'What? What is it?'

'Nothing.' She bit her lip, fooling no one. 'Where are they taking us?'

'Steadie. It's a radioactive reservation. It's mostly safe but there are no go areas so the Military steer clear.'

Ishbel began to laugh. 'I remember a time where you would run a mile from radioactive material.'

'Yeah, well, priorities.' I pointed to the cab wall. 'And these guys know what they're doing.'

She nodded and settled back, taking another swig of water. I told her about the kidnap and my stay at Steadie.

'Do you have no clue to her whereabouts?' I asked.

'No, and Monsieur Jacques has disappeared too.'

She shifted, knelt up, pulling a chess piece from her back pocket. When she held it up I could see it was a white queen.

'Did you place this in the wrong square as a signal – for me to find.'

'No. We never got as far as the tower. Why, what was wrong with it?'

'It's the odd piece from home, the one your father replaced.'

'But I don't understand. Where did it come from?'

She shrugged, 'I don't know, but that wasn't all. It was the set up. The king and queen in the wrong squares, the way I always confused them.' She squinted at me. 'I was sure you left it.'

I shook my head. 'Could it have been one of our surveillance guys? They watched everything at the Base.'

Ishbel shrugged again. 'Possibly, but they weren't that bright.'

She sat back. 'I thought it was you.' She rubbed the piece as she used to do with the pebble from her homeland. The pebble she gave to me to remind me she would be coming back to Black Rock for me. I had left it in Vanora's base in Freedom, along with my DNA passport. Would we ever get back there?

She put the piece in her pocket. 'No matter, I've found you now.' I could see why she thought it was a signal but to me she was clutching at straws.

*

The van rumbled over the rough road, every now and then we would be thrown from one side to the other. Each time I slid near the girl she backed further into the wall as if she wanted it to swallow her whole.

'There's something else, Sorlie,' Ishbel said after a while, her eyes closed, not wanting to meet mine. 'Merj is still alive.'

I felt my heart thud to my boots.

'How?'

She opened her eyes. 'He made it back to his homeland. They're healers and are busy fixing him up – as well as Scud.'

'He's in the same place as Scud?'

'Yes, and Kenneth. But I think he'll behave, he's still pretty wounded.'

'What are we going to do about him?'

'Nothing yet. He's safely out of our way but you'll need to watch your back and so will I.'

She told me about being on the beach that night, about throwing the butterfly bomb that maimed Merj.

'You saved my life.'

She shrugged. 'Maybe you would have beaten him fair and square, you were doing OK.' But we both knew what rubbish that was.

'Kenneth will alert us if Merj tries to leave. '

'Unless he sees to Kenneth first.'

The girl in the corner suddenly jerked from her place. She held her hand up to her mouth and retched.

Ishbel crawled to her and handed her the towel she had been given and made her sip some of her water.

'Come and sit with us, Reinya,' she said but the girl shook her head and glowered at me as if I were a rabid dog.

'What's wrong with her?'

'She's been through a bad time in the prison ship.' Ishbel lowered her voice. 'She's been caught. She went with her mother, to protect her. Her mother's dead and now I suspect the girl carries her reward for that care in her belly. She's only fourteen.'

'It used to happen all the time at the Base.' The words were out before I could stop them. 'It's so wrong.'

'Yes it is and yet all native women suffer the same threat.'

'You don't.'

She glowered at me, letting her native reserve slip. 'What do you know?'

Exactly, what did I know about her life? Even though she had lived with me since I was a baby, I knew nothing.

'What do you think we are fighting for?'

'What about the rest of the native army?'

'All of them. The injustice of what happens to our women, our children, our men at the hands of the Privileged. That is what we are fighting for.' Her amber eyes no longer had faraway trapped in them; they held the here and now.

I felt my face pink. She was right, I had gone to an all boys' academy where the norm was of porn cards, passed and pawed; chat and locker room boasts of what had been done to native girls. It was so wrong.

I looked at the girl curled in the corner. What was life like for her in the prison ship when even a Privileged boy wouldn't have been safe there? I knelt beside her.

'I'm sorry,' I said.

'Sorry for what? You never done nothin.'

'I'm sorry.'

I knew my Privileged genes were diluted but even so, Pa had been pure Privileged. Hadn't he been a decent man? And then it hit me. If the natives were to win this war, they needed Privileged sympathisers on their side. They need my Privileged side whether I wanted to help or not. I had no choice.

Ishbel

'They'll look after you here.' Sorlie said to Reinya. 'They took care of me.'

Poor Sorlie, he had so much to learn about women. That little Harkin had tried to attach herself to him like a limpet but the man Con had other ideas for her.

They were in a container fashioned into a home. It was basic but Ishbel was impressed with what she had seen so far of the set-up at Steadie.

'What are we going to do about Merj?' Sorlie asked when they all settled on the plastic furniture that crowded the room.

Ishbel sighed. 'Don't be such a worry wart.' She saw him flinch at her use of his father's common taunt.

'Don't put me down with that one, Ishbel, I see you're worried too.'

'Sorry.' It was funny being reunited with Sorlie. Ishbel immediately felt back on duty as his native, responsible for his well being. They had been separated for almost two quarters, ever since she'd taken him to Black Rock and handed him over into the care of his grandfather. Only two quarters and Sorlie had changed so much.

She'd deceived him with her motives and she now had to make it right. Things had gotten complicated, what with her mother's irrational behaviour and play acting at being a revolutionary. Sure, Vanora had orchestrated the Black Rock prison break but if Ishbel was honest it was Arkle who had been the brains behind that. Now from what Sorlie told her, Arkle was no more.

Sorlie had grown quiet after her worry wart quip. Ishbel rose to stretch her limbs and to look for Con and Dawdle. Harkin arched her back at her approach to the door, she looked like a cat ready to spit. What a strange girl. Her eyes were dark brown, almost black and her hair coarse. Ishbel had seen her likes before, hidden ethno genes.

'S'OK Harkin,' Sorlie said. 'Ishbel's my kin.'

Ishbel raised her eyebrow. 'Kin?'

And he started to laugh and patted his waistband. 'I carried my passport there for so long and then I found your paper that told me you're my aunt, Davie's daughter.' His face fell at the mention of Davie. 'Did you see him, dead?'

Ishbel nodded. 'Tell me.'

'It was an accident. I didn't mean to kill him. Scud will tell you.' Reinya shifted at the mention of Scud. She moved towards Harkin but Harkin melted into the wall.

'It was your name that tipped the balance. He'd already lost the plot of his mind but then I pointed out if he killed me you would be the only one left of his bloodline...'

'What did he say about me?' Ishbel knew it was a useless question. He would never have loved her. Her life had been a loveless wilderness.

'He didn't believe it at first but then he seemed to recognise himself in you. He was going to kill me, Ishbel. When I tried to stop him he blew his face off. I'm as good as a murderer.' His voice quivered but his face remained grim. He'd grown up so much.

'It sounds like he killed himself because of his discovery of me.'

'No, he was mad,' Sorlie said. But she could see he was lying. 'We have to leave him alone. He's destroyed so many lives. He's not destroying mine – or yours. We have to move forward and find Vanora and Jacques and find out what's going on. Find this Prince everyone is talking about.'

'Why?'

'Why? Are you crazy?'

'No.' Ishbel nodded towards Harkin and Reinya. 'Look at the mess of them. We could take them to Freedom. They would be safe there.' She smiled. 'You never wanted this life. Aren't you tired of all this?'

'Of course I'm tired of this. I want my old life back but that's gone.' He gnawed at the angry nail on his thumb and Ishbel could see he was tempted. He shook his head. 'No. What about The Prince? What about Merj, the Military? There are too many unknowns. How do we know we'll be safe?'

She whistled through the gap in her teeth. 'We can get the revolutionary operation going once we reach Freedom.'

'What operation? All the operatives on the ticker wall are disappearing.'

'What do you mean?'

Sorlie described the state of the wall, how worried Vanora had been about her disappearing empire.

'If The Prince is picking them off cell by cell, how long do you think it will be before Freedom is breached? Don't you see? He's taking over Vanora's operation. She thought it was the floods but it isn't. We met people fed up of waiting for Vanora to act. People who have been living in suspension for years. They've had enough and want action now.'

'What's happened to the boy who just wanted to sit at home playing with his wrestling station?' For the first time she noticed a dark shadow on Sorlie's upper lip and chin. His hardening jaw.

'I can't even imagine that life now,' he said without emotion.

'OK,' Ishbel had to fess up. 'Jacques had wanted to join forces with Vanora, that's why you made the trip. I called her down here for a meeting with Jacques. He said The Prince is growing strong. No one knows who he is and what his motives are. Jacques thought if the Noiri join with Vanora they can defeat the Military on Lesser Esperaneo then move over the channel to Esperaneo Major. The Capital is the prize. Jacques had it all worked out, but Vanora being Vanora would not be easily persuaded.'

'Then we have to find them.' Sorlie said.

'If they're still alive.'

'If they were dead, wouldn't there have been some boasting rumours? There's nothing, there isn't even a ransom note. And the Military seem to be pretty ineffective here.'

Ishbel rubbed her wrists where the ropes had chafed. He noticed. 'Their Transports were blown out of the water. Your man Dawdle had to take care of the boat guys.'

'I don't think we can trust Dawdle.' Ishbel said. He had disappeared as soon as they arrived at Steadie.

'I bet the Noiri can tap into the Military systems.'

'How do you know?'

'I keep my eyes and ears open.' He brushed his hair back from his eyes. 'Look, Ishbel, I didn't ask to be an outlaw. I know my parents are dead. Something happened to me on that island. OK, I'm an orphan.' He smiled then. 'Davie used to say, 'get over it.' Well, I have. I'm not just an orphan, I now have a purpose.' He walked to the door and pulled back the flap. 'Maybe it was being here. Look at those specials out there. They're safe here only because they're living on a radioactive site. But outside the reservation they're dead meat, and every now and then the Military don their protective suits and come in to crush them. We need to stop this, I see it now. The catastrophic change Pa warned me was coming is here. The DNA experiments will soon be rolled out, but that's only part of it.' He pointed to Reinya. 'And yes, we'll be safe in Freedom, but for how long and what about all the others like her?'

Ishbel began to smile. She had known he would shine in the end. She had brought him up well.

Ishbel heard dogs barking. Dogs? She hadn't heard them since her childhood. The natives in the North West Territories where she was born had kept dogs to pull their cargo sledges. But there had been a mass cull of dogs in Esperaneo in the past, when the Land Reclaimists came to power. The plan had been to preserve dwindling resources. Another short-sighted policy. They didn't understand that some of these domestic animals could have been put to work when fossil fuel was banned. Now wolves and bears were trained for illegal sport, always for profit.

Reinya was asleep. Harkin had given her something to drink. 'Betty will be along to take you to the canteen soon,' she said before she disappeared.

Sorlie sat in the corner, tapping into his comm. They only had one between them now and he'd been trying to contact Kenneth.

Ishbel stood when Dawdle entered. She wanted to punch him but knew they needed him.

'Where have you been?' she asked.

'He'll have been checking his consignment,' Sorlie said from his corner.

'Watch it, squirt.'

'What consignment?'

'They have my grandfather's books. They're more valuable than the rest of us put together.'

Dawdle reached down and hauled Sorlie to his feet. But Sorlie undercut him, twisted, hooked his left side and threw him over his shoulder. Dawdle sprawled on the floor looking surprised.

'Nice one, china,' he said, getting to his feet. He held out a hand to Sorlie who ignored it. 'The books were in the van I was kidnapped in. They belong to Ishbel so you better look after them.'

'Ah think ye'll find they're salvaged goods and in Noiri law they're finders keepers.'

Sorlie moved in but Ishbel stood between them. 'Stop!' Dawdle side-stepped and disappeared under the flap.

'How can you defend him?' Sorlie said as the tent flap slapped insolently back in place.

'He's good with Reinya and we need him.'

Betty came in. She hugged Sorlie. 'You came back. Come, come.'

Ishbel woke Reinya, 'Come on, we'll get you some food.'

Reinya stared and pointed at Betty. 'What?' Reinya said in too loud a voice. 'Is that one of those oldies?' Betty hirpled with exaggeration towards her. She hooked her arthritic finger at her and chuckled when she saw the young girl's horror.

'No need to be afraid, lass,' Betty chortled. 'Plenty more where I came from. C'moan, I've made you all some nourishing soup.'

'You should take it,' Sorlie said. 'It's delicious.'

As they walked from the tent Sorlie pointed to the buildings. 'There's the processing plant where they recycle plastic into yarn. And all sorts of products for the Noiri to barter.'

'Is it really contaminated?' Ishbel asked Sorlie as they walked across the duckboard to the big top.

'Yep. If the Steadie's stay, they're safe because they have adapted but if they leave they can get sick.'

'Is that not psychological?' Ishbel asked.

'It doesn't matter, it's what they believe.'

'What happens if we stay?' Reinya asked.

Sorlie shrugged. 'We may get sick but it could take years.' He tapped the monitor they'd been fitted with. 'They can tell with these. They've some medicine but I don't know what it is and if it works.'

Ishbel took one last look around the site. It was some operation and she couldn't help thinking Dawdle had a hand in it.

Dawdle was in the big top, deep in conversation with Con. Ishbel gently removed Betty's guiding hand from her arm and strode up to Dawdle. He held his hands up in apology.

'Settling in, Ish?'

'Just how powerful are you, Dawdle?' she asked. 'Do you know who kidnapped Jacques and Vanora?'

He rubbed his chin and looked as though he had all the time in the world. 'Give us a minute, pal,' he said to Con, who looked miffed at being dismissed.

'Who carried out the kidnap, you ask? Well aye, ah've an idea, but ah'd rather no speculate.'

'Do you know why, then?'

'Tae get thum out the way probably.'

'Are they dead?' Sorlie had come up behind. Ishbel could tell by the set of his jaw, he cared. He'd only just found his grandmother and despite her failings she was now his next of kin.

'Are they dead?' Ishbel repeated Sorlie's question. 'Tell him, he has a right to know.'

'Ah don't know.'

An old woman shuffled up to them and stepped between Ishbel and Dawdle. She shoved Dawdle aside, snatched Ishbel's hand and turned it palm up. She traced her finger along a line and a smile appeared on her lips. She dropped to her knees and kissed Ishbel's hand. The sound of tables scraping the floor filled the tent. Specials and natives crowded round.

'What?' Sorlie asked.

'Shsh, Shsh,' the old one said. Ishbel felt a tingle scrape her spine. Others peered at Ishbel's hand and knelt in supplication.

'Stop this.' Ishbel said. The crowd knelt back on their heels shocked. 'What's going on? Why are you treating me like this?'

Many produced from their pockets, and from around their necks, Celtic knots with the blue enamelled pearl at its centre; replicas of the one Dawdle owned.

'The messenger,' the old one said.

Ishbel felt a stab in her brain as if she had just swallowed an ice cube.

The old one took hold of a table edge and heaved herself to her feet. No one but Harkin moved to help her.

The woman patted Ishbel's side pocket. And she suddenly understood. She took out the chess piece that rested there. She looked at Sorlie and saw the colour drain from his cheeks.

'The ancestors are guiding you,' he said. 'I felt them on the island, I feel them here.'

Ishbel examined the chess piece again. Dawdle leaned against the tent wall as if bored but his eyes were intent on her actions. She held the piece to the light, she twisted the body. It moved. The natives gasped. The specials crowded her but the old women shooed them back. Ishbel twisted harder, pulled the head off. The audience ooh'd and aah'd. She tapped the upturned figure, a small roll of paper tipped out. The room held its breath. She unravelled it and smoothed it flat.

'It's from The Prince.' She felt something tighten in the silent specials. Even the natives retained an expectant quiet. She was aware of Sorlie standing by her shoulder.

'The paper is from the Penguin books in Black Rock's library,' he said.

'What does it say?' At last Dawdle spoke.

Ishbel read inwardly without expression then cleared her throat to read aloud, aware of how the words would sound.

'We have Jacques and Vanora. They will not be harmed if you do the following.

1.   Alert Base Freedom that no further action be taken against Esperaneo Major and Esperaneo Lesser

2.   The native Ishbel must travel to Base Freedom where the boy Sorlie will be released into her care

3.   Deliver Ishbel and Sorlie to Black Rock Penitentiary before the close of the third quarter

4.   Send the native Scud and the library of David Pringle to Base Freedom. This library is the property of Sorlie Mayben, no one else.

Failure to carry out these demands will result in the execution of Vanora and Jacques followed by the systematic elimination of the Noiri network.'

'He doesn't know you have left Freedom, Sorlie.' Ishbel said.

'But who is he?' Sorlie said.

Dawdle was shaking his head. 'Ah dinnae care who it is but ah tell ye this – the books belong to Noiri.' This was not going to be as easy as it sounded.

Sorlie

'Black Rock,' my voice, a shout amidst the silence. 'I'm not going back.'

Ishbel bit her lip. 'Yes you are, and Dawdle...'

'You're not going.' Dawdle's face was red as if the news had come as a shock to him.

'We are. And you're taking us.'

'Nut...'

Ishbel held her hand to stay his words. 'Yes. You were the one who said you knew who'd kidnapped them. You have the Blue Pearl badge, you know more than you're letting on, so just shut it and let's get this show moving.'

While Ishbel was having it out with Dawdle, Harkin sidled up to me. She seemed to have recovered from her siren fright and was back to the way she was when I was injured in the tent.

'You're going?'

'Not if I can help it.' Ishbel threw me a sharp look. I knew I would go even if she had to knock me out and carry me. 'Yes, I'm going.'

'I'm coming too.'

'You can't. Stay and look after Reinya.'

Ever since their arrival in Steadie Harkin had cared for Reinya; washed her hair, scrubbed her face almost raw, leaving a pretty apricot colour on her cheeks. Despite this Reinya still looked feral.

I knelt down beside Reinya. 'You have to stay here too, for a little while.'

She shook her head.

'You heard the note, just Ishbel and me. Your grandfather will go to Freedom, he may already be there with Kenneth.'

She rested a protected hand on her stomach. 'Uh don't want my baby to get sick.'

'It won't.' I pointed to her bar badge. 'You're in a safe zone. Harkin will make sure you stay safe.'

'Reinya,' Ishbel spoke. 'We'll send someone for you. We promised Scud we'd keep you safe and we will.'

'Ah'll come back for her,' Dawdle shouted from across the room. Whatever Ishbel promised him seemed to have worked because he was ordering specials to crate up the books and giving instructions over his comms to have them shipped to Freedom. He was smiling but a tick throbbed in his throat betraying how beeling he really was.

Harkin put her arm round Reinya like the little nurse she was. She smiled at me but I could see her hopeless tears behind the bravery. She stood on tiptoes and kissed my lips in full view of everyone. Reinya sighed and turned away. My throat closed in pain as I looked down into those chocolate eyes and realised I might never see her again. And I could see she understood she could never leave unless she chose to shorten her life and that was too great a price to pay for her freedom.

'I could always come back here,' I said. But she just smiled and shook her head.

*

Con led me to a corner of Steadie I'd never seen before. Specials were sifting through cargo containers, sorting a mountain of thin plastic gloves and bootees into clear and blue mounds. Con pointed to a fence post.

'You'll get a good signal here.'

I looked at my communicator that had been blinking on and off ever since he'd returned it to me.

'Why didn't you tell me before?'

'Because I wanted you out. I don't want to risk the State picking out an illegal frequency from here.'

'So why now?'

He shrugged. 'I still want you out but reckon the quicker you get in touch with your people the quicker you'll be gone.'

It took a while to boot. I knew what I had to do. The signal buzzed. The picture flickered and then I saw him, his smile splitting the screen and sending my heart into a black hole.

'At last!' Kenneth said. 'Where the devil have you been?'

I wanted to be with him. I wanted to tell him to his face so he could punch me if he wanted to. I tried to find a word to start with. I tried to find a smile. He noticed. He could see my face.

'How's Scud?' I asked, stopping his question.

Kenneth looked behind him. 'He's doing good. I'll text a full report to you now I know you're OK. Did you find Vanora? Is Ishbel with you? Where's Ridgeway? Let me speak to him. We had a secret signal but I haven't heard from him for aeons.'

'You have to take Scud to Freedom.' I told him about the ransom note and that we were going back to Black Rock. I told him about Steadie, I told him anything I could think of.

'Where's Ridgeway, Sorlie? Tell me.'

'I'm sorry...'

'Tell me, Sorlie, whatever, whoever, just tell me.'

'He's dead.' A shadow of pain passed his face and with it flew all his wasted lonely years.

He moved, maybe knelt down, I couldn't be sure. His breathing was faint, struggling. 'How?'

Ishbel walked across the patch of land towards me, then stopped. She stood stock still watching me. Waiting for me to finish what I had started.

'When Vanora and I left the Transport, it took off then exploded.' He rasped a sharp intake of breath.

'Why wasn't Ridgeway with you?'

'Vanora told him to go back.' I lost the image of him, I heard him roar, something crashed, I think I heard Scud's voice, at least Kenneth wasn't alone. The blurred face that returned to my screen had aged a hundred years, he was back in his cave.

His teeth clenched over his newly shorn beard. 'I'm going to kill her for this.' And he was gone.

Ishbel patted my shoulder. Poor Kenneth.

'Come on. Dawdle's craft has arrived. Let's go and get this done, whatever it is.'

When we sank below the waves I waited for Dawdle's pain, but it didn't come. 'Doesn't the pressure affect you?'

'Naw.' Then he twigged. 'Ah just cannae swim, never learned.'

I looked towards Ishbel, who shrugged a 'who cares'.

'Do you know who we're meeting?' I asked.

'Don't you?' At first I thought he was speaking to me but his eyes were on Ishbel. She took the chess piece from her pocket and twisted it round and round her fingers.

'It can't be.'

'Who?' I could feel my blood foam.

'You'll find out soon enough.'

The sub stank of diesel but was tidy and relatively clean. Not what I'd expected after seeing the state of the Noiri van I was trashed in. It was one of those tiny, stupid-looking orange things the Academy used to take us on Marine Biology field trips. We had a whole timetable of trips planned but after the second, when we ran into the vast plastic junk yard and our propeller was snagged on shredded blue rope and we nearly all died, the Academy cancelled the programme. It was pointless because we never saw any biological things, ever. I can understand how easy it is for Steadie to harvest their plastic from the ocean, there was an unlimited supply around the whole island. Anyway, the man Dawdle looked pleased with his sub.

'Is this it?' I said, more to piss him off and it worked.

'Sorry, your Majesty. The gold-plated Transport is having an oil change today.' His voice affected.

It might have been clean but it reminded me of the Transport

Ishbel and I travelled to Black Rock on the first time. Tired and worn out. It creaked and cranked but seemed to be watertight, even though it had to rest the engines every now and then.

'We'll never get there at this rate,' I said.

'Hold yer jets, pal. Peedle's never let us down yet.'

Ishbel was rooting around under one of the seats. She chucked a first aid kit across the floor then sat back on her heels when she had what she was looking for. It was a knot with a blue pearl in its centre.

'It's the same as the ones we saw at Steadie, when they all started going a bit weird,' I said. 'What is it?'

Dawdle stared into the murky depth that lay beyond the scored and scratched front shield. I saw his jaw chew on some words but he kept them to himself.

'It's the badge of the Blue Pearl Society. A secret organisation who once venerated Vanora. I suspect, based on the Steadie folks' behaviour, that this has now been appropriated by The Prince.'

'What do you mean appropriated?'

'He has managed to get them to switch allegiance to him.' She threw it at Dawdle. 'Isn't that right, Dawdle?'

'Look, dinnae ask me. Ah picked it up fae one o' the consignments. Ah thought it might be valuable. If ah'd known you were going tae bump yer gums about it every two minutes ah'd huv chucked it overboard.'

'Do you believe him, Sorlie? You've been in his company only a little while. Do you believe this fine upstanding Noiri man? No? Neither do I.'

Her dander was right up. She had certainly shaken off her native training in the months we'd been apart. She smiled, she growled, I might even see her cry one day but I doubted it.

'I wonder where all the people in Steadie got their badges? A community cut off. But they didn't look like fanatics, they looked like people clutching at straws. It's almost as though there's been a recent recruitment drive.' She moved behind Dawdle and placed her hands on his shoulders. 'Facilitated perhaps by someone who has easy access to all areas of our society, even those cut off.'

She squeezed his shoulders. I saw her knuckles turn white and the muscles in her right arm bulge. Dawdle didn't even blink but his jaw throbbed.

'Oh, and you never did explain how you know Merj.' She picked the knot from the dash where it had landed and shoved it in Dawdle's face. 'Does he have one of these too?' She closed her fist around it and shoved it between his legs so hard he gasped. I felt my eyes water in sympathy.

'Look, Ish you don't…' he choked

'You are up to your neck in this. What were you promised in return for your help?' She left him and sat on the floor where she could see his face.

'Did you arrange the kidnap?'

'No.'

'What about Arkle and Ridgeway?' I asked.

'No, we think that wis Purist insurgents. That wis the report ah got. They're starting tae become a right nuisance.'

'Report? From who?' Ishbel asked. He refused to answer. The memory of Kenneth's pain clung to me like a stale cologne that refused to die.

'Look, Ish.'

'Stop calling her Ish, her name is Ishbel.'

He left the controls and squared me. 'Ah can call her what ah like. She owes me big time and she knows it.'

It was like a slap across my face. 'What the snaf is that supposed to mean?'

'Don't listen to him, he's winding you up.' But the pinkness in her cheeks suggested some arrangement.

'She's not a piece of property.'

'That's rich coming fae somebudy who's treated her like dirt aw his Privileged life.'

There was no answer to that barb because it was true. 'She wanted tae get you tae Black Rock and this little beauty is the only means available.' He slapped the console.

'We'll pay you.'

'What with, books?' There was no sneer or joy in his voice, just business.

'So that was part of it too.'

'Listen son, since ah got in tow wi Ishbel ah've lost millions o' credits through lost business. Dae ye think ah operate a travel agent? No profit, no go, that's ma motto.'

'You're not interested in meeting The Prince then? From what Ishbel was saying it sounds like you might be working for him.'

'Ah work for no man. Ah'm a sole trader, pure and simple. If The Prince wants tae see me, he knows where tae find me, but it looks like today we'll aw be meeting him. Ah cannae deny ah'm no curious tae see if ma guess is correct.'

He scratched his chin for a moment and stared at the murk. Then he turned back to face us.

'Tell me, what dae ye think is more valuable? You and Ishbel or Kenneth and Scud?'

'What'd you mean?'

'A spoiled brat and his very capable and, may ah say, beautiful native or the architect of the DNA dilution and the success of that experiment. Ah know which one ah'd rather trade in. Or maybe he already hus the first prize and wants the second too.'

'Who?' He was maddening.

'He's only guessing, ignore him,' Ishbel said.

'You still dinnae get it, dae ye son?'

A small bell tinkled from the dash. 'We're here.' Dawdle jumped back into his driving seat. 'We'll surface just off the coast before we motor in. Just tae suss out what's what.'

The journey hadn't seemed real until I felt the ruffle of the wind in my hair as we emerged from the hatch. Salt nipped my nostrils and I was whipped back to my days at Black Rock and all the horrors they contained. We faced the penitentiary. Darkness had fallen while we'd been submerged and a sheet of low cloud had pulled down from the sky. It was raining – of course.

'It always rains here.' I said as if I was showing tourists my quaint ancestral home.

A small light still shone in the window of my cell as if the place had held its breath waiting for my return.

'How do you know it's safe?' I asked.

'Because we're expected, and if it wisnae safe we'd huv been blown out the water by now.' But Dawdle looked uneasy. 'Anyway, we've no choice.'

When Ishbel joined us in the hatch Dawdle made way for her but instead of taking the place she punched him in the mouth. His hand flew to stop the trickle of blood that appeared, he eased his jaw. 'What was that for?' he mumbled.

'You took my pill.'

'Ishbel, they're no going tae torture you here. They already huv Vanora. They're not the Military, ah'd bet my best van on it.'

Lights snapped a message from the castle crown, the ramparts where, in Davie's reign, guards patrolled, taking pot shots in the dark. It was impossible to see who sent this message but Dawdle seemed happy and returned the message with a handheld torch.

We dropped back down into the cab and he trundled through the shallower waters to the north of the island.

'What's in it for you?' I asked him. He'd already said 'no profit, no go.'

Dawdle seemed to consider answering then nodded. 'Monsieur Jacques,' he said. 'Ah've run a successful operation in Lesser Esp for years but it's becoming more difficult. The flood, y'know? Monsieur Jacques, he's connected. Ah need contacts in Major Esp. Although he has a base here, that was always the prize fur him. For me too, and The Prince. And if Vanora is smart, fur you too. So let's just get in there and get this done.'

'It's more than that though,' Ishbel said. 'What's Monsieur Jacques to you?'

Dawdle rubbed his neck.

'Come on Dawdle, spill. We're not going to tell anyone.'

I wondered what she was leading up to but stayed schtum. Dawdle looked uncomfortable.

'Let's just say when no one else wis around he wis there tae take care o' me until ah could take care o' maself.'

'So he brought you up?' she asked.

'Ah prefer tae think on him as ma patron.'

'And now you want to take over his operation.' She didn't even bother to hide her disgust.

'It's not like that, Ish. It's complicated.' But she wasn't listening, she was working a hole in her tooth with her tongue where her pill must have been.

'What about you?' I asked her to take her mind off the pill. 'What's your prize, Ishbel?'

She smiled – I'd broken the spell. 'I still can't get used to you calling me Ishbel. It was always 'native, do this and that.' Or 'you're in trouble, missy.''

Dawdle grinned and I felt my ears pink.

'Sorry,' she said, 'I'm just not used to being asked. I think it is the first time anyone has considered what I want.'

'Aw, come on, Ish,' Dawdle protested. 'Ah've been ferrying ye about aw over the shop.'

She ignored him and turned her amber eyes on me. 'I want to finish what Vanora started. When she returned to these shores from the Northern Territories she had it all planned. Her stash of gold and precious stones to finance her operation. She systematically recruited and set up her covert cells, found the best native brains credit could buy. She established Freedom as her base and managed a network of domestic natives to feed her hidden army. It took her five years to set up but she was focused and never wavered from that task. She knew what she had to do and did it.'

'So what went wrong?' I asked, remembering the unpredictable megalomaniac that I'd witnessed. 'The network is a shambles; cells festering all over the country, waiting and waiting for a day that never came. No wonder The Prince was able to scoop it up.'

Ishbel nodded. 'The problem is Vanora herself, she's a great organiser, and great on a small scale, but it all grew too big. She's a rubbish leader. She thought she needed to rule by The Art of War – always. Sometimes that might be necessary but most people were eager to get behind the cause. She made some mistakes. She put Merj in charge of operations.' Her face soured at the mention of Merj. I knew how she felt. 'When the Blue Pearl fanatics began to treat her as a celebrity she enjoyed it too much. She used to be in broadcasting, she always enjoyed the limelight.'

I remembered the T-map Vanora sent us with the plan of the prison break. It was pure theatre, but at least that worked.

'Vanora is and always will be a showwoman, which is fine in its place but she made too many mistakes. Many of the operations she ordered were not thought through and harmed natives on the ground.'

'Some were disasters,' Dawdle chipped in. 'Ah remem…'

'Enough….' And he shut it. 'You can't take the network she set up from her.' Ishbel continued. 'Many natives would not have their freedom or even lives if she hadn't acted when no one else did. We can't let The Prince waltz in and take that from her. She deserves her place. And she's my mother.'

'What about Kenneth?' She knew what I meant. By forcing Ridgeway to come with us for no apparent reason she had signed his death warrant and probably killed Kenneth with grief.

'She didn't know that was going to happen. We all take risks coming from Freedom. As I say, she makes mistakes. You asked what I want so there you have it.'

'It sounds like we all want the same thing,' Dawdle said. 'So in that case this should be easy.'

The hooded figure stationed on the jetty caught the rope and helped guide us in. He wore standard native civvies. I'd expected some sort of uniform to be worn by The Prince's guards. Vanora had insisted everyone in her network wear uniforms to give the impression of an army.

The rain was relentless. As we left the hatch the man hurried forward to help us up the slippery stone steps to a waiting three-wheeled buggy.

I dared a shuftie up at the penitentiary I'd been incarcerated in for months. From the sea it looked like a ruin. A castle crown perched on a mound with the penitentiary hidden underground.

There were many ways into the prison. When Ishbel had transported me here we had landed on the H pad and I entered through a roof door to descend that awful spiral stairway into the prison. The times when I'd been allowed out with Ridgeway, we'd gone from the corridor of my cell out onto the cliff face. The last time I had entered I'd shucked up a cooling water pipe into the reactor room. This time the guard who met us at the jetty trundled the buggy over a rough track towards huge gates that swung open on our approach. As we passed through I realised what a truly impressive castle this must have once been. The buggy stopped in a courtyard.

'We're being taken to a royal court,' I said. 'I remember from taught history of long gone monarchs. Is this what The Prince is about? Reliving the past?' Although I felt calm Ishbel took my hands to stop my worry wart scratching.

'We'll soon find out if it is a court,' she said. But it fitted the name and the use of chess pieces to send the message. More drama and symbolism, just like Vanora.

A thin light sliced into the rain-drenched darkness to welcome us. The smells of peat fire and a Monday morning soup pot filled the space.

'Yeas'll be after wantin to dry off, ah'm thinkin.' The man said in an accent of the water reffos. He led us to an ante-chamber, warm and light where towels and dry overalls hung beside showers.

Ishbel examined the clothes. 'The right size.'

'How do they know?'

'Who cares,' Dawdle said, stripping off. 'It's been years since ah've hud a decent shower.' He jumped into the cabinet uninhibited by his scrawny nakedness.

'You go first.' Ishbel said, trying to hide her irritation while I tried to forget the sight of his scrawny buttocks and the whip mark scars on his back. But my shock must have been obvious because Ishbel said, 'Lashings. They took place during the Purist Regime,' her voice low against the sound of the screams of jet joy pouring from the shower cabinet. 'The Land Reclaimist's stopped the practice,' she said.

'I wonder what he did.'

Ishbel shrugged. 'You didn't need to do much to be punished then.'

Dawdle emerged, wrapped in a towel, his hair dripping. I moved to go next then stopped and urged Ishbel to go first.

'A definite improvement,' she said as she stepped into the shower cubicle fully clothed, taking the largest towel with her.

As Dawdle and I waited for Ishbel to shower I asked him again.

'How do we know this is safe?'

He shrugged.

The corridors were wide and painted institutional green. As we passed one door labelled 'Infirmary' I stopped and recognised the long shape of the hall. The floor had been cleaned of the puddles of blood and the hospital beds cleared of their murdered occupants, but I could see traces of blood-letting; tiny pinpricks of blood missed in the clean-up and only visible to someone who had witnessed the massacre. I closed my eyes to wipe the image but it only made it worse. Ishbel put her hand on my shoulder.

'He murdered them all.'

'I know,' she said. 'Let him go, Sorlie. He's doesn't even deserve your memories.'

'Memories are the one thing the state cannot rob you of.' The mantra my mother used. Sometimes I wish the state could rob me. Wipe my mind clear in the same way as they cleaned this mess out.

'It looks like someone cleaned up. Davie's body will have been cleared out too, with the rest of the trash.'

I imagined I'd have been more frightened meeting The Prince but being back here dampened that fear.

Fear is a state of mind. I'd spent my whole time here in a varying state of fear.

One thing still niggled. Why was The Prince so insistent on Ishbel and me coming here?

Our guide led us from the infirmary, through the cell hall. All the doors were flung open just as we had left them, but the walls were washed and robotic machines were whooshing up and down the floors, polishing. It was as if the place was being preserved as a museum or being prepared for some other fate.

'Hey, this is some doss,' Dawdle said, looking round, fingering the fittings.

'Yep, top scrap value here,' Ishbel quipped.

'Now, Ish,' he said waggling a figure at her.

We passed the bottom of the metal stairway that led to the H pad. As my eyes travelled upwards my stomach twisted with the spiral of memory. So many unknowns. Since then I'd faced death and won. I could face The Prince. What was the worst he could do to me? Kill me?

That thought filled me with nothing but a regret. I wouldn't see Harkin again. Ma and Pa had been gone for months and even the ache of their death was cold.

'Bring it on,' I said to the echoing hall.

'That's the spirit,' Dawdle said.

We reached the museum hall that led to my grandfather's library. It had been cleared of its artefacts but the solid door with the plate-size handles stood slightly ajar. Our guide pushed and I waited for the hush of it to open and the smell of vanilla mixed with that powdery oldie smell of my grandfather and the books. It was all missing, gone and in its place was lavender and that got me, just as it always did. The smell of Ma, the smell of Vanora.

There was a warm glow from the room. I paused. I saw Dawdle and Ishbel look at each other like a pair of concerned parents, or were they wondering if perhaps this would be their last time together? Dawdle smiled, not his cocky smile but encouraging. And Ishbel tried not to return it but her eyes gave her away, softening from their usual hard glare she seemed to save just for Dawdle. She took my hand.

'It'll be fine,' she whispered as all three of us walked into The Prince's lair as one.

Vanora cooried in my winged chair pulled up to one side of the welcoming fire. She huddled in a cloak, dark circles panda'd her eyes, her hair faded even more than before. Where once she looked golden now she looked grey. Even the mulberry cloak could not brighten her complexion.

On the other side of the fire sat a man who stood when we entered.

'Jacques,' Ishbel bent to whisper in my ear. As he rose I thought he might hit the ceiling. What a height – imposing, Ma would have called him. His expression was grim as he tried to smile. He may have been of an age with Vanora, but his face looked modified false, an oldie pretending to be a senior. There was a dent in the middle of his forehead as if he had once been shot in the head and survived. He looked like a man who could stop a bullet.

He held out his hand. 'Ishbel, ma chérie, you came to rescue me.' And then he turned to me. 'Sorlie, enchanté.'

'What took you so long?' Vanora snapped, shuffling forward in her seat.

'Don't get up.' Ishbel said.

'Sorlie,' Vanora held her hand out past Ishbel, 'come here so I can look at you.'

'Are you OK?' Ishbel asked her.

'Yes, yes, we're well taken care of, aren't we Jacques? It's just this place is so cold. So bare.'

And she was right. The walls, once bricked with books were bare, the furnishings stripped.

'Where's The Prince?' I asked.

Vanora snorted. 'Well, that's the other thing.'

'I think you better sit down young man,' Jacques said.

'Why? What's going on?'

'Aye, come on Jacques, stop muckin about. Where is he? Ah've business tae attend tae, ken?'

Jacques moved to one of the bookcases. He nodded behind us. In the doorway stood a man in shadow, with only the fire flickering over his dark form. He stepped into the room and I felt a whoosh of dread spread through me.

'Merj?'

Merj is The Prince? I looked at Ishbel who had turned the colour of stodgy porridge. Vanora stared into the fire as if she had washed her hands of the situation.

Although he wore a patch over his eye and cheek and his arm hung a little stiffly off his body, he was the same man I'd met in this study all those months ago. The man I'd stabbed on the beach when he tried to capture me. The man Ishbel had blown up but told me was still alive. His smirk confirmed he was the same man. He was enjoying our confusion.

'Merj is The Prince?'

Vanora let out a massive sigh as Merj shook his head. A surge of relief washed over me.

'He's the delivery boy.' Vanora said.

'Yes, thank you, Vanora. I'm quite capable of talking for myself.'

Her sharp look sliced the air. 'Well get on with it then.'

'Take a seat, Sorlie. But before the show begins, there are two others waiting to join us.' Merj said ushering someone in from the open doorway.

'Hiya, wee man.' Scud grinned and tapped his nose in that maddening way of his. He looked almost human, with a definite air of Privileged remaining. His hair curled at his neck and his eyes shone with health; he'd even cultivated a small pot belly of comfort. Before I had a chance to welcome him a roar entered the room followed by a flash of blue cloak. Clawed hands hooked into Vanora's face and dragged her from the chair. Jacques reacted first. He yanked the figure off Vanora and threw him across the room. Ishbel moved in on her mother while I scrambled towards the figure in the corner. Kenneth roared again, struggling to his knees, untangling himself from his dramatic cloak. This time Dawdle was on him. Between us we restrained the foaming Kenneth.

Vanora opened her eyes. 'What…?'

'Shh,' Ishbel said.

'Sorlie.'

'Shh, he's here.'

'I'm going to kill her,' Kenneth bellowed as they pulled him to his feet.

Blood trickled from a cut on Vanora's forehead. Throughout the exchange Merj stood in the shadow, his expression hidden. He made no move to help.

'Come on, we can take her to my cell,' I suggested. Ishbel bundled her mother in her arms as if she were a pile of laundry and followed me along the corridor. It felt funny being back in these familiar surroundings. The same but with all the doors wide open, making a statement that we'll never be imprisoned again. Even the shuttered door to the outside anti-room lifted up some centimetres or so from the floor. This was the door Ridgeway had cranked up to take me outside. Poor Ridgeway. I couldn't help thinking Kenneth was right to attack Vanora for bringing about his unnecessary death.

I'd forgotten how white the room was. White and functional. Unlike the rest of the prison, this room remained untouched. The useless Beast workstation sat in place on the table, so obsolete even the Noiri refused it. And the starburst in the window, from the time I'd tried to break the glass with a brass lamp. What a dolt I'd been to think that would work. Scud followed us into the room and plumped a pillow as Ishbel placed Vanora on my bed. She lay so small, like a broken fledgling in a boot box. Scud handed me a swig bottle of puri water and opened the medi-kit he must have retrieved from his kitchen.

'Just like old times, eh?' he said but his grim expression showed me he was far from happy with this role.

'I'll do it,' I said, reaching for a cleansing wipe.

'No, best that it's me.'

He daubed the wound, applied a couple of stitches to her forehead. As he worked he turned to Ishbel.

'Where's Reinya?'

'Safe,' Ishbel said but a faint flush brushed her skin. 'Later,' she said to seal things.

233

He punctured Vanora's wrist with a medi-pen. 'She'll sleep now. We just need tae sit for a minute tae check for allergic reactions.'

'What is it?' Ishbel asked.

'A sedative with a healing element. Davie Boy always had some around in case Sorlie here got out of hand.'

'What? You drugged me?'

'Cool yer jets, we hardly ever used it.' Scud packed the kit and wandered to the window. 'This windae kept me alive. D'you know that?'

He swept down his body with a flourish of hands. 'Hey, look at me now.'

'You were experimented on.' I couldn't believe he could even come back here.

'Kenneth sorted that though, eh? Ah'm ready for anything now.'

'Anything?' Ishbel asked.

'Aye, this Prince malarkey. That Merj bloke, once he convinced Kenneth he was on our side, he gave us the gen on The Prince. Seems like he's sound as a pound. Has solid plans tae sort out the State once Vanora and Jacques buy in.' He looked out the window again. 'Peaceful plans, stop the pain.' When he turned around he was too slow replacing his pain with the cheeky expression.

'You know who he is?'

'No, but he knows me. Knows all about ma history teaching.' He nodded towards the library. 'Wants me tae set up teaching modules. Put the records straight.'

'Can you do that?'

'Aye. At least ah have tae try. Whole generations had only taught history. It's all lies and needs tae be fixed.'

'What happens if Vanora dies?' I asked.

'She's not going to die,' Ishbel said.

'But Kenneth hates her.'

Ishbel smoothed back her mother's faded hair. 'She's the symbol of all natives. We have to keep her alive.'

'She'll be fine. A bit shaken but she's a tough auld burd.' She looked so frail, I wish I had Scud's new Privileged confidence. 'And yet,' he continued. 'Kenneth knows how to stabilise the dilutions, so we'll need them both.'

'How did he do it?' I asked.

'Search me, but he and the souterrain folk did some stuff in a lab.'

'So they know how to do it too.' Ishbel asked. 'The reversal?'

'The stabilisation – not reversal.'

'What are you suggesting, Ishbel?' Although I didn't need to ask.

She shrugged. 'If we have to choose we have to choose.'

'Why not just keep them apart as Scud suggests?'

'Did you see him? He's lost his mind, like a rabid fox.'

'Vanora's not much better.' Ishbel rose to lift her hand to me but didn't follow through with a slap. 'Come on, you know that, Ishbel. They both need put away.'

'Enough.' Scud said. 'Ah can't believe you two.'

As if on cue, beyond the room came more shouts and shuffles. Scud shook his head.

'He's taking it badly. They had tae give him something when you first told him about Ridgeway, but it's worn off. All the way over on the moorlogger he's been spoutin murderous talk. Ah thought that was all it was – talk but, well.' He pointed to Vanora. His hand still had a tremor and I realised he was far from normal.

'How are you, Scud?' I asked.

'Much better.' He looked at Ishbel. 'Thanks tae Ishbel.'

She swept his words away with a nod. 'Can we leave her now?'

He took her pulse. 'Should be OK. Ah don't want tae miss the show.'

Kenneth had been bundled away by the time we returned to the library.

'How is she?' Jacques asked.

'She'll live,' Ishbel said with more bile than necessary. 'Where's Kenneth?'

'Restrained. In a cell. He'll stay there until you decide his punishment.'

'His punishment…'

'What about The Prince?' I stepped up to Merj. There was such a great difference in our height. It was incredible I'd come even close to beating him in a wrestling bout. I felt my shoulders hitch almost to my ears so I squared to him, pulling straight and tall. He smiled, charisma and charm cranked to the max.

'You realise I didn't have a choice?' he said. Was that an apology? 'I was under orders.' He touched his false arm. 'I bear you no grudge.' He nodded toward Ishbel. 'She's the one who caused the damage.' That wasn't true, I'd stabbed his cheek. I watched his thrapple swallow hard. All was not well with Merj. Conflict bubbled under his expression of calm. I stared at his one eye, letting him see he fooled no one.

'So what about The Prince? Can we move on? Where is he?' I said.

'Aye,' said Dawdle. 'Get on with it. Everyday ah'm involved with you lot ma business suffers losses.'

Jacques looked sharply at Dawdle but added. 'Oui, I agree, I have been incarcerated long enough. I understand the Purists insurgents are moving closer to the Capital. I need to advise my men. What does The Prince want from us?' He swept his arm round the room in a grandiose gesture. 'We are all here now. Non?'

'OK,' Merj said. He unclipped his reader from his belt and directed its beam to the wall above the fireplace. Fuzz, distortion and snow filled the wall. A high-pitched buzz squealed from the reader. He shook it and tapped it on his knee then tried again. Same result.

'Geez it here, let me try,' Dawdle said.

'No.' Merj hugged it to him. 'It's not working,' he said to the air then bent his head. He touched his ear where a small tympan lodged. He nodded. 'OK.'

'Who are you talking to?' I asked.

Merj straightened. 'We try something else.' He placed a small receiver on the floor and a holo smudged reality. Blurred at first and then a figure wavered, appeared and filled the room, larger than life size.

'Theatre,' I scoffed. 'Just like the thought map Vanora used to send us the escape plan.' But an eerie silence crept into the room, curling round us as the holo took shape. Ishbel put a hand on my shoulder and squeezed but it was too late, I'd seen it.

'Pa! It can't be.' My mind exploded with possibilities.

I ran into the beam and tried to grab it but it shifted and vaped. It was like trying to catch a rainbow.

'It's a trick!' My throat burned with my scream. 'Stop it.'

The vision's mouth moved but the words were lost in the ether. Broken, distorted, gone.

'Shut it off.'

'But the message...' the voice filtered through. His voice. '... must act...'

'Put it off.' Ishbel yelled. The first time I'd ever heard her lioness roar.

*

They must have given me something, one of Scud's pens, because I calmed even though I could feel the pain of sobs stabbing me in my breast bone. Or maybe that was the stab of betrayal I felt.

I couldn't look at Ishbel. Jacques gave me a drink of Mash and sat on the arm of the chair beside me.

'So The Prince – he is your papa?'

'My pa is dead.' The last time I'd seen him was the day he packed his bag and left to avenge my mother's death, to leave his Jeep keys for Ishbel to use, to take me to my grandfather.

Ishbel told me my pa, Dougie Mayben, had lost his mind after his wife's death. He'd killed Ma's commanding officer and was executed.

Ishbel had shrunk, hunkered down in a corner, staring at the spot on the floor where the holo had projected.

'You knew.' I accused.

She shook her head. 'No.' It was barely a word, just a breath. A single tear trickled from her eye. Tears from Ishbel. Impossible.

'I thought he was dead.' Her hand shook as she swiped the offending tear. 'I received instructions through the Military channel, followed by another, an encrypted instruction through an unfamiliar channel to get us past the guard. I'd no reason to doubt it. Why would I? It contained our secret word. It all made sense. He'd mumbled for weeks about a catastrophic change.'

A 'catastrophic change'. Yes, those were the words Pa used on our last trip away, just before Ma died.

Merj moved into the room from his shadow corner. 'Are we ready to try this again?'

'Aye, let's get going.'

'Dawdle!' Ishbel rose to her feet but still seemed small.

'Sorry Ish, but come on… it's a holo fur snaf sake. Could've been captured years ago.'

Merj placed the holo back into our centre.

Pa's dark clean shaven looks had been replaced by a ravaged face etched with pain lines, his hair faded. He'd changed but it was definitely him, only cored. I felt a knot in my throat start to strangle. I coughed.

'Why did you leave me?' I whispered.

'It's a holo, he can't hear,' Merj said.

'I'm not an idiot.'

When Pa's mouth began to move we all looked at each other. Merj did some adjusting with a remote.

'Wrong wave.'

Pa's voice boomed in the room. '…until I established an army. Once my son delivered the plug-in to Black Rock, his work was done.'

'I came to get you,' Merj said.

'Liar,' I hissed.

'The revolutionary army of Vanora have been ineffectual. By joining forces with the Noiri and Blue Pearl, the revolutionary capabilities will be enough to overpower the Capital and take the main prize of all Esperaneo. My commanders are already in place in Freedom. Part of the Noiri network has transferred to my command. Ladies and gentlemen, we either join to fight our mutual enemy or we fight each other and let the State win. My commanders will explain to you my plan. We must be ready to mobilise before next quarter; before the Purists take power and force some of our allies in the Land Reclaimist Party into Exile.'

Merj tapped the communicator and the screen vanished.

'No,' I said, amazed at how calm I now felt. 'Let him show himself. Where is he? Why a holo? If he wants them to help, why a holo?' I looked at Merj. 'Your reader, who were you talking to?'

I grabbed Merj's communicator wrist. 'Send him a message. Get him to come.'

Merj shook me off and unclipped the reader from his belt again and before he handed it to me he keyed it.

'Here. Ask him yourself, it works sometimes on handheld.'

The screen fractured then joined, more snow then it cleared and there he was smiling at me. The dial told me it was real time.

'Look at you – so grown up,' he said.

'Pa,' the word choked.

'Sorlie, I'm so sorry. I had no choice.' I looked at Merj. 'This is a trick, a recording like the other.' Merj shrugged. 'Ask him a question then.'

'Where are you?' Pa looked behind him. It was dark, faint candle light flickered in the background.

'It doesn't matter.'

'Why aren't you here in person?

'I wish I could be but I can't.'

'Why? Why did you leave me?'

'I had no choice.'

I wanted to throw the reader to the wall. 'Answer me. This is computer-generated isn't it? Not real.' We held each other's stare. He wasn't real. 'You're dead.' I bawled. He jerked back as my words slapped him. The face of my father faltered, and then I saw something I recognised behind him.

'Ask me anything…' I heard him say, but this time I did throw the reader to smash against the wall. I ran from the room.

I sprinted down the corridor, adrenaline burning off the sedative as I went. Past my cell to the large shutter door at the end. Scud was behind me. My fingers grabbed the bottom and strained. He helped and together it moved enough for me to crawl under. Scud groaned and struggled to follow. The anteroom was empty of outdoor gear. I didn't care. I yanked open the outer door, ready for it to be whipped from my grasp. How many times had I left this way with Ridgeway to search for the corncrake and Kenneth?

The stone steps were as slippery as I remembered but I slithered down them uncaring of the sheer neck-breaking drop beside me.

'Take care.' I heard Scud call from the top step.

I flew down the path, over culverts and rushing white water as I had done on my first trip out the prison. Wind and rain slashed my face, soaked my hair and clothes. The mist was low. I couldn't see far in front but I knew the way. My feet squelched. He was in the cave. I saw it, behind his worried face, the paintings on the wall. The ones Kenneth had created in his many lonely years here. He was in the cave. 'He's in the cave.' My feet beat time to the words. 'He's in the cave.'

Kenneth's arrow marker was still wedged into a cairn at the path junction. I scrappled down the steep slope. The sea was obscured by mist that rolled right down to the waves. I landed badly at the bottom and twisted my ankle. My ribs reminded me of my earlier crash. I rushed into the cave.

He wasn't there.

'Sorry' the note said.

The cave reeked of the loss of him. And still warm with the heat from Kenneth's nuclear battery heater, the flex unravelled since he had last been here. I ran outside. And heard the clank of boat engine disappearing into the distance.

'Pa!' I screamed. But knew he was gone. 'Why?' I hollered into the mist, hoping he would hear. He knew I was coming and left me again. Too embarrassed to face me.

'Sorry.' One solitary word written on a torn piece of plastic with some of Kenneth's homemade paints. I rubbed the plastic between my finger and thumb. Familiar and unnerving. It couldn't be. I licked my lips and tasted salt. I turned the note over and felt my heart shatter in my chest. The flip side was green, with a tiny corner of white. The distinctive livery was unmistakable. Steadie. No way would Kenneth have owned this when he lived here. Pa must have brought it with him. I folded it up and stowed it safe inside my overalls. Before I prepared to hobble back I rewound the battery flex and put everything right, it was the least I could do for poor Kenneth.

As fast as my twisted ankle allowed, I negotiated the climb on the uneven path. I was already soaked, I didn't want to risk the hypothermia card.

When I re-entered the prison, up the soapy steps and into the ante-chamber, I was not surprised to find Scud waiting for me.

'Sorry pal, nae hot shower this time but ah found you some dry gear.' He handed over an old pair of my prison overalls. They pinched at the waist and shoulder seams now. They sure fattened me up in Steadie.

'Find him?' Scud asked.

'No, he'd just left.'

'Uh huh, there'll be a reason.'

'He could have waited. He could have sent a signal.'

Scud slung an arm round my shoulder, something he'd never have been permitted to do in the time when I was pure Privileged and he was my native.

'There will be a reason, Sorlie, trust me. No man leaves his family without a reason.'

'Even when he's The Prince?' My head was bursting. How could it be Pa?

Scud led me through to the library where all were assembled with the exception of Kenneth.

Vanora was ensconced back in her chair, her face looking pasty against the strong red of her suit. Her skull strained against the skin, pushing her contours into dark relief. And she clasped her hands so tightly together her knuckles threatened to pop. Merj shadowed beside the oak door, one arm perched on an empty book shelf. Ishbel stood beside Dawdle as if they had at last made a truce. Monsieur Jacques sat by the fire cradling a goblet of Mash. They looked as if some great games master had arranged them in their corners ready for a play-off.

'Find him?' Merj asked with a straight face but I detected a smirk hovering just below the surface. Or maybe I'm just paranoid. This place did that to me.

'We've studied the very impressive plan The Prince sent out with the holo.' Merj went on adopting a grating teacher tone. 'And everyone is clear on their position, I believe.' Hamming it to the max. 'Jacques and Vanora have agreed to the terms.' Vanora sniffed at her former lieutenant's words. Merj whirled on her. 'Yes? No?' She lowered her head in a nod or was it a bow, but looked far from happy.

'Vanora, Ishbel, Kenneth and Scud are to return to Freedom to prepare for the northern assault.'

'Not Kenneth,' Vanora said, her hands tightening.

'He will be restrained. The Blue Pearl Commanders are in place there to help.' Merj was enjoying this.

'Jacques and Dawdle will mobilise their oligopolitical operations in Major...'

'We prefer tae call thum Ligos,' Dawdle quipped.

'As you wish. And Sorlie...'

'I'm going to Steadie.'

'What?' both Vanora and Ishbel sync'd.

'I'm going to Steadie.'

If he was taken aback Merj didn't show it. 'May I ask why?'

'Because I say so. I haven't agreed to The Prince's terms. Anyway, it's where he's headed, I'm sure. Pa will be in Steadie. ' Even as I said it I still couldn't get my head round the fact it was Pa and he was alive. The Prince was still a myth, another being. 'If he can't hang around to tell us his plan himself, why should we comply?'

'The Prince has instructed you be taken to a safe house.'

'Well I'm not going. And if he doesn't like that, well – tough.' As I spoke I noticed Vanora grow more uncomfortable. She had given in so easily. 'I choose to return to Steadie, end of story.'

'How...?'

'Dawdle can drop me off.'

'Heh, heh, ah might be headed the other way.'

'But you're not and you know it. You have some precious salvage to check up on.'

Dawdle gave a shuftie to Jacques. Did he know about the tower?

'You can't go on your own,' Ishbel said.

'He's not. Ah'm going too.' Scud had never left my side throughout this exchange. 'And when ah'm finished there ah'm coming back here. Sorry Ishbel but ah should never have left.'

'That is not in The Prince's plan,' Merj said in a jobsworth's voice.

Scud stepped up to Merj trying to look tall but only reaching his shoulders.

'Listen pal, who put you in charge? As Sorlie says, if your Prince cannae be bothered tae come speak tae us in person but send some minion tae dae his bidding, why should we follow his plan? Ah never signed up tae this.' Even though Scud's appearance had been altered, that sinister something I first spotted in him while he was my native in this prison rose to the surface and no amount of dilution could wash that menace out.

Merj bristled. 'Scud, you're of great value to the State. We can't allow you to just wander around.'

'Listen son, there's plenty others wandering around out there. They're just as valuable. Ah'll be safe with young Sorlie here.' He lifted his finger and stabbed Merj in his chest. 'And if what ah hear is right, this Steadie is one of the safest places in the State.'

'Reinya's there,' Ishbel's voice was small, as if she didn't want Scud to hear. His face flushed with shock.

'You should have told me, lass. Ah assumed you got her tae Freedom.' His voice low, almost a whisper, but the words clear.

Ishbel put her head down. 'I was going to. I just wanted to see how this played out first.'

Scud turned around to face me and tapped his finger to his nose. Sorted. No one was going to argue with this wiry wee man again.

As we made our way down to the jetty Scud said, 'Ah'm looking forward to seeing your pa again.'

'You know him?'

'Aye, your pa was one o' my students. A great historian he was before he joined the Military. Maybe that's what made him join. He knew history was the key. He's learned what works and what fails. He'll make a great leader.'

'Why didn't you tell me you knew him? All those months, in there, together, you never said.'

'Aw son, we both thought he was dead. Why rub salt in already weeping wounds?'

Ishbel walked down to the jetty with us. Suddenly Black Rock felt like the safest place in Esperaneo. We had retrieved our waterproofs from the guide but had abandoned the buggy, choosing to walk, crouched against the driving wind and rain coming off the sea.

Dawdle helped Scud into the sub first. He seemed quite jolly about Scud coming with us. 'Better disembarkation this time eh?' he said. 'And ye'll see yer wee lassie again. That's nice.'

Ishbel put a formal hand out to me, we shook as if we were equal strangers.

'I didn't know, Sorlie.'

'It's OK, Ishbel, I was upset.'

'Come back to Freedom once you've found him. We need you there.'

I nodded. She let go my hand and turned to Dawdle. If I'd counted the seconds of their silence I'd have lost count.

'Be careful Ishbel,' Dawdle broke first. There was a smile on his face. He held his arms out but when she didn't move he sort of flapped them to slap his sides in helplessness. He held out one hand, she hesitated then took it. He began to pull her closer but she broke free. Her face was soaked with rain, but when she flicked a look my way her stone expression melted momentarily. 'Take care,' she said to Dawdle. 'See you soon.'

'Take care, see you soon,' he repeated. 'That's good enough fur me.'

The Reunion

Dawdle tried to give Scud a sedative before submerging, to stop the pain in his ear, but Scud waved him away.

'The souterrain dwellers inserted a grommet while ah was being repaired.' He bit his lip and I could see the whites of his eyes. 'Ah want tae try it, see if it really works.'

'OK. Let's go then,' Dawdle said.

Scud sat in the corner biting his nails. I still couldn't quite get over the change in him. The last time I saw him he had morphed from native to Privileged, his stature, manner and even his voice had changed. Although he looked Privileged with his brown hair and walnut eyes, he was regaining his old mannerisms, and his speech was slipping back to the old Scud. It was good to have him back. As if he sensed my scrutiny he looked up and smiled and I saw his teeth were still broken and crooked. He tapped his nose. Sweat pricked his brow. I could feel the pressure in my ears so I yawned to make them pop. Scud put his hands up to his. He closed his eyes and began to mutter something under his breath. I couldn't hear what, perhaps one of those old prayer things folk used to chant. The engine chuntered then levelled to a thrum. Scud lowered his hands and grinned again. It had worked.

'This is going tae make such a difference tae our cause. Every native prisoner will have the chance tae be fixed of this affliction.'

Dawdle's eyebrow shot up in question. 'Have they patented it?' His expression twisted in calculation.

Scud chuckled. 'Well if they haven't ah'm sure someone will make a profit from it. Eh, Dawdle? It's the way things have worked since the beginning of mankind.' Scud shifted and stretched his legs in front of him. 'Who'd have thought things would have turned round like this,' he said to me. 'The last time ah saw you we were all thinking Vanora would save the world.'

'My grandfather knew. Even in his own madness, he said I was going out of the frying pan into the fire. He knew how mad Vanora was.' That may have been disloyal but as the words fell from my mouth a thought came to me. 'Scud, what if there's more of their genes in me than I want? I might be mad. I certainly feel like it sometimes.'

Scud shook his head, his solemn eyes to the floor. 'You don't understand. What they went through, that generation, my generation – the purge, the murders, the Separation of the Classes. The whole fabric of our society changed. It drove many mad. Your generation don't know anything else. Which is why you can take us forward into the revolution.'

'Is it a revolution?' I thought of all my taught history, the failed ancient revolutions of the past.

'Aye wee man, there's gonna be a revolution and you're right in the midst of it.'

If Scud had told me this on the first day we met I would have laughed, but now I knew more truth than I cared for.

Dawdle was mostly silent on our stop-start journey in the Peedle heap of junk. Scud told me a little about his family, his history. About Reinya and what had happened to them after he and Ishbel had left Black Rock together. The souterrain place sounded safe, almost as safe as Steadie. There was so much more to natives. Being brought up as a Privileged military kid, I knew nothing of them. They were just there to make my life easier. If all Privileged kids got to know their natives, surely they would want to help us change the system. A revolution Scud called it. Maybe he was right. The prospect of such a thing whizzed my head as we trundled toward Steadie.

'Dawdle, do you know if Steadie have access to FuB?' The State database may be useless but it might have some information on past revolutions. As if reading my mind, Scud shook his head.

'This isn't something you learn from books, wee man. But as ah say, yer pa'll know. He's a great military man as well as a great scholar. Just the man you need tae lead you.' Scud's face beamed with hope. 'This will be a fine and just revolution with your pa at the helm.' He stared into the distance. 'The trail o' tears is about tae end.'

A knot formed in my stomach at all this talk of Pa, the great saviour of the people. None of it was real. 'It's not really him. It's a trick.'

'Aye well, we'll soon find out,' Dawdle said. 'We're getting close tae docking. Batten down the earholes Scudster.'

As we emerged from the murky water we saw dull-light emerge. Grey skies hung over Steadie. A smir rolled off the sea peppering the windscreen with spray. There was no one on the jetty to meet us. It was eerily quiet.

'They're no expecting us so we'll creep in and have a lookie just tae make sure everything's kosher. We don't want tae hand yous two ower tae the Military.'

We docked under a pier and climbed up onto the plastic duckboards. As soon as we were over the beach Dawdle jumped from the boards and told us to do the same. My ankle still stounded from the sprain but I managed to sit on the boards and swing myself down to the sand. We crouched low and crabbed along the beach on the lea side of some dunes. When we were parallel to the hot building we crawled on belly to the boundary markers and looked into Steadie on an ordinary day. Specials were working at their task under the supervision of the oldies; lifting, carrying, sorting, silent. I searched the scene for a sign of Harkin but there was none. Scud searched with his eyes too, for Reinya no doubt.

'Looks OK,' I said. We all rose to move. Then the klaxon whawhaed. I grabbed Scud, we hit the sand. Dawdle was already down. 'Raid,' I whispered although the klaxon drowned every sound.

Like the last time the specials started screaming and were herded to the hot building. Where was Harkin?

And then I saw her running, her medic's graith strapped to her body, beside her ran Con. He carried someone in the same way he'd carried me there. 'It's Pa.'

'Oh Sorlie.' There was such pain in Scud's voice.

'What?'

'Fuck,' Dawdle said.

And then I saw. It was Pa, but it was only half Pa. One arm was slung round Con's neck the other missing, tears ran down his face as his body bumped against Con's back. His face contorted in a scream no one could hear.

'His legs. Where are his legs?'

'Oh son, he has no legs.' Scud put his arm around my shoulder but I pushed him off, turned and puked in the sand.

'That's his reason. He wasn't ready for you tae know.'

'Fuck,' Dawdle said again.

We lay in the sand while the biosuited unit, sent in to weed out oldies and specials, rampaged through Steadie. But I heard nothing. The image of Pa flashed through my mind over and over. And my words to Scud a short while ago. 'It's not really him. It's a trick.' But it was him. I just wished it was a trick.

'How?' I said as we lay in safety while chaos raged just over the sand dune barrier. Scud took and squeezed my hand and immediately let go. His native 'no contact' training still ingrained.

'Looks like mine damage,' Dawdle said.

'Or torture,' Scud added, preparing me.

The raid didn't last as long as the last one and the klaxon sounded before I was ready.

'I can't go.'

'Get up and get in there,' Dawdle said grabbing hold of both my lapels.

'Leave him be,' Scud growled. Dawdle dropped me as if I'd combusted. Scud held his hands out in front of him. They were free of blemishes with only a slight shake. 'Look at that. Remember all those times you saw me in a state in the prison, all the times ah nearly died, getting zapped, getting messages tae you.'

I nodded. I knew what he was getting at. 'I couldn't understand. I thought you were stupid, then realised you were brave.'

'Aye well, maybe stupid sometimes, eh? But d'you know what kept me going?' He thumbed to the land. 'The dream o' this, where we are now, on the cusp of revolution. Look at you, wincing over a sprained ankle. Did you see how much pain that man was in?'

'But how can he…?'

'Why do you think he came all that way to the island in that state?' I hung my head. 'Ah'll tell ye, will ah? It was so he could speak to you. He knew he could speak to you through that Merj's short range reader. We all thought he was dead. He's probably now the most wanted man on the planet and he came tae speak to you. Now get up there and reward him for that. None of this 'why did you leave me?' crap. That can come later. He had his reasons.' Scud stood up. 'And now ah have my granddaughter tae see.'

Dawdle threw me a look of disgust that I deserved.

We saw Reinya first, the blaze of her hair clashing with the green of the tent. She was tending to one of the specials, a little girl of about five; she cleaned a wound then pulled the child onto her lap, wiped her tears and gave her a cuddle. She looked up at us as we lumbered unhindered into the camp. Scud held his breath and stood petrified. And then she smiled and raised her hand to her forehead in a little salute and I thought I might need to catch Scud as he relaxed in relief.

'He's in Harkin's tent,' she said to me as if she had been expecting us. She pointed towards the midden.

It was the tent where Harkin had stopped that day she showed me round, where the boy stood in the doorway watching us. I knocked on the frame and when no answer came I pulled back the flap and entered. He was in bed but propped up. Thankfully his lower half was covered.

Harkin was rigging up drips. Pa noticed me first. Fleeting expressions of surprise, delight and then worry scudded across his face. He opened his mouth to speak and Harkin put a hand on his shoulder to stay him then whirled when she realised someone had entered.

She almost smiled, I'm sure. 'He's very weak. That raid took its toll.'

'It's OK, Harkin, let him in this time...' Pa's voice was a whisper of its former self.

She turned to me. 'I've given him a strong sedative. You can stay 'til he falls asleep.'

'What do you mean this time?'

Pa took a breath. 'I was here before...' but Harkin held up her hand.

'I'll tell him.' She turned to me but with a professional air. 'He wanted to see you, that first time. He was very sick, so I brought you down here before Con took you to the tower. He thought you were safe in Freedom. He didn't believe you were the injured boy brought here just after him. He had to be sure, so I brought you down for him to see.'

I looked at Pa and by his closed eyes I could tell she was telling the truth. 'We knew he was The Prince but we didn't know he was your pa. He didn't say.' She swallowed. 'He told us to take you to the tower to find Ishbel. Con wanted nothing to do with it. We...' she gestured to Pa. 'We had to convince him.'

She pulled a plastic chair from the corner and placed it by the bed. 'Sit.' And she left us.

We sat in silence for a few minutes but I knew time was short. 'I thought you were dead.'

'I know, I'm sorry.' His words came slow and weak. 'I thought I would be dead by the time Ishbel had taken you to your grandfather.' He swallowed. 'I never meant it to be like this, Sorlie. I went to avenge your mother's death. But by the time I reached her commander I realised it wasn't the answer. There was another way.' He shifted under his covers, pain washed over his face. I tried not to imagine how little was left of him. 'I'd been establishing the Blue Pearl network for many years. Your mother and I knew Vanora's plans weren't working. We planned to take over. And then.' He closed his eyes. 'Well you know...'

'Is she really dead?' This question I'd buried ever since I knew Pa was alive.

'Yes Sorlie, unlike me, she isn't going to make a miraculous entry back into our lives. She really is dead. I saw what was left of her.' His lips were cracked and raw, he licked them as he tried to smile. 'We are going to beat them, Sorlie. You and I.'

'But how? Why can't we stay here? Safe.'

He shook his head. 'No – it needs to end. It's all planned. We have the means. We only need to wait till next quarter. The Blue Pearl don't even need me now.'

I felt the panic whoosh through my body.

'You're not going to die.'

'No, not this time.' His eyes drooped, he was going to sleep.

'What happened to you, Pa?'

'I got careless. After we took Jacques and shipped him off to Black Rock we headed north to intercept Vanora.' He licked his lips. 'My boat was caught in the destruction of your Transport. It exploded almost directly above us, raining our boat with metal and explosives. I'm lucky, the rest of the crew perished. Our other boat picked me up and rushed me here.' His eyes closed, he shifted, every feature contorted with pain. He was doing it to stay awake.

'It's OK, tell me later.'

'No, no, you need to know. I didn't know Vanora had you with her. The men who kidnapped her panicked at seeing my boat explode. They shouldn't have killed the Noiri man. They should have checked the back.' He closed his eyes. 'I'm sorry, Sorlie.' I could hardly make out the words.

'What?' but he'd gone under.

And suddenly Harkin was at my shoulder. 'He said sorry.'

Harkin brought another chair and sat beside me. 'He was bad when they carried him in here. The healer was working on him when you were brought in. That's why we suspended you for over a week. Your injuries were not so urgent, but your father is strong, he recovered well from his operations. We transferred him to a moorlogger to recover on his way to Black Rock. He wanted to go there to speak to Jacques and Vanora through a short range device.'

'It didn't work.' Why did he put himself through so much pain? But I knew. Like me they would never have believed the holo on its own. He had to be there in person, but give the illusion of being whole and strong.

She took Pa's hand and enclosed it in both hers. 'I'm going to heal him, Sorlie. I can do it. We can make him prosthetics here, teach him to walk. Don't worry.' I looked at the tiny half man on the bed. It didn't seem possible he would ever be whole again.

'Thank you.' I looked at her lips, the lips I'd kissed when I'd left. I wanted to kiss her again, but something stopped me. The time, the place, the situation. Or was it the determination in her eyes, the way she held Pa's scarred hand in her small clasp.

Scud pulled the tent flap back and stood in the doorway, Reinya by his side.

'We are going tae beat them Sorlie. Ah know we are.'

This time I believed him.

Praise for Ways of the Doomed

"If you liked Divergent and 'that one about hunger', you're going to love Ways of The Doomed. Moira McPartlin's prose is rich but unpretentious, her storytelling, thumping. An exciting new voice in YA fiction." Helen FitzGerald

"Chilling, intelligent, and thought-provoking, this richly imagined vision of the future gripped me from the outset. Beautifully written with fully realised characters, vivid settings, and a clever and playful use of language, Ways of the Doomed makes for a thrilling read. I loved it! My only complaint? I can't wait for book 2."
Christina Banach, author of *Minty*

Moira McPartlin has created a scarily believable setting and populated it with mysterious characters and a teenage protagonist who is way out of his depth"
"Sue Wallman author of *Lying About Last Summer* (Zoella Book Club Pick 2016)

"Ways of the Doomed is a vision of a damaged future which resonates for today. Beautifully written, Moira has created a plausible futuristic world which we half-recognize with its historical echoes and imagined outcomes."
Alex Nye author of *Darker Ends*

ALSO BY MOIRA MCPARTLIN

THE INCOMERS